# THE ACTOR'S GUIDE TO
## *GREED*

**Books by Rick Copp**

THE ACTOR'S GUIDE TO MURDER

THE ACTOR'S GUIDE TO ADULTERY

THE ACTOR'S GUIDE TO GREED

Published by Kensington Publishing Corporation

# THE ACTOR'S GUIDE TO
# *GREED*

## Rick Copp

KENSINGTON BOOKS
www.kensingtonbooks.com

KENSINGTON BOOKS are published by

Kensington Publishing Corp.
850 Third Avenue
New York, NY 10022

ISBN 0-7582-0960-6

Printed in the United States of America

*For Rob—*
*thank you for opening my eyes to the world and so much more.*

# Acknowledgments

First and foremost, I would like to thank my wonderful editor John Scognamiglio for his tremendous talent and his knack for choosing spectacular New York restaurants whenever I'm in town.

Thanks to Michael Irpino for calling me up and quoting lines from the books.

Also I wish to thank Linda Steiner, who is the voice of Laurette; Joe Dietl and Ben Zook; Laurice and Chris Molinari; Joel Fields and Jessica Sultan; Liz Friedman and Yvette Abatte; and Milan Rakic. And to Marilyn Webber, Mark Greenhalgh, Lori Alley, Woody and Tuesdi Woodworth, David A. Goodman, Patricia Hyland, Craig Thornton, Sharon Killoran, Laura Simandi, Susan Lally and Priscilla Botsford, Dara Boland, Liz Newman and Brian O'Keefe, my deepest gratitude.

Special thanks must go to Michael Byrne for his enduring friendship and Vincent Barra for his wisdom, guidance and, of course, for sharing many, many good times.

And thank you Alan Burnett for allowing me into your incredible animated world.

My deepest love and appreciation to my parents Fred and Joan Clement; my sister Holly; and my phenomenal nieces and nephew, Jessica, Megan and Justin Simason.

I'd also like to thank my Writers' Group: Dana Baratta, Melissa Rosenberg, Dan Greenberger, Rob Wright, Allison Gibson, and especially Greg Stancl.

Also to my team of William Morris agents—Jonathan Pecarsky, Carey Nelson Burch, Cori Wellins, Ken Freimann, Lanny Noveck, and Jim Engelhardt—I am forever grateful for your unwavering support.

# Chapter 1

As I raced through the thick, foreboding woods, entangled in a maze of sharp tree branches and knee-high shrubs, I gasped and sputtered in a panic, disoriented and lost in my surroundings. It was dark and the air chilled my bones. I couldn't stop shivering. I darted my eyes back and forth, searching, so desperately trying to get my incessant wheezing under control. The last thing I needed was my lack of an effective exercise program to give me away. Taking cover behind an overgrown bush, I bent down and hugged my knees, praying he wouldn't find me. I took a gulp of air and held my breath. I heard some rustling branches as if someone were walking steadily toward me. A twig snapped. He was so close.

After a few tense moments, he mercifully retreated and all I could hear was the restless gust of the wind. He was gone. And I was still alive. Exhaling an exhausted sigh of relief, I stepped out from behind my hiding place and turned toward the direction of the campsite, where the others were waiting. Suddenly I stopped. There he was. Looming over me in a cartoon Elmer Fudd mask and wielding a sharp hatchet in his white-knuckled fist. He raised it above his head, and before I could let out a scream, he brought it down. Hard. So hard it cracked open my skull like a melon. Blood spurted everywhere. I stumbled back, shaking my head in utter shock and disbelief, grabbing my head and then staring numbly at my blood-soaked hands. I sank to my knees and raised my eyes in time to see Elmer Fudd swing the axe down again. I prayed that at any moment I was going to wake up from this horrible nightmare. But it wasn't a nightmare. It was real.

How could I ever have let this happen? How did I allow Laurette to talk me into taking this dreadful movie?

Charlie and I sat in the fourth-row aisle seats at the New Beverly Cinema, a run-down revival house near the Fairfax district of Los Angeles, for the world-premiere screening of *Creeps*, an exploitative slasher flick I shot last year in south Florida. I knew the project was completed on a shoestring budget, but actors always hope that sharp editing, some realistic sound effects, and a suspenseful score will somehow make it look a little better at the end of the day. No such luck. This piece of schlock was an unmitigated disaster. People were chuckling at my death scene. It was so silly and unbelievable. And it wasn't just the script or the way it was shot. It was me. I was awful. Completely over the top. Like Susan Hayward's wacky performance in *I Want to Live!* But Susan won an Oscar and went on to play juicy supporting roles in camp classics like *Valley of the Dolls*. This celluloid Titanic was going to sink my career. Or what was left of it.

Charlie knew I was on the verge of a breakdown. He gently placed one hand on my knee while stuffing a fistful of popcorn into his mouth with the other. I knew what he was doing. He was afraid I was going to ask him what he thought of my performance and figured a mouthful of movie popcorn would keep him from having to give me an honest answer.

The camera lingered on my crumpled, twisted, broken body for much longer than necessary, finally panning and stopping for a close shot of my separated skull. What a memorable big-screen debut. A ten-foot-high corpse in Technicolor. Mercifully, the film finally cut away from the flies buzzing around my dead body to a new scene as my ten-year-old son in the movie (played by a four-foot-high, Satan-possessed child star) wandered through the woods, worried about his dad, who had suddenly gone missing. The film's strapping, stoic, hard-bodied hero accompanied him.

I wanted to run screaming out of the theater, but the film's director was sitting directly behind me. Larry Levant was a rising young *artiste* full of creative promise that would instantly be washed away upon this clunker's release. He was in his early thirties, on the short side, with dark features and an intense gaze. With him was my manager, Laurette, a gorgeous, plus-size beauty who dwarfed him whenever they were together. They had found love on the set even though Larry never found a story for his movie. I wanted to yell at both of them for getting me involved in this mess. But when I spun around and was met with their expectant smiles, I simply gave my nervous director and my best friend an enthusiastic thumbs-up.

The film lasted another excruciating sixty-two minutes. Charlie shifted several times, especially at the gory parts. My boyfriend, Charlie, was a cop and saw blood and violence every day while investigating LA's underbelly. Accompanying me to the premiere of this movie was above and beyond the call of duty. And I loved him for it.

When the credits finally rolled, there was a smattering of applause. Most of the audience bolted from their seats and out the door before there was any chance of running into Larry and having to comment on the film. The cluster of executives from Sunbelt Films, a small, independent releasing company that unwisely chose to pick up this movie nightmare for distribution, offered a few perfunctory pats on the back to Larry, then clamped their cell phones to their ears and made their escape.

Charlie and I were stuck. We had agreed beforehand to accompany Larry and Laurette to the postpremiere party being held a few blocks from the theater across Beverly Boulevard at Starbucks.

Yes, Starbucks. Not the Skybar. Or Chinois on Main. Or Mortons. Or any other high-end LA hotspot the studios flock to for their numerous celebratory events. Sunbelt cried poverty when it came to hosting a party. Of course, this was after they saw a rough cut of the film. So Laurette, who refused to let the evening go by without some kind of festivity, organized a gathering at the nearest coffeehouse. She even sprang for pastries.

The handful of moviegoers who hadn't already dashed for their cars marched across the street. There was a somber mood in the air on this crisp, late-spring night. We were all thinking the same thing. What would we say if Larry and Laurette pressed us for our opinions on the film? Laurette and I had shared a years-long friendship based on honesty and I promised her very early on that I would always be up front with her, never hold back, never sugarcoat anything. And I expected the same from her. We had both zealously stuck to our pact. Well, almost. There was the time I traded in my BMW for a Prius in an effort to make an environmental statement and Laurette blindly leased a new Cadillac SUV that she had to fill up every time she made a two-mile trip to the nearest Nordstrom. Why make her feel bad? And then there was the time she made noises about her desire to adopt a toddler from China. I was concerned because the last thing she had to care for was a hamster she got when she was twelve that she forgot to feed for three weeks while she was busy mourning *A Flock of Seagulls'* failure to win a Best New Artist Grammy. I never said a word to her. Okay, so maybe fibbing about my true reaction to her boyfriend's new movie wouldn't be the first time I didn't stick to our honesty agreement.

As the small group of us poured into Starbucks, the workers with their black pullover Izod shirts and coffee-stained green aprons steeled themselves for a rush. Charlie and I were first in line, and I rattled off my usual iced venti sugar-free vanilla non-fat decaf latte. I know, I know, what's the point? Charlie spied an inviting maple-nut scone that was calling out to him and ordered a house blend to wash it down with. I declined a pastry because I'm an actor and we spend half our day comparing body-fat measurements. Charlie was on his feet all day, active in his work as a detective, and never worried about what he ate. It just made me feel better to know I refused to give in to my sweets craving. Of course, Charlie would inevitably offer me half his scone, and I would happily accept it. So in the end, it would all work out for me. I would demonstrate self-restraint *and* get half a maple-nut scone.

As we stepped aside to allow the next person in line to place their order, I heard a familiar voice behind me.

"Baby, don't even go there!"

That was the catchphrase I made famous during my five-year stint as a precocious troublemaker on a hit 1980s sitcom called *Go to Your Room*. It felt like a million years ago, but those five words would probably wind up on my gravestone right next to Gary Coleman and his signature catchphrase, "What you talkin' about, Willis?"

I plastered on a fake smile and spun around to see who just couldn't resist dredging up my cheesy past.

Wallace Goodwin, a bespectacled, balding, slightly paunchy sitcom writer in his mid-forties, beamed at me. Wallace had been a staff writer on my show for its entire run. He loved to claim credit for that snappy retort I used time and time again on any given episode. It was always so important for Wallace to let the world know he had come up with that immortal line that made such an indelible impression on American pop culture. He was convinced that some day it would be the deciding factor in his possible induction into the TV Academy Hall of Fame.

"I came up with that, you know," Wallace said, puffed up with pride.

"I remember." That's all I could think of to say.

Sitcom writers are a strange breed. They spend their lives cooped up on a studio lot in a bland, claustrophobic conference room with scuffed walls and stained rugs, eating most of their meals out of take-out Styrofoam at two in the morning as they pitch to improve bad jokes that rarely ever get better. They are also extremely competitive and hyperaware of how well other writers are doing. Who's the funniest? Who's the dead weight? Their entire self-worth is based on whether or not they can succeed in getting the show runner to laugh so hard he blows Diet Coke out through his nose.

After the show was canceled, Wallace went on to write for a string of successful shows, albeit no Emmy winners. He reached his peak in the late eighties by winning a NAACP award for a very special episode of a sitcom starring Marla Gibbs from *The Jeffersons*. Not bad for a middle-aged, white Jewish writer from New Rochelle. After that career high, his luck ran out. He snared freelance assignments on a few syndicated shows and at one point developed a pilot recharging the old *Knight Rider* franchise with a team of talking cars. He brought me in to audition for a gay minivan. By then, I was completely out of the closet thanks to a *National Enquirer* cover photo of me and a buddy making out at the LA Gay Rodeo. Wallace was hoping I could infuse my innate homosexuality into the personality of a screaming queen vehicle manufactured by Ford. He was polite when I came in to read for him, if not a little embittered by his circumstances. He wasn't exactly writing *Seinfeld*. After the audition, he assured me I did an admirable job, but in the end, wound up casting his fey personal trainer, who offered him a lifetime of free workouts if he gave him the part.

I never heard from him again until tonight.

"It's good to see you, Wallace." I wasn't lying. I had fond memories of those golden years of my childhood stardom. *Go to Your Room* was a seminal period in my life, and those of us involved in the show were like a tight-knit company of war-torn soldiers. We faced many battles together, lost some of our men, came back with a few scars, but were thankful we at least made it home alive.

"Great performance, Jarrod. I really enjoyed the movie a lot." Wallace obviously didn't get the honesty memo. His neck was beet red, a clear sign he wasn't telling the truth.

"You die very well," a woman's voice purred as Katrina Goodwin marched up with a bottled water and slid her arm through her husband's. Katrina was a raven-haired beauty, a former actress about nine years younger than Wallace was. She had guest-starred on *Go to Your Room* as the cheerleader friend of my older sister. Wallace had penned that week's script, and during our first run-through for the studio, she complimented him on his fine comedic writing. Wallace's script had been overhauled by the entire staff before the first reading, and there was only one line left from his original draft. "Hi, Mom." But nevertheless, Wallace accepted Katrina's gracious accolade and was smitten all week after that. The two became inseparable, but many naysayers suspected Katrina's motives. Especially after Wallace insisted the show bring her back as a semiregular due to her overwhelming chemistry with the rest of the cast. Everyone else on the writing staff failed to see her potential, but Wallace was undeterred. Every story line he pitched and every script he turned in featured that sweet-natured, batty, and mammary-stacked cheerleader friend. And amazingly, the viewers responded. Mostly the teenage boys, but hey, that's exactly who the show was designed for. Then Katrina started hanging around the set during the weeks she didn't even appear in the script, and it soon became clear she and Wallace were an item. The crew placed bets that she would bolt by the end of the season, but she stuck around, and even after the show was scrapped, they stayed together. And remarkably, after all these years, Wallace and Katrina Goodwin seemed as happy and in love as the first day they met.

Katrina touched my arm, and with the utmost sincerity, said, "You look happy, Jarrod. You don't know how happy that makes Wallace and me."

Wallace nodded vigorously in agreement. Of course, he automatically agreed with anything his beloved wife said.

"I am happy." I smiled. "I may not be so happy after reading the reviews of this movie, but hey, we've all been associated with a lot of crappy projects. You've got to pay the mortgage, right, Wallace?"

Wallace stared at me blankly. In his mind, everything he ever did was art that was simply misunderstood. I remember him telling me at my audition that his *Knight Rider* redo was a quirky, intelligent reimagining of the franchise, and critics be damned if they weren't smart enough to see that. Wallace wasn't about to group himself with me, whose only critically hailed project since the good old days of *Go to Your Room* was a memorable turn as an earnest rookie cop gunned down in the line of duty in an Emmy-nominated episode of *Homicide: Life on the Street.*

Katrina bristled at my unintentional slam aimed at her husband. She was very protective of him. I had to backpedal fast.

"So what show are you working on now, Wallace? Any sitcom would be lucky to have you."

Katrina relaxed. I had tactfully sidestepped the land mine.

Wallace scoffed. "I haven't done a sitcom in years. I got tired of the grind. It was time to stretch myself as an artist." Writer speak for "No one will hire me, so I have to scramble and find something else to do."

"Writing movies?" I said.

"No. Why waste my time in features? Writers get no respect in movies. Studios go through more on one film than a stuffy nose goes through Kleenex."

Maybe if Wallace worked on his analogies, he would get more work as a writer.

"If you come out of sitcoms, the movie execs look down on you. It's tough out there for writers," Wallace said, almost growling.

"It's even worse for actors," I said, trying to offer my own perspective on the hardships of carving out a lasting career in Hollywood. "You get pigeonholed from one role. For years, I tried to break out of that child-star box they put me in, and then, when I finally prove I can do drama as a young adult on that *Homicide* episode, all the casting agents say, 'We saw him as the cop, but can he do comedy?' Everybody forgets I had my own sitcom!"

Wallace was looking blank again. He had been enjoying his rant, and as actors are prone to do, I had shifted the attention from him onto myself.

Katrina pouted, annoyed that I would so blatantly steal the focus from her husband.

More backpedaling. "I'm just saying, I know how frustrated you must be."

Wallace shot a glance at his wife, as if to say, "Can you believe this guy?" Then plowed on. "I socked some cash away after the *Knight Rider* fiasco. Took some time to regroup, consider what it was I really wanted to write, and you may not believe this, Jarrod, but—"

"Wallace wrote a play," Katrina chimed in, excited and proud of her husband.

There was an awkward silence. Clearly Wallace wanted to tell me this exciting news himself. He glared at Katrina, but her enthusiasm was bubbling over with such intensity, she didn't even notice.

"It's a murder mystery. Wallace's agent absolutely loved it. He said Wallace is going to be the next Ira Levine."

"Who?" I said, recognizing the name as my dentist on the West Side, not a famous playwright.

"Ira Levine," Katrina said, obviously put off by my stupidity. "The guy who wrote *Deathtrap* and *Boys in the Band*."

"Levin," Wallace hissed. "Ira Levin. And it wasn't *Boys in the Band*, it was *Boys from Brazil*."

"Whatever," Katrina laughed. "It was about homosexuals in Rio."

I bit my tongue.

Wallace sighed. "*Boys in the Band* was about homosexuals in New York. *Boys from Brazil* was about breeding young boys to be Nazis."

"Were the Nazis gay?" Katrina said, completely serious.

"No!"

I quickly intervened. "What's your play about, Wallace?"

The tension immediately drained out of Wallace's face. He loved talking about his work. "It's set at a bed-and-breakfast in Manchester, England. A rainstorm traps the guests in the house for the weekend, and one of them is an escaped killer. No one knows who it is, and the bodies start piling up, and there is a detective from America who ultimately exposes the killer—"

"Turns out it's the Danish countess with a split personality," Katrina said.

Wallace's face flushed with anger and he turned to his wife. "You just told him the ending."

"Well, you can pretty much guess it by the end of the first act," Katrina said.

"No, you can't!"

Somehow I remembered these two much happier. In one more attempt to defuse the situation, I said, "Sounds very Agatha Christie."

It didn't work. Wallace spun around and barked, "No! She was all about the puzzle. My play is a deep psychological portrait of a mind gone mad!"

"It was fun to research too," Katrina cooed. "We traveled to England, met with some psychiatrists, even took lessons at the shooting range so Wallace could conceive a plausible murder."

"I learned I don't like tea and crumpets, despise head shrinks,

10

and I can't shoot a rifle worth shit. Katrina fared much better," Wallace said with a thin smile.

Katrina reached into her bag and pulled out a copy of the script. "Wallace was hoping we'd run into you tonight," she said. "He wants you to read his new play."

"Why should he bother?" Wallace huffed. "You already told him the ending."

I snatched the script from Katrina. "I'd love to read it," I said, hoping to make a fast getaway soon. I glanced over to Charlie. He was half done with his scone and about to dive into the other half. This was a disaster. I was stuck with these two lunatics, and I was going to miss out on him offering me half of his scone!

I was just about to pry myself free when Katrina said, "We'd like you to be in it, Jarrod."

This stopped me in my tracks. "It's getting produced?"

Wallace beamed. "Yes. We got the financing last week. Rehearsals start a week from Monday."

"Here in town?" I said.

Wallace shook his head. He wasn't about to tell me. He wanted me to guess.

"Broadway?" I said, straining to hide my incredulity.

He shook his head again.

"London! The West End!" Katrina said while clapping her hands excitedly.

Wallace narrowed his eyes so hard they almost disappeared. "I wanted him to guess, Katrina."

"Sorry," she said without a hint of remorse. I got the feeling Katrina wasn't as dumb as she pretended to be. She just liked pissing off her husband.

"Are you serious?" I said.

"I brought your name up to our producer, and he went wild," Wallace said. "He thinks you're prime for a comeback. British audiences adored *Go to Your Room*. They all want to see what you look like now. They'd flock to the theater in droves."

Macauley Culkin did a play in London, and it reignited his whole career. A flashy role in an edgy independent film. A funny turn on *Will & Grace*. He was back on the map. This play could do the same for me.

"Who would I play? The American detective?"

Wallace almost laughed but caught himself. "No. His gay valet."

"Wallace said he was visualizing you in the role the whole time he was writing it," Katrina said, resting her head on Wallace's shoulder. After an uncomfortable moment, he flinched and she moved her head upright again.

The gay valet? It sounded like Wallace wanted to cash in on my tabloid notoriety. But honestly, I didn't really care. I had always dreamed of appearing on stage in the West End. The same dusty old theaters graced by the likes of Sir Laurence Olivier, Sir John Gielgud, Dame Judi Dench, and supermodel Jerry Hall. All the greats!

I noticed Charlie raise an eyebrow as I talked in hushed tones with Wallace and Katrina. He knew we were conspiring about something and was curious as to what I was getting mixed up in now.

I told Wallace I would read the play tonight and give him a call first thing in the morning. A part of me didn't even have to read the play. I knew I was going to England. This was fate. I didn't know which notion was more outlandish. Me on a London stage or Wallace Goodwin's name on the marquee.

As I left Wallace to scold Katrina for giving away his precious ending, I bounced back over to Charlie, snatched the last piece of scone out of his fingertips, and popped it in my mouth.

"You really think you deserve that for leaving me here alone all this time?" Charlie said.

"Wallace wrote a play. And he wants me to be in it."

"I thought you said Wallace was a hack."

"I never said that. He just needed to stretch himself creatively to demonstrate his real potential." Of course, I probably did tell Charlie at one time that I thought Wallace was a hack. But actors are adept at rewriting history when there is a part at stake.

"So is it going up at one of those little theaters on Santa Monica Boulevard?" Charlie said.

I shook my head. Like Wallace the sadist, I wanted him to guess.

Charlie's eyes lit up. "Broadway?"

"London!" I couldn't contain myself. "I'm doing a play in London!"

Charlie smiled, genuinely pleased. "That's great, babe." But then, the issues involved in this decision began sprouting up. "How long will you be gone?"

"I'm not sure yet. I haven't even read the play. I may hate it."

But we both knew I'd love the play. No matter how bad it was. In my mind, I was already on that plane with my passport and a London walking-tour guide.

I swiveled around and spotted Laurette and Larry at a corner table, sipping extra foam lattes and sharing an oatmeal raisin cookie. Laurette had her hand over Larry's, and I presumed she was reassuring him that his new movie had some artistic merit and was not going to be a career killer.

I leaned down and kissed Charlie on the forehead. "Be right back."

Racing over to Laurette, I blurted out, "I've been offered a play in London!"

Laurette glanced up at me as if she didn't hear me correctly. "I'm sorry?"

"Wallace Goodwin wrote a play—"

"That hack wrote a play?" Laurette said.

"Keep your voice down," I hissed. "He's right over there."

Laurette left Larry to sulk over his film's reception, promising to return soon. She grabbed my arm and dragged me outside so we could have a little privacy.

I filled Laurette in on all the details, and she squealed with delight. She knew how much this meant to me. She knew what a great opportunity this would be for my career. And she knew in a matter of weeks she would be on a shopping spree at Harrods.

"Sweetheart, this is sensational news," she said. We both looked back inside to see Wallace and Katrina in deep conversation with another couple. Wallace was grimacing as Katrina spouted stories animatedly. I wondered if Katrina was revealing the ending of Wallace's play again just to get his blood boiling.

"I never thought he had it in him," Laurette said. "You never know, I guess. He could be the next Ira Levine."

Unlike Wallace, I chose to let it go.

"You'll be great," Laurette said. "Just great."

"Now, I don't want this conflicting with any jobs you may be working on lining up for me."

Laurette stared at me, not sure how to respond.

"You know, there might be another film on the horizon or a recurring role on a series that you were going to send me out on . . ." I was losing steam. I could see it in her eyes. "Nothing, huh?"

Laurette didn't want to hurt me, so she tried to be diplomatic. "It's really a bad time for everybody. Pilot season is months away. Movies are going after big names right now . . ." It didn't work.

"So flying off to London is probably a good idea?"

"Absolutely," she said. "Besides, Larry and I are leaving for Maui in a few days. We'll be gone for three weeks. So I won't be lining up auditions for you anyway."

"Three weeks? But he'll miss the opening weekend of his movie!"

Laurette leaned in, and whispered in my ear. "That's the idea."

Poor Larry. When I met him he was indestructible. And after a mere twenty-seven-day shoot in south Florida, he was now a pariah. I knew what he was about to go through. I had weathered the ups and downs of a stormy Hollywood career myself. You just keep trudging on, never giving up, and one day, destiny might shine on you and you're rewarded with a second chance to recapture the glory of the past. Most people give up and move on to a new path. But a few of us diehards remain steadfast gluttons for punishment.

"This play couldn't have come at a better time for you," Laurette said. "It'll perfume some of the smell you're going to get from this stinker of a movie."

She was right. Wallace Goodwin's stage thriller was looking to be not only a dream come true, but also a much-needed career move.

Wallace Goodwin's play *Murder Can Be Civilized* wasn't half bad. I didn't find it to be a searing psychological portrait of a mind gone mad by any stretch of the imagination. Wallace's artistic claims were a bit exaggerated. But as a light romp that poked fun at the clichéd Agatha Christie murder-mystery conventions, it worked brilliantly. Sometimes perennial unemployment can really hone a writer's craft. The secondary role of the gay valet was also a surprise. It wasn't a stock role by any means. Damien Sheffield was a blisteringly sarcastic, ruggedly sexual, and dangerously cunning concoction full of bravado and swagger. He was hiding a multitude of juicy and scandalous secrets, which bubbled over at the worst times. And he didn't even get knocked off until late into the third act. So I was looking at a wealth of time onstage.

I finished reading the script just after midnight, keeping Charlie awake by spouting aloud some of my character's more colorful lines. When I finally put the play down, Charlie had already dropped off to sleep. Our Pekingese, Snickers, was curled up at the foot of the bed snoring softly. I was going to be up all night, my mind racing at the exciting prospects of a new career in the theater. This was the break I had been waiting for.

The following morning, I rang up Wallace and told him how much I loved the play and wanted to do it. He had already been in contact with his London producers to alert them to my interest. Within an hour, Laurette had received an offer, and by lunchtime, the deal was closed. I was to report to the old Apollo Theatre on Shaftsbury Avenue in London on the following Monday. Laurette and Larry postponed their Maui getaway a few days to allow her some time to finish up the details of the contract.

After that, the news just got better. In a stunning coup, the producers locked up Academy Award–winning actress Claire Richards for the leading role of the countess. Claire was one of the star students at the Royal Academy of Dramatic Arts in the late seventies and then went on to start up the internationally renowned Cheek By Jowl repertory company that boasted such names as Kenneth Branagh, Stephen Fry, and Emma Thompson. During her tenure there, she played a number of career-making Shakespearean heroines. In the mid-eighties, she made a seamless transition to film, appearing in projects alongside an impressive brood of hard-drinking, well-respected English actors such as Michael Caine, Peter O'Toole, and the late Oliver Reed. Toward the end of the eighties, she adopted a flawless American accent to play a farm wife left alone by her husband's suicide to battle land grabbers, tornadoes, and a shifty con man played by Aidan Quinn. The film *Songs from the Heartland* garnered seven Academy Award nominations. It won two. Best score and best actress in a leading role. Claire Richards was Hollywood royalty. And I was about to be her costar in Wallace Goodwin's play. I didn't know whether to scream for joy or throw up from nerves. How was Claire Richards going to react to the news that she was sharing the same stage with Jarrod Jarvis? The only award I had ever gotten for acting was from some child-development organization for convincingly playing a bed wetter during the fourth season of *Go to Your Room*.

I decided to put my reservations aside and prepare for my extended trip overseas. Luckily I was so busy renewing my passport and shopping for a new "serious actor" wardrobe at Fred Segal, I barely noticed the savage reviews that hit the papers on the day *Creeps*, a film by Larry Levant, opened in two hundred theaters. I did manage to catch a few of the choicest sound bites. "This film gave me the *Creeps*. And not in a good way!" screamed *USA Today*. "I was hoping the axe-wielding killer would step off the screen and put me out of my misery!" declared Rex Reed. And in a nod to my appearance in the film, Richard Roeper of *Ebert and Roeper* said, "Baby, don't even think about going to this movie!"

The film opened well below the top ten moneymakers for the weekend, barely grossing a quarter of a million. We would be gone from multiplexes within a week. But I didn't care. *Creeps* would soon be just a distant unpleasant memory. In a few days, I would be sharing a bottle of scotch at Kettners with Ian McKellan and Maggie Smith and swapping war stories about our show-business experiences.

I had committed to four weeks of rehearsals and a three-month run. The producers would put me, my fellow castmates from abroad, and the Goodwins up at the swanky Savoy Hotel in Covent Garden during the duration of the play. I was ecstatic. This was shaping up to be my best job ever. I couldn't imagine anything going wrong. Of course, whenever I say that, something usually goes wrong. And this time, it shook my entire world.

# Chapter 2

It was an idle Tuesday. Less than a week before I was scheduled to leave for London. Laurette and I were having lunch at Dalt's, a chain restaurant located across the street from Warner Brothers in Burbank that boasted an artery-clogging menu of comfort food. Laurette and I made a pact before we picked up our menus to order salads for our entrees, but caved to the temptation of noshing on their delectable fried onion rings as we debated on whether to get the stir-fry salad or the chicken Caesar.

Laurette had faxed the signed contract to the producers in London that morning, so we felt an impromptu celebration was in order.

"What am I going to do with you gone for so long?" Laurette sighed.

"You're coming over to see me, right?"

"Of course. But I can't stay the whole time. I have other clients, you know."

I always forgot about Laurette's other clients. Most actors prefer believing their manager's entire life is solely dedicated to finding them employment. It helps us sleep at night.

"I'll try to fly over for opening night after we get back from

Hawaii," Laurette said, dipping a thick battered onion ring in a small paper cup of ketchup and then tossing it in her mouth. "And of course I'll do a little shopping, but we're only talking a few days."

The harsh reality of this job was finally settling in. No Charlie. No Laurette. No Snickers. And no Diane Sawyer on *Good Morning America* to update me on all the world's overnight news as I shaved and did my sit-ups in the morning. I could only hope the British version of Diane would be as warm and soothing when I woke up and flipped on the TV.

"Four months is an awfully long time to be over there," I said.

"You'll have a blast," Laurette said. "You probably won't even want to come home when it's over. The Brits love kitsch. They *all* remember *Go to Your Room*. That crappy show is syndicated everywhere! You'll be a guest on Graham Norton, and the whole country will fall in love with you."

Graham Norton was an openly gay, outrageously funny talk-show host Charlie and I watched religiously on the BBC America cable network and more recently on Comedy Central. My name had just enough camp value to possibly get me a spot on his show. But I was getting ahead of myself. I hadn't even started packing yet, and already I was sitting on a couch next to Hugh Grant chatting up Graham.

"How does Charlie feel about all this?" Laurette said. She knew Charlie had issues with long separations and had been uncharacteristically mum on the subject of me flying the coop for four months.

I shrugged. "I think he's resigned to it, as usual. But he did promise to take a week off from work and fly over for the opening."

"Oh, good. Then I'll have a travel buddy."

"Larry's not going to come?"

Laurette shook her head. "He's close to signing a deal for a Disney movie. And preproduction starts the day after we get home from Maui."

My ears perked up. *Creeps* was a complete and utter disaster. How could this be? Laurette was reading my mind.

"I know, I know, but the studio's desperate. They've got a small window for one of their teenage girl stars, and it's an easy shoot, and they loved Larry's first independent film. I think they're all turning a blind eye to his latest opus because they need to get this movie out quick to coincide with the girl's new pop album."

Welcome to Hollywood. The only place in the world where people fail and then get promoted. I was happy for Larry. He was a decent guy, a vast improvement over Laurette's last disastrous relationship. I'd call him later to congratulate him and inquire about any characters in the new movie that might be right for me. That's what actors call multitasking.

I was suddenly distracted by the television over the bar. Dalt's was a wide space packed with oversized booths and tables. Laurette and I were seated at the window next to the neon green reversed letters that spelled out "Dalt's" for the passing cars on Olive Avenue. The restaurant's bar was clear across the room, but thanks to the laser eye surgery I had performed on me three years ago, I had a crystal-clear view of the TV screen. And what I saw was like a kick in the stomach. There was a news bulletin regarding a violent police shoot-out in Westwood Village, a once-illustrious neighborhood just south of the University of California, Los Angeles campus that lost its upscale luster after a gangbanger shot a bystander standing in line for a movie some years back. Charlie had left the house this morning and told me he was tracking a homicide suspect who worked at a mystery book shop in the Westwood area. The man was suspected of murdering his live-in lover, but the police were having trouble pinning the crime on him. Charlie had been assigned to the case just over a week ago and was working overtime to accumulate enough physical evidence to warrant an arrest.

Laurette noticed me staring and shifted around in her seat to see what I was watching so intently. After a few moments, she spun back around.

"Where's Charlie?" she said.

I pointed to the television screen. Laurette nodded as her mind raced.

"I think you should call him."

I fumbled around for my cell phone before realizing I had left it in Laurette's car. Without waiting for me to explain, Laurette fished hers out of her purse and handed it to me.

I kept staring at the TV screen in a mild state of shock as I began punching numbers into the phone. Two cops down. A suspect holed up in the bookshop armed with a rifle and three hostages. Charlie was going to be okay. Charlie was going to be okay.

Charlie's deep, gentle voice answered. "This is Charlie . . ." A wave of relief washed over me until I realized I had gotten his voice mail. "Leave a message after the beep."

I waited and then, in a measured tone, I spoke, trying desperately to conceal my panic. "Hi, sweetheart, it's me. Been thinking about you. Call me when you get this. Hope you're having a good day." I wanted to kick myself. Hope you're having a good day? What kind of lame way was that to end the call? Whenever my mind was clouded, I always managed to blurt out something stupid.

Lunch was over. There was no way Laurette and I would even be able to pretend everything was fine. She signaled the waitress to bring us our check, then slid out of the booth, dropped a few bills onto the table, and headed for the door. I followed her in a numb state. She didn't have to tell me where we were going. I knew. Westwood Village.

We climbed into Laurette's Cadillac SUV and barreled out of the parking structure below Dalt's and ten floors of office buildings. Laurette decided it would be faster to head over the hill by way of Coldwater Canyon, a stretch of road over a mountain dividing Los Angeles and the San Fernando Valley. But there was construction near the top of the hill just south of Mulholland Drive, the famous scenic road along the top of the mountain and namesake of David Lynch's weird cult movie that incredibly garnered a few Oscar nods. Traffic was backed up, and it took the better part of an hour to finally break past it.

I tried calling Charlie's cell a few more times with no luck. I just kept getting his voice mail. We rode in silence. Laurette tried to break the nervous tension by turning on the radio, but neither of us was in the mood for Ryan Seacrest's relentlessly chipper, metrosexual, thinly veiled fey personality, so she quickly shut it off.

I had left four messages. Usually by now Charlie would call back. He was never without his cell phone. And even if he was swamped, he would take the ten seconds to ring me back and tell me he would talk to me later. The nerves in my gut continued to grow and expand.

We reached Sunset Boulevard, where Laurette turned right, pressing her foot on the accelerator and weaving around the slower drivers as we raced toward UCLA, took a fast left on Hilgard, a street running parallel to the campus, and shot south toward Westwood Village. Only a few blocks away, my cell phone finally rang. Laurette and I exchanged hopeful looks. I took a breath and answered the phone.

"Charlie?" I said.

"No. Ned Winters."

Ned was Charlie's partner. He was about ten years younger than I was, in his mid-twenties, fresh-faced, eager, and unabashedly homophobic. Or at least he was until he was partnered with Charlie. Two weeks in, Ned asked Charlie if the picture of me on his desk was of his brother, and Charlie, almost absentmindedly, replied, "Nope. Boyfriend." Within minutes, Ned had put in for a transfer. The thought of a gay dude watching his back was unsettling to say the least for the Kansas City native until Charlie saved his life in the line of duty. Ned froze up on a rooftop downtown as they closed in on a sniper. Ned ordered the sniper to drop his rifle. The suspect complied, but simultaneously reached for something tucked away in his belt. Ned waited too long. Charlie didn't. Charlie took the guy out with one shot. One more second and he would have had the opportunity to fire at Ned and probably kill him. Ned cancelled his transfer request. His then girlfriend Rita, a gorgeous young Latina social worker who is a huge fan of *Queer Eye for the Straight Guy*, also contributed enormously to Ned's newfound enlightenment over the last few years. Now we double date.

"What's up, Ned?" I asked warily.

Silence. At first I thought I had lost the call. My cell phone always cut out at the most crucial point in a conversation. I was forever cursing Verizon Wireless.

"Ned?"

"Jarrod . . ." Ned's voice trailed off. He was still with me. And my heart stopped.

"What, Ned? What? Where's Charlie?"

"He's been shot," Ned said, choking up.

"Where is he?" I was fighting back tears now. This was like a bad dream. One I had been having ever since Charlie and I started dating.

"We're at UCLA Medical Center," Ned said. "They just wheeled him into surgery."

I didn't need any more details. Those could come later. I just had to get to his side.

I turned to Laurette, who didn't need an explanation to know what was happening. I told her to get us to the hospital.

"We'll be there in a few minutes," I said to Ned before ending the call. I bit down on my lip, determined not to lose it. Charlie was going to need me, so I wasn't about to unravel.

Laurette, on the other hand, was a complete mess by the time we parked in the covered parking structure adjacent to the hospital. She was sobbing uncontrollably, and I squeezed her hand as we raced up the walkway to the main entrance. I knew she hated herself for not being a pillar of support, but Laurette was an emotional powder keg ready to burst into tears at any given moment, even during a very special episode of *Everwood*. We charged up to the information desk, found out on which floor they were operating on Charlie, and hurried toward the elevators.

It was the longest three-floor ride I ever endured. Laurette grabbed a tissue out of her purse and wiped away her tears, sniffling and apologizing for not being stronger. I gripped her hand and raised it to my lips and kissed it softly. When the elevator doors opened on our floor, we both took a sharp inhale of breath to steel ourselves for what was to come before stepping out.

The overhead fluorescent lighting was blinding, and the steady procession of nurses and attendants bustling back and forth was confusing and disorienting. I had no idea where to go or what to do.

"Jarrod," said a familiar voice from behind me.

I turned to see Ned, his eyes red and puffy, walking toward us. He instinctively grabbed me and hugged me. We stood there embracing for what seemed like an eternity. Ned didn't want to let go. He was almost as upset as I was. When he finally stepped back, tears welling up in his eyes again, he knew what he had to do.

"We've been closing in on this suspect for a week. Charlie got a warrant, wanted to search the bookstore where he worked. The guy seemed almost happy to oblige, but when we started looking around the back storage room, we heard him cocking a gun, and before I knew what was happening, he was firing at us.

I ducked behind a box of books. Charlie was out in the open. There was nowhere for him to go. By the time I got my gun out and started firing back, Charlie was down." Ned broke down. "It was my job to keep an eye on the guy. But I didn't. I blew it."

Laurette collapsed in a chair and buried her head in her hands.

"How bad is it?" I said, still fiercely determined to keep my cool.

"One bullet in the right arm. Another in the left leg."

No vital organs. This was a good sign.

Ned brushed away the streaming tears on his face with a forearm. "And one in the chest."

Everything was dizzy. I had to grab Ned's shoulder to keep myself steady. It didn't seem real to me that Charlie might die. That after three years of a sometimes euphoric, sometimes maddening, always loving relationship, he might leave me.

Ned felt compelled to continue even though I had stopped listening. "Somebody heard the shots and called the police. A unit was already in the area, so they arrived within seconds. They managed to distract the shooter long enough for me to drag Charlie out a back door. There were a couple of people still in the store, so he kept them as hostages. He fired a warning shot and hit a patrolman out front. They've been trying to reason with him since then, but the guy's a nutcase."

"Do you have any idea how long he's going to be in surgery?" I said.

Ned shook his head. "They haven't told me anything."

Down the hall the hostage situation was playing out on a TV mounted on the wall. Word was out that the suspect, cornered and desperate, finally turned the gun on himself. The two hostages ran out of the store physically unharmed but emotionally spent. The ordeal was over. Mine was just beginning.

Once the reporters on TV began verifying Detective Charlie

Peters as one of the shooting victims, my phone began ringing nonstop. I shut it off and stuffed it in my back pocket.

Hours passed. Ned's wife, Rita, joined us and brought takeout from a Greek diner across the street from their apartment building in Silver Lake. The four of us sat in the hallway, quietly contemplating the worst-case scenario of this unexpected tragedy.

Laurette stepped away to call her boyfriend, Larry, to update him on the situation. I called my parents in Florida to break the news. Though my mother, Priscilla, always struggled with me being gay, her love for me was unwavering, and her love for Charlie was equally unshakable. She tried to remain calm for my sake as I relayed the details. My father, Clyde, was the more emotional one of the duo and wept so hard on the phone, my mother asked him to hang up the extension because she couldn't hear what I was saying. Talking to them was a comfort for the simple fact that it took up time and provided me with a few minutes of relief from my anguished thoughts.

Daylight slipped away, and we sat in the off-white, sterile halls of UCLA Medical Center. Finally, a few minutes before midnight, a young Asian doctor, no more than thirty-five, short and compact, burst through a pair of metal swinging doors and marched toward us. Ned sprang to his feet, signaling to me that this was the man trying to save Charlie's life.

"I'm Dr. Lee," he said, his face tight, almost unwilling to give me any hint of Charlie's condition. "Which one of you is Jarrod?"

I stepped forward. My stomach flip-flopped like a trout on the deck of a fishing boat. Sweat beads formed on my brow. I was squeezing Laurette's hand so hard I half expected it to break.

"I am," I said, my voice cracking.

"Charlie's asking for you," Dr. Lee said with a warm smile.


Although Dr. Lee was able to remove all three bullets, Charlie remained in the hospital in recovery for three days. When I was finally able to bring him home, he was still in a lot of pain and was confined to his bed. I instantly became a doting Florence Nightingale, running to the pharmacy to stock up on his prescribed pain-relief medications, fixing his favorite meals (okay, picking up the phone and ordering his favorite Indian food dishes for delivery), and making sure the TV remote was within his reach so he could absentmindedly flip between ESPN and MSNBC.

During his surgery, I had plenty of time to consider life without him, and I was determined never to let that happen. Even the possibility of losing someone you love can shake you at the core and force you to reexamine your priorities. Which was why I was totally caught off guard early Friday morning when Wallace Goodwin called me.

"Hey, Jarrod, just checking in. Katrina and I are on Virgin Air. Which airline are you flying?" he said.

"I'm sorry," I said. "What are you talking about?"

"Your flight to London on Sunday," he said, a bit perturbed by my distant tone.

"Wallace, didn't Laurette call you? I'm pulling out of the show. I can't leave town right now."

I was standing in the bedroom a few feet from Charlie, who was watching Lester Holt's midday news update on MSNBC. We both loved Lester with his broad shoulders, chocolate skin, and commanding voice. But even Lester couldn't hold Charlie's attention. He was more interested in my conversation with Wallace.

"I'm sure you're aware that my boyfriend was shot in the line of duty," I said, turning my back to the patient and lowering my voice.

"Yes, I saw it on the news. But I heard he's on the mend," Wallace said. "So what's the problem?"

"Someone needs to be here to take care of him," I said. I was about to ask Wallace if he would still go to London if Katrina had been injured. But after seeing their ferocious bickering at Starbucks, I already knew the answer.

"Jarrod, I think you should still go," Charlie said.

I spun around and vigorously shook my head at Charlie. He wasn't thinking clearly, a good sign that the painkillers were doing their magic.

"Wallace, I can't really talk now," I said.

"I'm serious," Charlie pressed on. "I want you to keep your commitment to the play."

He was delirious. Had I accidentally doubled his dose of medication?

I stared at him a moment before returning to my conversation with Wallace. "I need to call you back."

"Jarrod, you have a contract," Wallace wailed before I hung up on him.

I turned to Charlie. "What's all this about? You trying to get rid of me?"

"Yes," Charlie said matter-of-factly.

It was like a sharp slap across the face. "Why? What did I do?"

"You've been wonderful. I've never seen such a dedicated, hardworking nursemaid, who hovers over the patient all day and all night, full of good cheer and kind words, and I have to tell you, babe, it's driving me nuts!"

Snickers, who was curled up next to Charlie on the bed, lifted her head as if to nod in agreement.

"I just want you to be comfortable," I said.

"I get that. And I appreciate it. But I miss my boyfriend. The self-absorbed, sarcastic, career-obsessed former child star that I fell in love with," he said with a sly smile. "And believe me, when you always put my needs first, it's like I don't know you anymore."

I didn't know whether to hug him or hit him.

"Who will take care of you if I go?" I was already warming to the idea, since it meant so much to Charlie.

"I already called Isis. She's available. And back in Cairo she worked part-time as a candy striper at an American GI hospital."

"How long have you been plotting to get rid of me?" I said, still not sure if his burning desire to get me out of the country was a good thing.

"Since the moment you blew off a callback for *Crossing Jordan* to go buy me a new bedpan," he said. "That's just not right."

I looked him over, trying to determine if he was just saying all of this because he didn't want me moping over giving up the play in London. But he was dead serious. I had gone overboard trying to take care of him because I was so frightened by the prospect of not having him around anymore. I was suffocating him, and he was just trying to come up for some air. And the best way for him to do that was to make sure I was on that plane to the UK on Sunday.

"So you're sure Isis will move in and be here at all times?" I said.

"Yes," he said. "She predicts I'll recover in no time."

Isis was not only a dear friend but also a dead-on psychic whose accuracy rate was astounding.

"Did she happen to mention if the play is going to be a success?"

Charlie broke into a wide smile. "He's back!"

He was right. My boyfriend was healing from three bullet holes in his body, and I still couldn't resist inquiring about my chances for a big career comeback.

After a little more protesting on my part, Charlie laid down the law. I was going to call Wallace back and reassure him that I would be at the Old Apollo on Monday for the first cast read-through of the play. Isis would move in to tend to Charlie's needs, and if he made significant progress in his recovery during the next month or so, both of them would eventually fly over to see the show before it closed.

But if I had known I would encounter more violence abroad than from the horrific shoot-out in Westwood Village, I never would have agreed to the plan.

# Chapter 3

I almost missed my British Airways flight from Los Angeles to London because I lost track of time going over my long list of instructions for Isis, who would be de facto nursemaid in my absence. I wanted Charlie to be well taken care of while I was gone, and Isis was one of the few people I trusted to get the job done right. The day before, we had made our biweekly pilgrimage to Price Club, where she stocked up on bottles of soda and canned goods and wrapped meats that would feed a small Iraqi village. I swore I wouldn't have blinked twice if one day I found out Isis was part of some survivalist militia group who packed their basements with food and ammo, waiting for the right opportunity to overthrow the government. Isis spared no expense (especially since the bill was going on my American Express card) to ensure Charlie's comfort. She bought four packages of Snickers bars (twenty-four per package) since she knew they were Charlie's favorite (so much so we named our dog after them). She also splurged on fresh linens, a small library of best-sellers, and a brand new TiVo machine so Charlie could rest and still not miss the week's newest installment of Donald Trump's runaway hit *The Apprentice*.

With Isis moved into the house and the cupboards fully stocked, I felt safe kissing Charlie good-bye and climbing into the chauffeur-driven Town Car for the forty-five-minute ride to Los Angeles International Airport. Unfortunately, I unwisely suggested to the driver he take the Hollywood Freeway to downtown and change to the 110 freeway south, which hooks up with the 105 Imperial Freeway that is a straight shot to the airport. Figuring downtown would be a ghost town on a Saturday night, I was startled to discover that Justin Timberlake was playing the Staples Center, and traffic was at a standstill as hordes of teenyboppers and their parents clogged the freeways in both directions. I nervously watched the precious minutes tick away as the frustrated driver pounded on his steering wheel, muttering curses under his breath.

When we finally made it to the international terminal at LAX, I had less than an hour to make it through check-in and security and onto the plane. Compounding my unfortunate situation were three heavy-duty Samonsite bags crammed with three months of clothing and skin products. If I missed this flight, I would have to wait until morning to catch the next one, and that would put me into London dangerously close to the time I was to report to the theater.

I didn't have time to call Charlie as I was herded through the security checkpoint and ushered to the aircraft for immediate takeoff. Luckily the producers had sprung for a business-class seat, so I was able to stretch out and flip through *Us* magazine as the plane taxied for takeoff. After a brief pause, we shot down the tarmac, lifted up, and sailed over an endless sea of twinkling city lights before jetting out over the Pacific, looping into a turn, and heading east.

There was still a gnawing feeling in the pit of my stomach that I shouldn't be leaving Charlie in his condition. But he was so insistent and almost happy to see me go. I guess I had been a wee bit insufferable after landing this high-profile play, not to mention more than a little overbearing when he arrived home from the hospital. With worried thoughts of Charlie swimming around in my head, I was out within minutes. I hadn't planned on sleeping during the entire flight, not with a new Al Franken book to laugh my way through. But not only did I miss the shrimp cocktail and beef Wellington, the free-flowing merlot and most importantly, the hot fudge sundae, I squinted my eyes open to sadly discover I had slumbered through most of a Sandra Bullock romantic comedy the in-flight magazine described as "uproarious" and "delightful." Okay, so that wasn't much of a tragedy. But I do like to keep abreast of what my fellow actors are doing. I smiled to myself, wondering if Sandra Bullock would be jealous that I was appearing in a play with the incomparable Claire Richards. Who wouldn't want to share a stage with such a theatrical legend? Of course, I would no doubt be willing to switch places with Sandra if it meant garnering just one of her fifteen-million-dollar paydays.

When the 767 touched down at Heathrow on a late Sunday afternoon, it was chilly and cloudy with spotty rain. Typical English weather. After a brutal couple of hours waiting in line at customs, securing my three oversized bags, and fighting off some German tourists for a taxicab, I settled back for the ride into London. I had only been to the city twice. Once when I was fourteen and we shot a TV movie in London based on our hit sitcom. It was all the rage at the time. All the shows were doing it. *Family Ties Vacation* and *The Facts of Life Down Under* (which was a publicly demanded sequel to the widely popular *The Facts of Life Goes to Paris*). Ours was cleverly titled *Go to Your Room at Buckingham Palace* and had to do with our vacationing family unraveling a convoluted plot to discredit the queen of England. We were so busy shooting a tightly packed fifteen-day schedule I never got to explore much of the city's offerings. A few years later, when I was nineteen, I figured it was time I "bummed around Europe" but I only briefly skirted through London.

There was a cute twenty-five-year-old Austrian named Arno who was waiting for me in Salzburg with promises of a memorable *Sound of Music* tour, so I wasn't about to waste a week bopping around jolly old England.

Once *Murder Can Be Civilized* was up and running, my plan was to make use of my free time and really see the city and its surrounding areas. My father's side of the family dated as far back as the Boston Tea Party. They originally fled the mother country to escape exorbitant taxes, which is what some in my family still attempt to do to this day. I had a deep familial connection to the British Isles and was anxious to soak up all it had to offer. My father, Clyde, a fervent genealogy buff, had e-mailed me the names of family members whose descendants might still be living in villages north of the city. I had printed out his information and stuffed it in my luggage. There was a lot to do while I was here.

The taxicab pulled up to the famous landmark front entrance of the Savoy. I was blown away by its opulence. I had read up on this historic hotel that opened its doors to the public in 1889. Throughout the following century and beyond, the Savoy sparkled with glittering parties and hosted a number of dignitaries and celebrities such as Sir Winston Churchill, Eleanor Roosevelt, Charlie Chaplin, and more recently, U2.

After I checked in, Arthur the friendly bellhop, in his late seventies and wearing a dusty gray suit with black stripes and a thin charcoal tie, entertained me with a bouquet of colorful stories as we rode the elevator up to my floor. He claimed to have been working at the hotel in the mid-fifties on the day Marilyn Monroe held a press conference at the Savoy when she came to Britain to star in *The Prince and the Showgirl* with Sir Laurence Olivier. He also said he once brought up a bottle of champagne to Elizabeth Taylor, who spent the first night of her honeymoon at the hotel with Nicky Hilton.

Once Arthur's shaky hand inserted the key into the old-fashioned lock and pushed open the door, I followed him inside to find a deluxe suite with a plush king-size bed, fresh flowers and fruit on an antique oak table, and a breathtaking view of the river Thames. We were going to have to sell out every last performance if the producers were ever going to recoup the pounds spent on this room.

Arthur leaned in conspiratorially and said, "I'm not supposed to talk about other guests, but this is the room where Elton John stayed once."

"Really?" I said, a fool for gossip. "How was he?"

"A total gentleman," Arthur said. "But one night he answered the phone while running his bath. These baths fill up fast, mind you; there was a flood, which caused considerable damage to the rooms below!"

"Oh my," I said, anxious to e-mail this tidbit to all my friends back home. Arthur then launched into a litany of amenities at my disposal, and after a long-winded speech stretching well beyond the time it took Halle Berry to thank all the African Americans who helped make her Oscar win possible, Arthur was finally ready to take his leave. I overtipped him, mostly due to his generous Sir Elton story, and after he finally left I began to unpack.

I was thrilled with the abundance of closet and drawer space to put away a three-month wardrobe. Once that was done, I calculated just how late or early it was back in Los Angeles and picked up the phone to dial an operator and phone home to Charlie. Before I got an answer, there was a knock at the door. I was hoping Arthur remembered another juicy bon mot, perhaps a Bette Davis temper tantrum because room service put mayo on her club sandwich or Madonna getting noise complaints from the adjoining rooms while having nasty sex with Wesley Snipes. I was ready for anything. But when I opened the door, the last thing I was ready for was to be staring into the smiling face of Claire Richards.

"Jarrod, darling, you made it!" she said as she planted a perfectly theatrical kiss on my lips and swept into the room carrying a bottle of Dom Perignon. "Is this a bad time, love?"

"No . . . I mean . . . no," I stammered like a shy schoolboy.

Claire was much smaller in person, barely five feet four inches. On screen she had such a commanding presence, her tiny size was rather disconcerting. Her hair was cut short, she wore a sleeveless white blouse and flower print skirt, and several gold bracelets jangled on both wrists.

She lifted up the bottle of champagne. "I'm just down the hall. I told them to ring me up when you got here so I could pop by and offer a proper hello." She pointed to the label. "Nineteen eighty-five. A very good year, apparently." A bottle of Dom Perignon from the eighties had to be worth in the high hundreds. I searched around for some glasses as I tried to get used to the idea of splitting a bottle of champagne with the incredible Claire Richards.

I heard a loud pop, and white foam flowed out of the bottle and all over Claire's arm. She let out a hearty laugh as she marched into the bathroom, grabbed a fluffy white towel off the rack, and started wiping herself off. I managed to secure a pair of wineglasses from above the minibar as Claire shot a fast series of questions at me regarding my flight, my opinion of the accommodations, my excitement over the play. I kept my answers brief simply because I was still in a state of shock over Claire's magical appearance in my room.

Claire filled up our glasses to the rim, then plopped down on the bed and crossed her legs. Her print skirt slid up and I got a clear view of her extraordinarily well-preserved and impressively toned gams. Claire might have been in her late forties, but she had a youthful vitality, a soft face with nary a wrinkle, and a jaw-dropping, incredibly sexy body. If I were straight, my mind would be working overtime trying to figure out how to get her under the covers in a horizontal position.

She tapped her glass to mine. "Here's to us finally working together, Jarrod."

At first I thought she must be confusing me with someone else. Another cast member, maybe. But she said my name. Jarrod. How many other actors named Jarrod could she have worked with? She downed her champagne and instantly poured herself another. After gulping down a generous sip, she turned her sparkling hazel eyes in my direction.

"Baby, don't even go there!" She waited for my reaction, and then howled with laughter.

She knew it. She was familiar with my catchphrase. This was too much.

I must have pleased her with my stunned reaction because she continued guffawing until her glass was empty and she had to focus on filling it up again.

"I'm surprised you even know about the show I was on," I said, still in a mesmerizing haze of admiration and abject fear.

"Oh, I never saw it, love. I just did my homework when I heard you'd been cast."

Of course. Somehow I couldn't imagine Claire Richards delivering a spellbinding performance as Lady Macbeth at the Old Vic and then racing home to watch the episode where I shoplift a squirt gun from the local department store.

"But I think it's utterly charming," she said adding a slight lilt to her elevated English accent. I loved that accent. In fact, I always imagined dating a Hugh Grant or a Jude Law, someone oh so very British, and attending tea parties and pheasant-shooting weekends like in *Gosford Park*. That was long before my world changed forever when I met meat-and-potatoes Midwestern boy Charlie Peters.

Claire pounded me with more questions involving my career. She appeared genuinely interested, and it scared the hell out of me. How could this living legend be at all interested in my humble career scraps? But she was, and it made her eminently likable. Within minutes, we had polished off the '85 bottle of Dom Perignon. Claire scooped up the phone and ordered three more bottles. Luckily, she made sure to charge the cost to her own room, so there was nothing to compromise my pleasant buzz.

After what seemed like an endless Barbara Walters interview, with Claire peppering me with questions, I managed to turn the tables and grill Claire about her own life and career. She filled out her résumé with enough outrageous anecdotes and sexual escapades to make even Arthur the seen-it-all bellhop blanch. Some of the biggest names in show business were supporting players in the life of Claire Richards. The drunker we got, the more graphic Claire's descriptions became, and at one point she made me promise to take a certain knighted actor's astounding penis size to my grave. By midnight, we were best friends. And sloshed. The room was spinning, and when I stood up to open the last bottle, Claire had to grab my arm to keep me from falling over. We erupted into a fit of giggles.

Suddenly there was a loud rapping at the door. I covered my mouth, fearing it might be some snotty English lord or uptight duchess from next door put out by our loud partying. Claire gripped the bedpost and hauled herself to her feet and stumbled toward the door. I hid behind the swath of nylon curtain that draped down over the window overlooking the Thames.

Claire looked back at me as she reached for the door handle, snorting as she twisted it and flung open the door. Standing there was a towering figure of manhood, a muscular young stud in a tight-fitting tank top and sweatpants, arms ripped, and longish wavy auburn hair that flowed down just above his shoulders. I was so struck by his impressive stature and handsome face, without even knowing who he was I was ready to invite him inside.

Claire, in what I considered a bold move even for her, reached up with her hands, clapped them against his cheeks, and pulled his face down low enough for her to kiss him. Claire slobbered all over him until he finally stood erect, leaving her pursed lips behind.

"Darling, this is Jarrod, the boy I was telling you about."

Boy? God, I loved her.

The man looked me over, unimpressed. His eyes flickered to the four empty champagne bottles that littered the room, and he grimaced before grunting a reply.

Claire swung back around in my direction and as she fluttered toward the bed she slurred, "This is Liam, my boyfriend."

He was at least twenty years younger than she was. You go, girl.

Liam offered his hand. "Liam Killoran."

I shook it, my hand disappearing in his giant paw.

"Liam was one of my acting students when I taught a class at the Royal Academy last year. Who knew a one-day stint as a guest lecturer would result in me meeting my soul mate?"

She batted her eyes seductively at Liam, who replied with a tight smile.

"God, the minute I saw him in the window, I just knew I had to have him," she said. I could see why.

"It's late, Claire. You have to be at the script reading in a few hours," Liam said. He wanted to break up the party. Now.

I looked at the clock. It was three in the morning. This was not good. I had been so swept away by my indoctrination into the wonderful world of Claire Richards I had completely forgotten why I was even here in the first place. I had a job to do, and it started at eight in the morning. Not only would I be fighting jet lag, I would be operating on four hours of sleep.

Claire sighed as she took one final swig from the champagne bottle and set it down on the dresser. She shuffled over to me, wrapped her arms around my waist, and kissed me full on the mouth. I was facing Liam, whose face flushed with anger. As

Claire pressed her lips against mine, the seconds ticked by, and I kept one eye on Liam. He looked as if his head was ready to explode.

Claire finally pulled away, patted my cheek with one hand while squeezing my butt with the other, and then slithered back to Liam. He grasped her elbow and steered her toward the door. She wrenched her head around as Liam forced her out the door.

"Good night, sweet prince," she said as Liam slammed the door behind them. And thus ended my first night in London.


When I awoke a scant three hours later to the sounds of a Rolling Stones classic on the clock radio, my head felt like it had been pressed through a meat grinder. The lingering aftereffects of a veritable fountain of champagne was a steady throbbing that not even a couple of Tylenol tablets and a blistering-hot shower could dull. I threw on some jeans and a polo shirt and slipped on a pair of docksiders and hurried out the door clutching my *Murder Can Be Civilized* script.

I quickly consulted my *London Visitor's Guide* for the best walking route. After that, it was a short twenty-minute stroll along the busy Strand, filled with shops and department stores, through the beautiful converted flower market of Covent Garden, into the bustling arts scene in the heart of the West End. Finally, I turned onto Shaftsbury just a few blocks away from the old Apollo Theatre. As I hustled through the rush-hour crowd, I hit the home-access button on my cell phone and clamped it to my ear as a lone signal shot out across the world to connect me to my life thousands of miles away.

After several rings, a harried, familiar voice picked up. "Yes, what is it?"

"Isis, it's me," I said, shoving a finger in my free ear to block out the car horns and sirens of early-morning London.

"Who?" she said, sounding hurried and uninterested.

"Jarrod."

There was a slight pause as she considered my unexpected call before she answered in an anguished whine. "It wasn't my fault!"

"What? What wasn't your fault?"

"Charlie's fine. He just twisted his ankle when he fell down the stairs."

"Charlie fell?"

"The doctor said it could've been a lot worse."

My head was spinning from both my overindulgence in champagne and this latest revelation from Hollywood.

"Where's Charlie now?"

"He's in the backyard with the physical therapist. He's very cute, by the way."

"Charlie?"

"No, the physical therapist. Well, Charlie is too, but you should see Chad. What a hunk."

"I really didn't need to hear that detail," I said. "How did he fall?"

"He wanted some water and went against my instructions and tried walking up the stairs. The bullet wound started to hurt and when he went to touch it, he lost his balance."

Our house was inverted, meaning the living room, dining room, den, and kitchen are on the top floor, with the bedrooms located on the lower level.

"Where were you, Isis?"

Another long, considered pause.

"Isis?"

"Don't be mad."

"Just tell me."

She sighed. "There was a sale at Kmart on Martha Stewart pillow cases. I just couldn't pass it up."

"I told you not to leave him alone!"

"I know! But they were 30 percent off. You and I both know that doesn't happen every day. And we need to support Martha after she had to serve that horrific jail sentence."

"Isis . . ." I said, mustering up an admonishing tone.

"I told Charlie you wouldn't want me to go, but he insisted. He promised me he'd be fine. But I heard your voice scolding me the whole time, which is why I rushed to get there, so the scratch is partly your fault."

"Scratch? What scratch?"

"More of a dent, really. I drove your Prius. You said I could."

"In the event of an emergency!"

"You don't call a 30 percent off sale at Kmart an emergency? I got some new sheets for you too!"

"What happened to the car?"

"I was so worried about getting home to Charlie, I guess I wasn't concentrating on my driving and didn't see that steel pole . . ."

I took a deep breath. "How bad is it?"

"It's just the back end of the car. You barely notice it. At least when you're standing in front of the car. I don't care what the witness said. I didn't crush the whole bumper."

"Crushed? A witness used the word 'crushed'?"

"Yeah, but he was a big drama queen."

"Isis, I don't want you driving my car again."

"Don't worry. I'm never getting behind the wheel again. Besides, it's making all kinds of funny noises now. Doesn't seem safe to me."

I took a deep breath and exhaled. *Stay calm. Stay calm.*

"I have to pick up Snickers at the vet later today," she said. "But don't get excited, I'll take a cab."

"Vet? Snickers is at the vet?"

"Didn't you get my e-mail?"

"I just got here last night!"

"She got into that package of candy bars we bought for Charlie. Ate every last one."

"Chocolate is toxic for dogs!" I yelled.

"I know. That's why I didn't want to take any chances and took her straight over to the emergency room at the pet clinic. But Dr. Aboulafai looked her over and said she'll be fine. He just kept her overnight for observation."

I wanted to ask clairvoyant Isis why she hadn't predicted any of these disasters *before* I left. I could practically feel her quaking on the other end of the phone. I had put her in charge of my home, and she was botching the job. But I wasn't about to make things worse by chewing her out. Dealing with stress wasn't her strong suit.

I stopped in front of the entrance to the Apollo Theatre. "Okay, I'm at my first rehearsal, so I better hang up now."

"Break a leg," she said and giggled. "Then you and Charlie will have a matching set."

"I thought you said he twisted it!"

"He did! It was a joke!"

"I'm not sure I'm going to last four months here with everything falling apart back home."

"You need to calm yourself, Jarrod. I have everything under control back here. Trust me. Besides, you may not be there for as long as you think."

"Why? What do you see? Is the play going to be a disaster?"

"No. But someone's going to leave it early."

"You mean quit? Who?"

"Is there a Connie? Or Clara?"

"Claire? Claire Richards?"

"Yeah, her. She's going to leave."

"Why? What's going to happen?"

There was empty air. I assumed Isis was channeling her spirit guides to get me more information. I was wrong.

"Chad is coming up from the backyard with Charlie now, Jarrod. I have to go and see if he needs anything. He's so damn sexy. Bye!"

Click. She was gone. And I stood paralyzed on Shaftsbury Avenue, my life back home in Los Angeles crumbling.

There was nothing much I could do from here. Laurette was in Maui with Larry. My parents were in Florida. My sister was in Maine. I had to put my faith in Isis and pray she could eventually pull her act together.

It was time to meet my director and fellow castmates. When I entered the theater, I was hit with the choking smell of cigarettes. Most of Europe has yet to adopt America's no-smoking policies in public places. A long cardboard table and chairs were set up on stage with a stack of scripts in the middle. Coffee and assorted pastries had been placed on another table off to the side. Wallace self-consciously talked to Claire as she poured herself a cup of java. He was as starstruck by her as I had been. Liam watched him from a third-row seat, a scornful look in his eye. I wondered if he was capable of smiling.

I recognized the other players who huddled in a circle, getting acquainted, near the front of the stage. Our esteemed director Kenneth Shields, bright, full of energy, and a rising star according to the London theater crowd. Kenneth was in his mid-thirties, boyishly handsome, and despite his receding hairline and doughy build, had managed to date a number of beautiful English actresses—most of them named Kate, from Winslet to Beckinsale. Kenneth was a terrific talent, and from all accounts, he was acutely aware of that fact. Still, I was excited to work with him and knew if anyone could get a decent performance out of me, it would be him. Kenneth was chatting up two of my costars, the flamboyantly gay Sir Anthony Stiles and the strikingly handsome Akshay Kapoor. Sir Anthony, a dusty, graying, weathered old coot, had a spotty career that was decaying rapidly until he officially came out as a homosexual. Suddenly he found himself cool again. All the hot directors wanted him on their marquees. I had read about his resurgence with a religious fervor since it had obvious parallels to my own public coming-out. I knew less about Akshay, a dashing East Indian man in his late twenties, around six feet, with wavy black hair gelled to perfection and a heart-melting, manipulative smile that showed off the most faultless set of teeth I had ever seen. Wallace had told me that Akshay was a big star in his native Bombay, appearing in a number of Bollywood movie musicals. More recently he was cast in the leading role of Andrew Lloyd Webber's personal salute to his homeland, *Bombay Dreams*. Akshay was, in a word, stunning, and I couldn't help but notice all the women, not to mention a few of the men, continually stealing glances his way.

Wallace spotted me out of the corner of his eye and waved me over. My stomach was flip-flopping as I made my way to the stage.

As I walked up onto the stage, Claire, who harbored not even a trace of a hangover from the night before, threw out her arms and grabbed me in a tight hug.

"So good to see you, you sexy beast!" she said, without even the slightest hint of sarcasm.

Liam shifted in his seat and let out an audible groan.

Claire's declaration drew everyone's attention and I felt all eyes in the room sizing me up and down.

Kenneth ambled over and shook my hand and offered a half smile as he said, "I look forward to working with you, Jarrod."

Sir Anthony was right behind him. I stuck out my hand to shake, but Anthony pushed it away and hugged me. He also squeezed my left butt cheek, just as Claire had done when I first met her. Was this some old English theater tradition I was unaware of? Or was I blessed with two famous admirers? Only time would tell.

Akshay nodded in my direction but kept his distance. Was he just aloof, or did he consider me beneath him? I had prepared myself for the possibility of my fellow actors looking down on me. I was a lowly sitcom star, and one from the eighties at that. Of course, I thought my troubles would come from the revered Claire, but she was the one who blurted out my familiar catchphrase upon meeting me, thrilling me beyond belief. So if Akshay was going to be the one to give me attitude, so be it. I could handle him.

Wallace trotted over and clapped me on the back. "Is this fucking cool or what?"

"Isn't Katrina coming for the reading?" I asked Wallace.

He scoffed. "Please. She said she already knew the ending so she was going to visit some museums, which is total bullshit because I caught her pilfering three of my credit cards from my wallet. She's off shopping. We won't see her until well after dark."

I nodded, still trying to squash my nerves. The first reading of the script was about to start, and though I had spent a whole week going over my lines, trying to nail my intention and emphasis, there was the very real possibility that I would be exposed as a fraud once I uttered my first few words.

Wallace prattled on about how he and Katrina were happily ensconced at the Savoy, how they dined with the producers the night before, how excited everybody was, but I let his rambling bounce right off me. I was too busy concentrating on not passing out.

Kenneth cleared his throat and clasped his hands together. "All right, everyone, I think we should get started."

The moment of truth. I kept telling myself, "Please don't be bad. Please don't be bad." I took a seat between Claire and Sir Anthony. Claire smiled at me and squeezed my knee with her hand. I turned to Sir Anthony. He did the same.

Akshay sat on the other side next to Wallace. Kenneth stood at the head of the table. There was an empty seat across from

me. When I left LA, Wallace had phoned to tell me that the crucial role of Lady Quagmire was still left to be cast. Offers had gone out to acting goddesses Dame Judi Dench and Dame Maggie Smith, but both had turned the role down flat. It was a delicious role, full of hilarious one-liners and showy moments, but alas, it was a small supporting role.

Kenneth broke into a smile. "Welcome to our first day of rehearsals for *Murder Can Be Civilized.* I'm very excited about this production. It's been my dream to work with most of you here."

Most of us? I had no delusions that he was including the prepubescent star of *Go to Your Room.* My insecurities were slowly coming to a boil.

"Now as you know, we've had quite a time casting the Lady Quagmire role, and I feared we might have to postpone the production. But our producers called in a favor, and it is with great pleasure that I can tell you our casting is complete."

Kenneth raced over to stage right, as if some grand entrance had been preplanned for the read-through. He shot out an arm and like a footman introducing the queen, bellowed, "Please welcome to our little company Dame Sylvia Horner."

I gasped. Out loud. Sylvia Horner, though nearly eighty, w still a vibrant presence in the theater. She shuffled out like a s ingenue, her white hair pulled back in a tight bun, bowing a curtseying demurely as most of the cast erupted in enthusias applause.

She looked frail, her tiny frame hunched over and her b hands begging for the ovation to stop. In a scratchy, weak vc she said, "I am overcome by your reception. I am just so pi to be included in such a distinguished company of actors."

It was all an act, of course. Sylvia Horner was at heart a ti and enjoyed mauling lesser actors who dared invade her lowed space.

Sir Anthony leapt to his feet and kissed her hand. Not

outdone, Akshay kneeled at her feet and stammered on about what an influence she had been on him in his youth and to this very day.

I stayed in my seat. Not out of disrespect, but out of complete and utter paralysis. Sylvia was going to be sitting directly across from me, watching me as I read my lines from the play. I wanted to go home. This was too much pressure.

Sylvia kissed Kenneth on the cheek and took her seat. She winked at me. I nodded, a frozen smile plastered on my face. Everybody was smiling. Everybody except Claire. She was ashen faced, trying desperately to hide her fury. This was an actress who had just been sandbagged. She was undoubtedly assured she would be the only living legend to grace the cast. I'm sure the producers thought it a wildly brilliant idea to bring Claire Richards and Dame Sylvia Horner together onstage at last. But they knew what Claire's reaction would be, and nobody had the balls to tell her beforehand. The task was left to the show's director, and he chose to downplay the ramifications by saving the announcement until it was too late.

Once all the fanfare revolving around Dame Sylvia's entrance died down, Kenneth got down to business and launched into the stage directions that set the scene and got the play off and rolling. Luckily my first line wasn't until page fifteen, so I had time to brace myself and prepare. Dame Sylvia had the first line, and she took her time getting it out. She wanted everyone to savor the moment. A line reading from the great Dame Sylvia Horner.

"I say, isn't it time for tea and crumpets yet?"

Genius. A toss-off, but so full of power and presence. The only problem was, she had the disturbing habit of spitting when she spoke. And not just a thin sliver of saliva here and there, either. She lobbed huge balls of white, foamy spit! I dodged the first one but got nailed in the nose and right cheek with two more hits. I was going to need a towel after her lengthy speech

in the second act. As a courtesy, the management would have to provide umbrellas to the first three rows of the audience.

I also could smell the gin on her breath from across the table. Her slow, deliberate line reading wasn't because she was making a meal of the text. Her eyesight was blurry from extreme intoxication and she was having trouble homing in on what the words actually were. What was it about aging English actresses and their unadulterated love of alcohol?

Claire sat motionless. Her face was masked with indifference, but internally, it was obvious she was ready to blow up and attack someone. Hopefully I wouldn't get caught in the line of fire when the time came. She was never going to stand for this. She would quit before she allowed Dame Sylvia to steal her thunder. This must have been what Isis saw in her premonition.

And as I leaned forward to grab a napkin so I could wipe the spittle from Dame Sylvia off my face, Sir Anthony reached around behind me and pinched my butt. I flashed him a scolding look. He replied by pinching it again.

We were off to a rollicking good start.

# Chapter 4

Over the next week, rehearsals for *Murder Can Be Civilized* became a free-for-all for boorish behavior. Dame Sylvia and Claire not surprisingly despised each other and went out of their way to make each other look bad. I took copious notes, hoping to one day write a memoir of this juicy experience. The diva feud at the Apollo Theatre would undoubtedly rival the divine quarreling between Bette Davis and Joan Crawford in the early sixties when they shot the camp classic *Whatever Happened to Baby Jane?* Most of the company took Dame Sylvia's side because Claire's antics were wildly out of control. If fresh flowers weren't delivered to her dressing room each morning, she would stalk out of the theater and back to the Savoy until the situation was rectified. She made a habit of undercutting her costars by sighing loudly or shaking her head in disgust if she felt their line readings were not up to snuff. Kenneth, who seemed so powerful and in control at the first script read-through, slowly disintegrated and by the second week was Claire's personal lapdog. He knew she was the star and would get butts in the seats on opening night. Dame Sylvia, though just as revered, was a supporting player. This was Claire's show. Claire knew it. And she was going to remind everyone of that fact every minute of every day. But she threatened to quit so many times, the producers got nervous and set about finding an understudy just in case she stormed out right before a performance.

There was only one person in the entire company who managed to escape Claire's devastating wrath. Me. For some reason, she found me "captivating" and "hilarious." She would sit in the back of the theater, a cigarette dangling from her mouth, when I was up onstage, quaking in my Nike Air Jordans and mumbling my way through my scenes. If one of my lines was just the slightest bit humorous, I would hear Claire guffaw in the back, clapping her hands and bellowing "Good show, Jarrod!" in her thick, scratchy upper-crust British accent.

This quickly isolated me from the rest of the cast. Dame Sylvia, who couldn't remember my name anyway, had no use for an American has-been. Akshay, distant from the beginning, just seemed to snarl whenever he saw me, as if my mere presence was insulting to him. Sir Anthony was afraid to talk to me out of fear his idol Dame Sylvia would disapprove. This, of course, didn't stop him from continuing his habit of pinching my ass whenever no one was looking. Wallace, who sat quietly behind the director and was still in a state of disbelief over the fact that his little stage thriller was actually on its way to an opening night, wisely chose to ignore me. So did his wife, Katrina, on the few occasions she showed up at the theater with a dozen shopping bags dangling from her arms to check on our progress.

But the one person harboring the most venom toward me was our esteemed director, Kenneth Shields. I coasted during the first week with very little to do. As we blocked the scenes, Kenneth appeared annoyed every time he had to address where I was going to stand. It was as if he would have preferred cutting my part out entirely. This did not inspire my confidence. In fact, if it weren't for my devoted fan Claire Richards, I probably would have fled back to LA and Charlie after the first week. We worked on scenes where I had one or two lines, so I was able to melt into the background and stay out of Kenneth's eyesight. But I knew my big scene was coming up, where Sir Anthony's character confronts me about my sordid past. It was the scene that most excited me about the part, but I was acutely terrified on the day we were scheduled to block it.

Kenneth had excused Claire for the day before we began to work on it. This was not a good sign. Without Claire hovering in the back, protecting me and applauding my efforts, Kenneth would have free rein to humiliate me. Of course, there was the possibility that I was just being paranoid. But it is very unusual for an actor to be paranoid. Not.

The theater felt disconcertingly quiet with only four of us left. Sir Anthony and I stood onstage while Kenneth and Wallace were seated in the middle of the third row.

Kenneth had his face buried deep in the script. He never looked up at me. "All right, Jarrod, go ahead."

"Where do you want me?"

Kenneth raised his eyes for a brief moment and sighed. "Where you are is fine."

I launched into my first line and got no more than four words in when Kenneth hurled his script to the floor. "Good God, Jarrod, do you think you could possibly give the lines at least a smidgen of life? Can you do that for me, Jarrod? Can you?"

I just stood there, not sure how to respond.

"What, Jarrod?" Kenneth said, sighing.

"Nothing. I—"

"We open in less than two weeks. You've given me nothing. Nothing! Do you need four cameras and a studio audience of laughing hyenas in order to act? Is that it?"

"No," I said, resisting the urge to leap off the stage and strangle him with my bare hands until his dismissive, judgmental eyes rolled up in the back of his head.

"Good. Now start again," he said, throwing Wallace an "I told you so" look. Wallace shrugged. He wasn't about to take responsibility for getting me cast.

This time I made it through a whole sentence before I was interrupted.

"Holy Christ, you're abominable! Did you spend *any* time going over the script before we started rehearsals, Jarrod, or are you naturally this flat?"

"You haven't given me a chance to—"

Kenneth sniggered. "You had five years of chances to hone your craft on that excruciatingly bland situation comedy of yours."

Wallace sat up, much more offended than I was. He had been dining out on that credit for years, and this snooty Brit was making light of its lasting impact on American pop culture. Wallace had a skewed view of the importance of *Go to Your Room*. But he bit his tongue, deciding to stay out of the fray.

"I'll be honest with you, Jarrod," Kenneth said.

"You mean you haven't been up to now?" I said.

This caught Kenneth by surprise. I was actually talking back and my sarcasm was obvious. I could tell he was mildly impressed, but he didn't want to give me any props. "You were not my first choice for this role. In fact, you were not my second, third, or fourth choice. Directors often have to make casting compromises in order to get other actors like Akshay who they know will shine. So the bottom line is, love, we're stuck with each other, and it is now my mission to bring you to a point where you won't embarrass me, the company, and yourself."

"Got it," I said, determined not to let him see me crumble in front of him.

Wallace had a look of pity on his face. So did Sir Anthony. But neither had the balls to come to my defense.

"Try again," Kenneth hissed.

I took a deep breath and exhaled. He let me go a bit further, maybe half a page of dialogue. Sir Anthony even got to respond. But I knew he was simply lying in wait, ready to pounce.

"Dear Lord, this is hopeless!" Kenneth barreled down the aisle, leapt up onto the stage, and grabbed me roughly by the forearm. He dragged me up behind some furniture on the set away from Sir Anthony.

"I'm changing the focus of the scene. I want Sir Anthony down front and you cowering back here. Maybe this way, the audience won't notice you so much."

I shook his hand off my arm and glared at him.

"Go ahead, love. Quit," he said with a sly smile.

That was his plan. He wanted me to walk. Probably so he could fill the role with one of his buddies from his theater company. He was about to get his wish.

I opened my mouth to tell him exactly what I thought of him and his direction when a booming voice from the back of the theater cut through the momentary silence. "Enough!"

It was Claire. She had come back.

"You egotistical, manipulative little prick," she screamed as she shot down the aisle to confront Kenneth. "How dare you speak to an actor like that!"

"Claire, he simply doesn't have the chops to do this," Kenneth said, turning to Wallace, hoping he would back him up. Wallace, who quivered whenever Claire came within three feet of him, avoided all eye contact.

"Jarrod is a pro. More than *you* will ever be. You have no right to treat an actor of his stature this way, never mind a novice. I have half a mind to quit myself," she said.

"Try to understand, Claire. I don't have time to coddle actors who are not up to the task. I'm under a lot of pressure to get this show ready in time for the opening," he said.

"He's up to the task. And you know it," she said. "And if you don't start treating him with the respect he so richly deserves, I will go straight down to Fleet Street and spin such an entertaining yarn to all the tabloids about King Kenneth the tyrant, you'll be a leper to every respectable name actor in London."

I had no doubt Claire would make good on her threat. This play was all about her, not Kenneth.

Kenneth considered his options in about two seconds, then spun around to face me and through gritted teeth said, "I apologize for getting us off on the wrong foot, Jarrod. I promise to be more sensitive in the future."

"Thank you," I whispered, still stung by his blistering remarks.

"That's a good start," Claire barked. "I will think about other ways you can make up for your atrocious behavior later."

Of course, the irony of the queen of atrocious behavior saying this was not lost on any of us. Still, I wanted to kiss Claire Richards for rushing so valiantly into battle to save what was left of my tattered ego.

Kenneth nodded, shot an irritated look at Wallace for staying mute through this whole ordeal, and then offered me a forced smile. "All right, Jarrod, why don't we begin again?"

"No!" Claire yelled and waved me to join her. "No actor can be expected to perform after such a ruthless attack on his talent. You can start blocking the scene tomorrow. Come, Jarrod. I have a bottle of 1990 Chateau Mouton Rothschild one of my ex-husbands sent me in my dressing room. I think we could both use a drink."

I figured a fancy bottle of French red wine was just the cure for my shaken confidence. Especially one that was worth about a grand.

Kenneth nodded, giving me the all clear to leave. But he grimaced as Claire took my arm and we headed for the side door that led to a hallway of dressing rooms. As I opened the door for

Claire, she whipped back around and barked, "By the way, Kenneth, the reason I came back to the theater was to inquire as to whether or not you have secured a walk-on part for Liam."

"Um, no," stammered Kenneth, "I haven't asked the producers yet."

"Don't ask them, my dear. *Tell* them." Claire sailed through the door. Out of the corner of her mouth she said softly, "Slam it."

With all my might, I shoved the door closed with a bang. Claire smiled proudly. "It's always good to punctuate your point."

Claire's dressing room was filled with programs and mementos from her past triumphs on stage. And despite her very loud demands for fresh flowers every day, there wasn't a bouquet in sight. There was a plain partition and a rack of clothes off to the side and a plush purple love seat to the left of the door. Claire had erected a wine rack on the wall that held twenty-four bottles. Three were left. We had only been rehearsing a week and a half. Claire was giving her rival Dame Sylvia the lush a run for her money.

Claire popped the cork of her vintage bottle and poured us both glasses. Instead of stopping halfway, she filled them to the brim. When we toasted, streams of red wine spilled over the side and onto my hand.

"To a dazzling success for both of us," she said and then set her glass down. She began nonchalantly unbuttoning her blouse. I instinctively turned away.

"Don't turn away, darling. Behold!" And with that she tore the flimsy blouse off, revealing two remarkably well-preserved breasts.

"Nice," I said, for lack of anything else coming to mind. "Very nice."

Claire pushed me down on the love seat. More wine flew out of my glass and onto my Banana Republic khaki pants. "They're yours if you want them, Jarrod."

She pressed her bare breasts against my face almost to the point where I couldn't breathe. I was still stunned that such a big star was so blatantly putting the moves on me. I muttered an unintelligible reply, my mouth smothered by her milky white flesh. She pulled back a little in order to hear what I was trying to say.

"Come again, cutie?" she said with a warm, seductive smile.

"Claire, I'm gay."

"Oh, isn't everyone just a little bit gay?" And with that, she buried her mouth over mine and ripped my shirt open with her hands. She began rubbing my chest and squeezing my nipples. I tried protesting again, but her tongue was in the middle of a sword fight with mine.

Neither one of us heard the door open. But I quickly sensed another presence in the dressing room. I flicked an eye upward to see Liam, clutching a fistful of peach carnations and boiling with rage, standing over us. Without saying a word, he dropped the flowers, grabbed Claire by the neck, and yanked her off me. Then he reached down and wrapped his big calloused Irish workingman's hands around my throat and started to choke the life out of me. Claire struck him from behind with her balled-up fists, battering him mercilessly, but he was in the zone. He didn't feel a thing. He was entirely focused on killing me.

Before losing consciousness, I knew I had one chance to save myself. I brought my leg up and slammed my knee into his groin hard enough to knock the air out of him. He loosened his grip, allowing me to grab his arms and twist them. He howled in pain, and before he had the chance to recover, I punched him hard across the face. Liam went down, writhing and groaning on the floor. Living with a cop gives you an added advantage when it comes to self-defense. Not to mention five years of scene combat class.

Claire, fuming, kicked at his sides. "You big Irish oaf! How dare you come barging in here like that?" Claire knelt down, scooped up the discarded carnations, and began whacking Liam in the head with the bouquet. "And how many times do I have to tell you, I hate peach! Give them to Sir Anthony! He loves peach carnations!"

As Liam moaned an apology, I quietly slipped out the door to leave the two lovers to quarrel. Let Claire explain what happened. It didn't matter. I had already made a lifelong enemy out of Liam Killoran.

As I made my way down the hall, I bumped into a gorgeous brunette with a perky little body too small for her electrifying, luscious lips. "Hi, I'm Minx."

"Of course you are," I said with a droll smile, perfecting my James Bond cool.

"I'm Claire Richards's understudy," she said.

I was somewhat taken aback. Little Minx was in her mid-twenties, more than twenty years younger than Claire was. Then I realized Wallace had originally written the role for an ingenue. But when Claire agreed to do the play, no one dared age the character up. That would steer everyone in the prickly direction of having to acknowledge Claire's advancing years. So Kenneth probably decided to ignore it and just use a very thick make-up base on Claire to melt away as many years as possible.

"I'm Jarrod. It's nice to meet you, Minx."

"I am just so thrilled to be a part of this production. It's been my dream to appear on a West End stage." Then with a wink, she said, "So how is Claire's health? Do you think she might be susceptible to colds or anything like that?"

"She seems fine," I said, knowing the evil thoughts swirling about in Minx's pretty little head.

"Drat. Well, I need to jump-start my acting career, and this play is the perfect vehicle. So if Claire doesn't fall ill at some point, I may have to kill her."

I laughed, but a little voice deep inside told me this girl was dead serious.

# Chapter 5

Minx's hopes for a sudden illness were dashed when on opening night, Claire arrived at the theater looking robust and healthy and ready to take the stage. We had suffered through a rocky dress rehearsal the night before. Dame Sylvia couldn't remember her lines due to acute intoxication. Liam mangled his one walk-on line. Sir Anthony was threatened with a harassment suit by a cute, wiry, and very heterosexual twentysomething stagehand. Akshay kept blocking me from the audience during our one scene together just to piss me off. And our director, Kenneth, got the shakes considering the possibility that this production would bring an abrupt end to his once-promising career. We all held our collective breath hoping the old adage would prove true: a bad dress rehearsal always means a good show.

Since I didn't make my first entrance until the third scene in the play, I was the last one to head into make-up. I decided to grab some alone time in my dressing room and pray to the almighty gods that I wouldn't somehow screw this up. Kenneth begrudgingly admitted I had come a long way from those inauspicious first rehearsals and was now on a par with the rest of the cast. Still, I had no illusions about ever working with him again once this production closed.

I passed Minx, who paced nervously up and down the hallway, eyes clamped shut, wishing Claire would trip and fall and fracture her leg at the last minute, thus allowing her to go on in her place. I flashed her a brief smile and hurried on, afraid if I paused for even a second I would be stuck in a vapid conversation with her. I slipped into my dressing room and was happily surprised to find an opulent gift basket filled with wines and cheeses and crackers and chocolates all wrapped in clear cellophane. I picked up the gift card that was tucked inside the red ribbon that tied it all together and beamed with joy.

The note read *I ache all over, and not because of the bullets. I miss you. When are you coming home? Love, Charlie.* My eyes welled up with tears brought on by a sharp pang of homesickness. I had been gone a month, and I desperately missed my better half. But I wasn't going to cry. I had a show to do.

Stuffed in a corner behind my clothes rack was a big grocery bag of gifts. Two bouquets of flowers. A box of chocolates. Some Giorgio Armani aftershave. A bottle of scotch. I lifted it up in my arms and headed out the door. My mother, Priscilla, had begun a long-standing tradition during my days on *Go to Your Room*. At the start of each season, we would arrive on the set bearing gifts and dispense them all to our fellow cast members. It was a nod of gratitude for their enduring love and support and dedication to the show. Of course, I strongly felt that this motley crew of drunks and has-beens deserved nothing from me. Claire was the only one who had even shown me a modicum of respect during the last weeks, but it was a tradition. And I always felt it was bad luck to thumb your nose at tradition.

I stopped first at Akshay's door and knocked. "Hi, Akshay, it's Jarrod." I heard him inside on his cell phone. He stopped talking for a moment, and then resumed his conversation. He didn't deem me worthy enough to even bother opening the door. I set the bottle of aftershave down in front of the door and secretly hoped he would come out and step on it, crushing it with his bare feet and cutting himself. I moved on to Dame Sylvia's and knocked heartily for fear she might be passed out in a stupor. She opened her door a crack, inspecting me with one eyeball.

"Yes?" she said with obvious disdain.

I thrust the bottle of scotch out to her. "Opening-night gift. From me to you." Her hand shot out, snatching it from me like a grabby, snot-nosed little schoolboy. She inspected the label and sniffed.

"Thank you," she said and slammed the door.

I arrived next at Minx's dressing room. I figured why not include the understudy. She was just as much a prisoner at the Apollo as we were. But as I raised my knuckle to rap on her door, I envisioned myself getting dragged inside and forced to listen to her incessant girlish babbling. And I had to be in make-up soon so I softly knelt down, slid the box of chocolates quietly up against the door, and tiptoed away. She never even knew I had been there.

Only two to go. Sir Anthony and Claire. The gay pervert was next. I sighed, pulled myself together, and strategically took a position that would make it very difficult for him to pinch my butt. I knocked. When the door was flung open, I gasped. Standing before me was Sir Anthony. Stark naked. Like Baby New Year.

"My dear boy, how good of you to drop by," he said with a proud smile.

"I was . . . um . . . I just wanted to . . ."

He leaned in conspiratorially and then glancing down at his groin region, whispered, "Mighty impressive, I know."

He could have been telling the truth. Frankly, I didn't know. I refused to look.

"Would you like to come inside?"

"No, I just wanted to give you these," I said, thrusting a bouquet of multicolored carnations at him.

"They're absolutely gorgeous!" He made a big display of sucking air through his nose and savoring the melodious odor. And then, with a hand over his heart, he bowed to me. "Thank you, dear, dear boy."

He put his hands on his hips and jerked his pelvis outward, daring me to take a gander. But I still refused. I kept eye contact with him.

"Well, I know it's only a few minutes before curtain. I don't want to disturb you. You probably need some alone time to get ready and centered and all of that."

"Oh no, I don't need to be alone. In fact, I'm entertaining." He leaned in close to me again. "One of the many male acting students from the Royal Academy that I've taken under my wing. I'm sure you understand," he said with a wink.

"Oh, yes. Perfectly," I said, desperate for an escape.

"In fact, right now we're doing a few warm-up exercises. Would you care to join us?"

"No, not me, but thank you. I'm warmed up already."

"You certainly are, Jarrod. In fact, you're very hot."

I let out a fey giggle that I felt ashamed about. But this guy was making me extremely nervous.

"Are you certain you don't want to join the party? My boy has abs you could set a table on."

Flustered, I shook my head. "I have to get these flowers to Claire."

Sir Anthony perused my selection. "Traditional red roses. Very wise. I was afraid you might slip up and try to deliver her something of a peach color."

"I'd never make that mistake," I said, grinning, before whipping around and heading off down the hall. I could feel Sir Anthony's eyes undress me from behind before his guest distracted him and he disappeared back inside his dressing room.

When I arrived at Claire's room, I could hear a commotion inside. Instead of knocking, I pressed my ear to the door. I heard someone groaning. No. Not groaning. Moaning. Someone was moaning. No, wait. Two people. Two people were moaning. It wasn't going to take Sam Spade to figure this one out. Claire and Liam were engaged in their own brand of warm-up exercises. I smirked to myself and set the roses down. If anything, I was discreet. I turned around and started back to my dressing room when I stopped suddenly. Standing in the wings watching patrons file into the theater and take their seats was a fully clothed and agitated Liam Killoran. His face was all red. Thoughts of having to deliver even just one sentence in front of a live audience was causing the novice actor to break out into hives.

He was perspiring and sucking on a cigarette, even though smoking was banned in the theater. As I passed him, I said softly, "Don't worry. You'll be great."

He eyed me with contempt. "Fuck off." He practically spit the words at me.

I should have told him the love of his life was doing just that in her dressing room with someone else, but a cooler head prevailed. In the interest of company harmony I would keep that little secret to myself. I simply shrugged and moved on.

I had to wonder, though. Who was Claire sleeping with besides Liam? I must admit I felt a tiny pang of jealousy. I thought I was the only one besides her Irish lover that Claire had designs on. But she was a celebrated star, oozing charm and confidence. She could have anyone she wanted. I took a quick inventory. Kenneth and Wallace were nowhere to be seen. I had heard Akshay inside his dressing room. And Sir Anthony, well, let's say he was easy to rule out as a suspect. Of course, it could have been just about anyone. The young, delicious stagehand that Sir Anthony had been torturing with his undivided attention. Or the married lighting guy whose eyes sparkled every time Claire smiled his way. Claire had been around long enough to know it was imperative to make the guy in charge of lighting your new best friend. He is without question the ultimate authority on how you look.

The mystery of Claire's moaning man would have to wait. Holly, the frizzy-haired young female theater intern from Oxford, raced past me, frantically speaking into her walkie-talkie. "Two minutes to curtain," she said as she rounded the corner. It was show time. And the nerves in my belly decided to let me know that I was about to pass out from fright.

I was done with make-up by the time Claire swept onto the stage to thunderous applause. The play had been a bit sluggish up to that point, with only Dame Sylvia wringing a few polite laughs from the expectant audience. But Claire's entrance breathed life into the proceedings, and it was infectious. It raised the cast to a higher level. They had no choice. They had to keep up with powerhouse Claire or risk disappearing into the scenery. By the time I made my entrance well into the first act, the audience was enthralled with the entire show. There was polite applause from the few fans that remembered me, but even the modest audience reaction was enough to cause Akshay to visibly flinch with scorn.

After a shaky start, I got my bearings and managed to infuse the seedy character of Damien the valet with just enough sleaze and sarcasm to win instant admiration from my detractors. I was getting laughs. Big ones. This one performance was going to make this difficult ordeal completely worth it. I was on a roll. By the time I reached my big confrontation scene with Sir Anthony, I had hit my stride. I was having a ball. The audience was with me. The lines were slipping off my tongue as if I were coming up with them off the cuff. Everyone, even Claire, was caught off guard. This was going to be the most memorable night of my life. But unfortunately it would not be due to my crowd-pleasing performance.

I died right on cue in the third act, from multiple stab wounds administered by a heartless killer, just like in *Creeps*. But this seemed a far more highbrow death. When the lights went down between scenes, I quietly stood up and slipped offstage. The stagehand assisted me in removing my bloodstained shirt. He handed me a fresh pullover, and I slipped it on as I stood in the wings and watched Claire's dramatic final scene. This was the linchpin moment of the piece. Claire's character has solved the murder and unmasked the killer, who turns out to be Akshay's character. Claire stabs him with the same knife he used to kill my character, Damien. Akshay, the shameless ham, took almost a full minute to die. But Claire ultimately triumphs and the ruthless killer is finally vanquished. Just as the audience has been lulled into a sense of security, believing that the murderer has finally been dispatched, Claire, the last character left standing, opens a door to exit. The lights dimmed, marking the end of the play. The audience sighed with relief. But then, at that moment, a gunshot rang out. The audience screamed. And Claire, clutching her stomach, blood seeping through her fingers, sank to the floor. It was Wallace's surprise ending. The killer had vowed to do away with Claire and rigged up a shotgun that would fire off a round the minute anyone tried to leave the room. Claire had forgotten that one detail. His vow to murder her even if he had to reach out from the afterlife. It was a chilling end. Not for the faint of heart. And Claire pulled it off beautifully.

The curtain came down. There was a brief moment of silence and then an eruption of applause. We all gathered in the center of the stage and joined hands. I was between Akshay and Dame Sylvia. I was supposed to be between Claire and Dame Sylvia. That was how Kenneth had staged the curtain call. Akshay glared at me, and then grabbed my hand as the curtain rose. I looked around. Where was Claire? And that's when I saw her. She was still lying on the stage in a pool of fake blood. And she wasn't moving. The audience laughed uproariously at first. They thought it was one more ghoulish trick from the fiendish mind of the playwright. Until they noticed the cast onstage staring at

Claire's lifeless body in disbelief. The laughter died slowly and then disappeared altogether.

I took a step toward her. "Claire?"

I knew the moment I saw her dull, glassy eyes staring up at me. Claire Richards was dead.

# Chapter 6

Kenneth, who had been watching the performance from the back of the theater, ran up to the booth and ordered his two technical assistants to lower the curtain. The audience was confused as to why Claire didn't get up to make her curtain call, but nevertheless filed out of the theater, completely oblivious to the shocking and horrible truth.

An ambulance arrived within minutes. But despite the best efforts of the paramedics to revive her, Claire Richards was declared dead. We were all asked to return to our dressing rooms until the police could question everyone. Although the cause of death was still to be determined, the police wanted to at least conduct a preliminary round of questioning in the event that they might have a homicide on their hands.

As I sat alone waiting for them to get to me, I choked back tears. I just couldn't believe it. My theatrical hero, my drinking buddy, my staunchest ally, Claire Richards was dead. The thought of it was devastating. My head swirled with theories as to what happened. Claire Richards was perfectly healthy before the show, full of energy and vigor and ready to conquer the London critics. And by the end of the play, she was a corpse. This didn't make any sense.

The prop gun had been checked and did indeed fire blanks. So Claire did not die of a bullet wound. Maybe it was a heart attack or stroke. She was a big drinker, just like her bitter rival Dame Sylvia. But because Claire's death was so mysterious and I am, after all, an admitted conspiracy theorist, I instantly jumped to the conclusion that foul play had to somehow be involved. She certainly didn't lack enemies with a motive. Almost everyone in the company despised her. Her Irish bully lover, Liam, could have discovered the same secret dalliance I had stumbled upon earlier when I tried delivering flowers to her dressing room and exacted his own brand of revenge. Then there was our director, Kenneth. Claire had pretty much emasculated the guy throughout the entire rehearsal process, which might have pushed him to a point where he decided to strike back. Minx the understudy, of course, had very clear reasons to want Claire out of the way. The stage-diva rivalry between Claire and Dame Sylvia might have finally reached an ugly head. Neither Akshay nor Sir Anthony displayed any overt hostilities toward Claire, but that didn't prove their innocence.

I had all night to mull over the possibilities because the police questioned me last. It was six-thirty the following morning and I was fighting to keep my eyes open. The severe detective inspector, a blond woman in her fifties who had no time for any smiles or pleasantries, sat me down in my dressing room and hovered over me in a blatant attempt to intimidate me into cooperating fully and spilling everything I knew.

"I'm Detective Inspector Sally Bowles," she said.

"You're kidding me," I said, followed by a quick burst of laughter.

Her eyes narrowed. The joke was lost on her at first. "Yes," she said.

"Like Liza Minelli's character in *Cabaret*?"

She sighed. "Yes."

Bowles gave a withering glance to her partner, a pudgy man in his mid-forties too small for his suit, who stood steadfast at the door to the dressing room in the event I might try to bolt. He nodded and then jotted something on a notepad. I presumed he was writing, "Suspect is gayer than a picnic basket."

"I suppose you get that a lot," I said.

"Only in certain circles," she said and then abruptly turned her back to me and said something to her partner that I couldn't hear. He grunted and wrote some more on his pad.

"Could you describe your relationship with Ms. Richards?" Sally said, her back still to me.

"Good. Very good," I said. "We got along quite well."

"How well? Did you share intimate relations?"

I let out another quick burst of laughter. "I'm gay."

One more nod to her pudgy partner. Suspicions confirmed. She locked eyes with me. "You still didn't answer my question."

"No. I did not sleep with her."

"Someone claims you did."

I shook my head, irritated. "That would be Liam. He assumed we were. But nothing ever happened between us. Ever."

"He said he walked in on the two of you having sex."

"He's wrong."

"He said you were on top of her, your shirt was open, and you were kissing."

"She was on top of me. But she was the one who ripped my shirt open, and yes, she was kissing me. But I was trying to pull away. Claire said she wanted to make love, and I explicitly told her I was gay. That didn't seem to deter her and that's when Liam walked in."

Sally wasn't satisfied. She frowned as she stared at me, trying to read my eyes to see if they flickered from her gaze, a sure sign I was lying. They didn't.

"Are you saying Claire's death wasn't from natural causes?" I asked Bowles.

"We don't know yet," she said.

Bowles decided to batter me with more questions. An hour's worth, in fact. Questions about my career, my life with Charlie, my history with Wallace and Katrina, my relationships with Kenneth and the rest of the cast. She had me recount the timeline of activities leading up to the performance. I didn't hold anything back. I confessed all the backstage minidramas that went on during the rehearsal process. Sally listened with rapt attention as if engrossed in the latest episode of England's classic soap opera *Coronation Street*.

She was thorough and determined, and by the end of the questioning, I had a newfound respect for Detective Inspector Sally Bowles. She reminded me of the glorious Helen Mirren, who played a kick-ass, flawed but brilliant detective in the *Prime Suspect* detective series. Cold, distant, but fabulously British. As we wrapped up, I could sense she was slowly beginning to warm up to me. She even smiled slightly as she shook my hand and thanked me for my cooperation.

"So, do you think Claire was murdered?" I said.

"Like I said, we don't know at this point," Sally said. "Autopsy's going to be conducted tomorrow. We'll have more information then. We just wanted to talk to everyone while the events are still fresh in everyone's mind. Just in case."

If this had been anyone else, the police would have undoubtedly waited for the autopsy results before interrupting their suppers and dashing over to talk to everyone. But this was Claire Richards. A national treasure. They were doing their homework early.

Sally nodded to her partner and they were halfway out the

door when it dawned on me that I had forgotten the juiciest detail of all.

"There is one thing I think you should know," I said.

Sally spun back around, her interest piqued.

"I believe Claire was sleeping with someone else connected to the play."

"Who?"

I shrugged. "I didn't see him. But I heard them going at it when I stopped by her dressing room before the performance. I assumed it was Liam, but then I saw him hanging around backstage right after that. So it couldn't have been him in there with her."

She made a note of it, thanked me again, and then left.

At last I was free to go. All I could think about was finding my way back to the Savoy and crashing into bed for some much-needed sleep. Kenneth had announced that the show would go dark for the following few nights until all the facts surrounding Claire's mysterious death could be sorted out.

As I wandered through Covent Garden towards the Strand, still distraught over Claire's untimely passing, I stopped at a newsstand. The morning editions were out. I snapped up copies of all of them, grabbed some Starbucks coffee, and hustled back to my room to see what the critics had said about the world-premiere performance of Wallace Goodwin's *Murder Can Be Civilized*.

The first headline read, "Murder May Be Civilized but Sitting Through This Play Is Most Certainly Not." It got worse. "The Only Murder in This Disaster Worth Championing Is the Audience Offing the Playwright." None of us escaped the wrath of the critics. I was described as "relying on my situation-comedy bag of tricks to muddle my way through." Maybe Kenneth had been right. Sir Anthony was blasted for being the most effeminate military figure this side of Gomer Pyle. Akshay was described as startlingly sexy but hopelessly stiff. And in the most ironic review of the batch, one critic cried, "Claire Richards, though bursting with talent, alas died unconvincingly in the final moments of the play." Boy, would that reviewer feel stupid when word got out.

Only Dame Sylvia escaped the knives of the critics unscathed. No one dared to touch her. Whatever she did was breathtaking, spellbinding, riveting, and always a tour de force. One critic damned the play but praised Dame Sylvia for being a real trouper for putting up with it all. The production was a cataclysmic failure. I was actually starting to believe during the performance that we had a hit on our hands. How could I have been so wrong? But the real issue was not how long we were going to squeak by before audience apathy shut us down. The big question was what the hell were we going to do now? Our leading lady was dead. Would Minx take over? Would the producers just cut their losses and get out?

Although the morning papers didn't have time to print the announcement of Claire's death, the Internet and television news programs were all abuzz. Clips of all of Claire's movies were played on every breakfast chatter show. Big stars like Michael Caine and Anthony Hopkins were roused from their beds and forced to show us their stunned though still-sleepy reactions.

I sat on the bed in my room at the Savoy and watched the coverage as if I hadn't actually been there, as if I was a mere spectator like the rest of the world. Hours went by when I should have been resting. But I couldn't tear my eyes off the television.

My phone rang, shaking me free of my TV news overdose. It had to be Charlie. He must have just heard the news. I picked up the receiver.

"Charlie?"

I heard a man's wailing voice. He was sobbing, obviously wracked with grief. I was still hoping it was Charlie and that he was calling to beg and plead with me to come home. He missed me more than he ever imagined he would and didn't want so much distance to ever separate us again. But sadly, it wasn't Charlie.

"Jarrod, this is so awful, so incomprehensible."

It was Wallace Goodwin.

"I know. I'm just kind of numb over the whole thing."

"How could this happen?" He broke down, sobbing.

"They're going to conduct an autopsy. The police will find out how Claire died soon enough."

"No, I mean the reviews," Wallace said. "They're so vicious, so mean-spirited."

How silly of me to assume Wallace was devastated over Claire's death and not over the universal pan of his first theatrical effort.

"I don't know, Wallace."

"It's like they saw a different play. I thought it went pretty good . . . Well, except for Claire dying and all. Katrina thinks we should file a lawsuit against the critics for gross misconduct—"

I hung up. I couldn't help myself. Wallace was a reminder of the rampant self-absorption in show business, and I simply couldn't handle it at the moment. I would call back later and apologize, say we were somehow disconnected. But now was not the time to commiserate over some lousy reviews.

I ordered up a roast beef sandwich from room service, un-plugged the phone, took a long, hot bath, and then curled up in bed and slept for what felt like days. By the time I was ready to face the world again, I received a note to report to the theater. Some decisions had been made.

I dressed quickly and headed out the door. I passed the news-stand and stopped suddenly. The *London Times* was reporting on its front page that Claire Richards's death had been caused by a massive stroke. So it wasn't a murder. I felt a wave of relief wash over me. During the two days I had stayed in my room sleeping off the past month of stress and nervous tension, I had a series of unsettling dreams that someone in the cast was a murderer and that I would eventually be the killer's target. This wasn't so far-fetched, considering my history. I had played amateur detective on several homicide cases, much to the chagrin of Charlie. But at least this time it was a death from natural causes. I bought the paper to absorb more of the details as I headed toward the Apollo Theatre on Shaftsbury. The autopsy appeared to be very conclusive. It didn't make losing Claire any easier. Funeral services were being arranged. More stars were commenting on their absolute shock and devastation over their fellow artist's demise.

I entered the Apollo through the backstage entrance. It was eerily quiet. No one was milling about. There were no lights on. I looked at the note slipped under my door and noticed I had misread the time of the cast call. It was nine-thirty, not nine o'clock. Now I had a half hour to kill before everyone else arrived for the meeting. I lumbered down the hallway to my dressing room when I heard some rustling. At first I thought it might be Sir Anthony entertaining yet another one of his young male acting students with a swimmer's build from the Royal Academy, but his door was shut. The commotion was coming from inside Claire's dressing room next door. I debated on whether I should just ignore whoever it was and use my time to call home and check in with Charlie. But my curiosity, as usual, got the best of me. I quietly tiptoed over to the door, which was open. Pushing it open, I saw a figure in a leather jacket and jeans and wearing a red ski mask rifling through Claire's belongings.

Every instinct told me to run. It's never a good idea to confront a thief. I had guest-starred on too many detective shows where someone stupidly calls attention to themselves by saying something like, "What are you doing here?" panicking the bad guy and then getting knocked out or something. Anyone with half a brain would just get the hell out of there.

"What are you doing here?" I said.

Surprised, the red-masked thief bolted upright and stared at me. Then he rushed me, shoving his hands against my chest, knocking me over. My head hit the floor with a sickening thud. And I felt the boots of my assailant stomp over my chest as he raced out the door. Then everything went black.

# Chapter 7

As I slowly awakened, I felt a sharp unrelenting pain in my side like someone kicking me in the ribs. As I forced my eyes open, I saw the sharp toe of a cowboy boot swinging toward me. It struck me again. Someone *was* kicking me in the ribs.

"Get up," a low, gravelly voice commanded.

I looked up to see the scowling, flushed face of Liam Killoran. If his hardened expression weren't so full of bile and contempt, he would have looked rather dashing in his corduroy sports jacket, white shirt open at the collar, and skintight Levi's jeans.

"What are you doing in Claire's dressing room?" he said, reaching down, grabbing a fistful of my shirt, and hauling me to my feet. I stumbled, still woozy from cracking my head on the floor during my fall. My knees gave out. Instead of letting me fall, Liam grabbed me by the arms and hurled me onto Claire's purple couch, the same one he had found the two of us draped over a few days earlier.

"I got here early," I said, rubbing my head and checking for blood. "I heard someone in here. I came in and this guy attacked me—"

"I didn't see anyone," Liam said as he glanced around the room for any valuables that might be missing.

"He knocked me out and then ran."

"You're making this up! Tell me what you're up to!"

By now the rest of the company had arrived and were drawn to Liam's booming voice echoing out of Claire's dressing room. A small crowd quickly gathered outside the door. Minx. Sir Anthony. Akshay. Wallace. Kenneth. Everyone but Dame Sylvia, who I assumed was still at breakfast downing her seventeenth Bloody Mary.

Kenneth stepped forward. "Liam, what's going on here?"

"I found Jarvis in here sprawled out on the floor. He says he caught a thief going through Claire's things, but I don't believe him."

"Okay, Liam, you caught me red-handed. I had to have something of Claire's to remember her by, so I arrived early to loot her dressing room, but when I heard you coming, I bopped myself on the head with her Oscar to make it look like I was attacked. Kudos to you for cracking the case, Inspector Clouseau," I said, waving him away.

Minx giggled. "You're so funny, Jarrod."

Okay, so it wasn't a ringing endorsement, but I was in no position to turn away an ally. Even a backstabbing opportunist like Minx.

"Thank you," I said.

"What did this alleged thief look like?" Akshay said, unwilling to believe me for even a moment.

"I didn't see his face. He was wearing a red ski mask," I said.

Sir Anthony's eyes brightened. "And his physique? Was it strong and imposing?"

"I didn't notice. It all happened so fast," I said.

Wallace, who had been hovering in the back of the group, couldn't take it anymore. "Look, as long as nothing was stolen, can we get back to the task at hand? We need to discuss what we're going to do about the show."

Kenneth nodded to Wallace, motioning for him to keep his cool, and then he turned to me. "Would you like to file a report with the police, Jarrod?"

"What for?" Akshay said, folding his arms and offering me a disdainful look. "The only crime committed here was his performance last night."

I wanted to punch his flawless, dark-skinned, handsome face. Knowing what was inside made the outside far less attractive.

"Jarrod's obviously been assaulted," Kenneth said, in a surprising show of support. "He has a right to find his assailant."

"No, forget it," I said. "There's been enough drama already. I'm just glad I showed up before he was able to take anything."

"Her Academy Award is missing," Liam said, frantically searching through Claire's dresser drawers. "She kept it behind her wardrobe partition, and it's not here." He pointed an accusing finger at me. "You said you didn't see him take anything."

"I didn't," I said.

"But you just made a joke about the thief stealing her Oscar!" he said.

All eyes were on me.

"It was a coincidence," I said. "I swear he didn't have anything in his hands when he rushed me. Maybe he had already stuffed it inside his jacket."

Kenneth sighed, then flipped open his cell phone. "Holly, call the police and have them send someone down to the Apollo. I'm afraid there's been a robbery."

"I say we check Jarvis's dressing room straight away to see if he's got it stashed in there," Liam said, his eyes bulging and his fists clenched.

"What do you have against Jarrod?" Minx said. All the men, with the exception of Sir Anthony, anxiously turned and looked at her, their eyes settling happily on her flimsy silk clinging dress that could have easily passed for lingerie from Victoria's Secret.

"*He* knows," Liam said before pushing past the company and charging out the door. There was an uncomfortable silence.

Kenneth finally spoke up. "What did you do to him?"

"He thinks I was sleeping with Claire."

The room erupted in raucous laughter. I would have been offended if I hadn't found the notion so absurd myself.

Kenneth raised his hand for order, and the guffaws slowly subsided. "All right, calm down, everyone. We have much to discuss."

Minx held her breath. This was it. Her moment of truth. Would the show go on? Would she finally have her chance in the spotlight?

"There are a million reasons why we should shutter the show and all just go home," Kenneth said.

Minx let out an audible gasp. I could actually hear her entire world starting to crumble.

"First and foremost, our leading lady has passed away. Calls are already pouring into the theater requesting refunds. It seems with Claire dead, so is audience interest."

I wasn't upset in the least. This had been a trying, emotionally draining experience, and the sooner I got back to Los Angeles and home to Charlie, the happier I would be.

"Not to mention we've been hit with less than kind, no, more like passionately negative reviews," Kenneth said. "The producers want to pull the plug."

I thought Minx was going to faint. Sir Anthony cupped his hand underneath her elbow to keep her steady.

I felt for Minx but was happy to be free of this thespian asylum. I was halfway out the door, anxious to return to the Savoy, pack my bags, and head straight for Heathrow.

"However," Kenneth said, a sly smile creeping across his face, "I have convinced them that in Claire's honor, we should go on."

Minx squealed with unabashed delight before catching herself and adjusting her joy to the somberness of the circumstances. Wallace was ecstatic his show was given a last-minute reprieve. Akshay showed no emotion whatsoever. And Sir Anthony pinched my butt.

"Funeral services for Claire are planned for the day after tomorrow at Westminster Abbey. It should be quite a star-studded event, not to be missed. I hear Sir Elton John might make an appearance, maybe even sing a song," Kenneth said, completely unaware of his own astounding insensitivity. "Performances will resume on Sunday with the matinee. Minx will be taking over Claire's role."

Sir Anthony raised a crooked, bony finger. "Excuse me, Kenneth. No offense to Minx's talent, but wouldn't it be wiser for us to drum up another big name in the role to boost box office?"

Kenneth nodded. "We already thought of that and called every actress in town. No one wants to touch this play."

"It's not the play, right?" said Wallace in a pathetic show of insecurity. "They just don't want to have to fill Claire's shoes. Right?"

"Absolutely," Kenneth lied.

Minx stood there like a delicate, withering flower, the euphoria of her victory slowly draining away thanks to the callous words of her director. But she smiled through her pain. I felt sorry for her.

Kenneth finally noticed Minx and cupped her face in his hands. "You'll be great, love. Just do it as we rehearsed and the audience will adore you."

Kenneth's wispy, stick-thin, and gawky young assistant, Holly, poked her head in the dressing room. "Kenneth, the police are on their way."

"Good. Let's clear out of here so they can do their job when they arrive, everyone," Kenneth said as he marched out, followed by Minx and Sir Anthony, leaving only Akshay and me.

Akshay turned to me and smiled. "You know, Jarrod, the only member of the company who was absent during all of this was Dame Sylvia. She would certainly have cause to swipe Claire's Academy Award. She despised her and has never won one herself. Perhaps she was your attacker."

"I wasn't attacked by an eighty-year-old woman, Akshay," I said, trying to maneuver around him to get out the door. He blocked my path.

"Oh, I'm certain she could take you in a fight any day," he said.

"Maybe so. But I have no doubt I could whip your curried ass," I said, not backing down.

Akshay and I stared at each other, neither of us wavering, not for a second. Finally, Akshay scoffed, shaking his head as if I was inconsequential to him, like an irritating little gnat, and walked out the door. I hated him more than ever.


Kenneth hadn't lied about the memorial service at Westminster Abbey for Claire Richards. It was packed with royalty. And not just British royalty. Hollywood came calling too. Tom Cruise showed up. So did Tom Hanks and wife Rita Wilson. I was seated two rows behind Sir Elton John and Dame Judi Dench. Prince Charles and new wife Camilla Parker Bowles arrived with much fanfare and were seated directly behind Claire's immediate family, including two brothers, their wives, and assorted nieces and nephews. Sir Michael Caine paid tribute to the wild and uproarious actress with hilarious tales of their days trying to crack each other up while performing *As You Like It* at the Old Vic. Nearly a dozen of Claire's costars, directors, costumers, and producers lined up to sing her praises. Liam, acknowledged by

Claire's family only as one of a long line of her boy toys, gamely tried to deliver a hastily written eulogy, but he was so inconsolable, so distraught, that Sir Andrew Lloyd Webber had to escort him back to his seat after only a few opening words.

Outside the church was a madhouse. Reporters jostling to get shots of the famous attendees. Thousands of mourning fans kept at bay by a veritable army of police officers. News crews from all over the world blocking the streets with their vans, falling over themselves to cover this sad, unsettling, still-unexplainable loss. Claire's last public appearance was a powerhouse of pomp and circumstance. Not even the most inventive publicist could have planned such a spectacle. On this dark, cloudy, gray day in Great Britain, Claire's accomplishments and reputation could not be denied, not even by Dame Sylvia, who was unable to attend because of a head cold that would miraculously disappear by happy hour. Claire Richards was one of a kind. And I missed her terribly.

No one was battered by Claire's legacy more than poor, naïve little Minx, who bravely took to the stage the following day, blissfully unaware she was walking into the lion's den. None of us seriously expected her to live up to Claire. But we were totally unprepared for just how awful she was. Her quaking nerves got the best of her. She butchered her way through the play's text, dropping lines and confusing her fellow actors, nervously wrapping her curly brown hair around her index finger when she wasn't speaking, and finally wandering offstage to consult the script midway through her climactic speech. I later learned that Claire had casting approval over her understudy and purposely chose a bad actress to ensure that if she were unable to perform there would be no show. Of course, poor Claire never took into account the event of her own death.

As I watched Minx's agonizing performance from the wings, I caught sight of Wallace standing in the back of the theater, weeping as his wife Katrina gently patted his back, trying to comfort him. It was over. We all knew it. And then, when Minx finally died on stage, the audience whooped and hollered. They were thrilled that both the star of the show and the audience themselves were all finally put out of their misery. Minx knew she had blown it. The show had been such a stink bomb that the actors almost didn't bother with the curtain calls. We were busy consoling Minx when the curtain was raised for our bows. Half the audience had already begun racing for the exits as if a raging fire were sweeping through the theater. The remaining patrons, in a show of abject pity, offered tepid applause.

I could see Kenneth up in the booth on his cell phone, already begging his agent to line up a new gig and fast. He had two separate alimonies to shell out.

It had been quite a ride. Although I had been beaten up by my director, looked down upon by a majority of my costars, and ruthlessly ravaged in the press, I wouldn't have traded this experience for anything. I could fly home knowing I had not only befriended but also won the respect of Claire Richards, a theatrical legend. It was worth all the heartache and pain of the past month. The memory of our brief time together would be something I could relish for the rest of my life.

I had already cleaned out my dressing room that morning, expecting the worst, so all that was left for me to do was say my good-byes and hightail it back to the Savoy. But as I began my procession down the corridor of dressing rooms, I realized the only person in this entire company I had any affection for was dead. I didn't need to subject myself to that fake "I would love to work with you again" ritual actors put themselves through in an effort not to burn any bridges. So instead I just walked out.

It was a crisp, cool night in London and as I strolled back to my hotel, I pulled out my cell phone and called Charlie. There was no answer. Isis didn't even pick up. I thought that was strange. I knew Charlie was quickly bouncing back through a rigorous physical-therapy regimen with the studly Chad, but it was a bit early for him to be out carousing on the town with Isis. I decided to try calling him again later.

As I glided through the opulent, historic lobby of the Savoy, Arthur the friendly bellhop in his trademark dusty gray suit with black pinstripes called out to me.

"Good evening, Mr. Jarvis," he said, waving a shaky hand at me.

"Hello, Arthur," I said.

"How did your show go?"

"We closed."

"Oh. I didn't even get a chance to come see it."

"Consider yourself lucky," I said and made a beeline for the elevators.

"Your friend has arrived. He's upstairs."

I stopped cold. "Friend?"

"Yes. I let him into your room. I hope you don't mind."

"Arthur, I wasn't expecting a friend."

Arthur's face fell. "Oh, dear. Please don't tell the manager. I could get sacked for this."

Someone had conned their way into my room. And I was betting it was the red-masked thief. What did this guy want? I grabbed Arthur by the arm and dragged him with me up to my room. I knew the frail, teetering old man would be useless to me if the situation got violent, but I figured at the very least there was safety in numbers.

When we reached the door, I pulled out my key and quietly inserted it into the lock. Before turning it, I pressed my ear against the door. I couldn't hear anything.

"What if he's got a gun?" Arthur said, his whole body shaking.

I put a finger to my lips, signaling him to keep his mouth shut. Then I silently, slowly turned the key and opened the door a crack. Peeking through, I saw that one bedside lamp had been turned on. A tall, physically imposing man stood at the foot of the bed, his back to me, and he was rummaging through my suitcase.

That's when Arthur dropped his ring of keys and alerted the intruder to our presence.

# Chapter 8

"Hey, babe, I forgot to pack toothpaste, and you seem to be out. Got any more in your suitcase?" Charlie said, his eyes twinkling as Arthur and I stood in the doorway. Our mouths dropped open to the floor.

Arthur, in an adorable show of bravado, stepped in front of me, waving his unsteady finger at Charlie. "Security is already on their way up, so you better not try any funny business."

"Arthur, it's okay, I know him," I said.

"Oh," Arthur said, almost disappointed that our exciting, heart-stopping adventure was over. "Is he a relative?"

I smiled at Charlie, overwhelmed and relieved to see his gorgeous face in my hotel room. "Yes."

"Brother?"

Arthur was a regular Tim Russert out to get the full story. If he really wanted to know, so be it.

"Boyfriend."

Arthur sized up Charlie. It was tough to know how an eighty-year-old English codger was going to react to a happy American gay couple. It might be a little too modern for him to handle. But I was guessing that Arthur had seen it all during his countless years at the Savoy and wouldn't blink twice at this minor revelation.

But he did blink. Actually, it was more of a wink. And then he nudged me slightly in my still-sore ribs and whispered, "Good for you. He's hot."

Son of a gun. Arthur was family. I tipped him ten pounds, and after one more long, languorous look at Charlie, he quietly bowed out of the room to give us privacy for our long-awaited reunion.

I threw my arms around Charlie and kissed him softly on the mouth. He stiffened a bit, still feeling the pain from his injuries. I instantly pulled away.

"I'm sorry, I didn't mean to hurt you," I said.

"No, don't worry about it. I'm feeling stronger every day. A few weeks, and I'll be back 100 percent."

"What are you doing here?" I said, as if I actually cared why he had come. I was just so thrilled he was here in London and in my hotel room.

"I promised to come see your show at some point. There's been so much press back home on how Claire's death will affect the future of the production, I figured I better hightail it over here fast before they shut it down."

"You're too late," I said.

Charlie arched an eyebrow. "Already?"

I nodded. "I'm afraid you came for nothing."

"That's not true," he said wrapping his thick arms around my waist and pulling me close to him. "We're together."

Charlie and I spent the next hour lying on top of the luxurious king-size bed, entwined in each other's arms, talking. I prattled on about how miserable the cast and director were to me, how Claire was my one ally, how shocking her death was, and how relieved I was that this ordeal was finally over. Charlie updated me on our beloved Snickers, who was so put out by my prolonged absence that she had begun to make repeated statements about her annoyance by peeing all over the house. Isis spent half the day chasing the little Pekingese around while clutching a roll of paper towels to clean up after her. Isis was in way over her head. She had never counted on just how time consuming and challenging the role of nursemaid would be. Charlie noted that a good psychic would have seen the difficulties coming a mile away. He was never a big believer in the art of clairvoyance, but he tolerated my utter devotion to it. And he highly valued Isis as a friend.

After we caught each other up, I jumped off the bed and stuffed all my clothes in a suitcase. I told Charlie we could be checked out of the Savoy and on our way to Heathrow in less than an hour. He came up behind me as I struggled with the zipper on my Eddie Bauer carry-on suitcase and nuzzled my neck.

"Look, I just got here. Let's stick around for a few days, see the sights, have a real vacation," he said.

I wanted nothing more than to just go home after a brutalizing month in one of my favorite cities in the world. But I had been here alone, without Charlie, working on a doomed project. Perhaps tooling around London with my significant other would be the perfect antidote to the harsh experience I had just endured. Not to mention the fact that Charlie rarely took a vacation from work and this might be the only opportunity for us to enjoy one before he returned to the department from his medical leave. The Savoy was already paid for through the week by the producers, so why not?

London boasts some of the best Indian restaurants in Europe. And since Charlie and I were huge fans, even planning a whole night of our week around Indian cuisine, I suggested we take a taxi to east London and dine out on chicken tikka, vegetable curry, and several orders of meat samosas. Charlie was all for it.

After a quick shower together, we threw on some fresh clothes and headed out. Arthur tipped his hat and offered us a conspiratorial wink as we passed by him in the lobby. We were just about out the door when a familiar voice stopped us.

"Jarrod," Akshay said, hailing us down a few steps from the gold-plated door that led to the street. "I didn't want you to leave before I had a chance to say good-bye."

I was stunned. Say good-bye? This Bollywood beefcake bastard despised me. Why on earth would he take the time to say anything to me? But it quickly dawned on me that while Akshay was speaking to me, he never took his eyes off Charlie.

"Good-bye," I said and then tried to hustle Charlie out the door.

"Can I give you a lift to the airport?" Akshay said, smiling, his pearly white teeth a startling contrast to his smooth, flawless brown skin and wavy black hair.

"No, thanks," I said. "We're not flying home. We're just going out to dinner."

"I see," Akshay said, not even bothering to glance my way. Then he shoved a perfectly manicured hand out and grabbed Charlie's. "I'm Akshay Kapoor."

Charlie shook his hand. "Charlie Peters."

"My boyfriend," I hastily added.

"You make a very handsome young couple," Akshay said, full of warmth and charm that I had never seen before.

"Thank you," I said, completely stone-faced.

"Where do you plan on dining?" he said, finally wrenching his eyes off Charlie and resting them on me. "Perhaps I could steer you in the right direction."

I didn't want him to know any more, but there was no stopping Charlie. "You know any good Indian restaurants you could recommend?"

Akshay lit up. Here was his opportunity, and he immediately pounced on it. "My family owns a cozy little place in Little Bengal. I'm sure you would love it. Very festive, and the food is superb, if I do say so myself."

"That's okay, Akshay," I said. There was no way I was going to spend the evening in a restaurant owned by anyone remotely connected to this creep.

"I could take you there myself, as my guests. It would be an honor for me and my family to treat you both to a full-course traditional Indian dinner."

Before I could open my mouth, Charlie jumped at the invitation. "We'd love to. Thank you."

Charlie was always looking to save a buck, so this was the ideal situation for him. What could possibly be wrong with a free dinner and a handsome host? I didn't like this. Not one bit.

Before I could protest, Akshay swept us out the door and into a waiting taxicab. Within minutes we were pulling up in front of a modest building with a large glass front and "Muhib Indian Cuisine" painted over the window. It was squeezed in between two other Indian restaurants. The place was packed inside, and there was a crowd of people milling about on the sidewalk, waiting for tables to become available.

Akshay paid the driver and ushered us through the door past the long line of waiting customers. A stout East Indian woman in her late fifties, with long, graying black hair pulled back into a ponytail and wearing a colorful orange and red assemblage of traditional Indian garb wrapped around her padded figure, hustled up to us and grabbed Akshay in a bear hug.

"Akshay, you didn't tell me you were coming by tonight," she said in an English accent that betrayed only a hint of her Bombay roots.

"I brought some friends," he said, introducing Charlie and me to the woman, who turned out to be Akshay's mother. She smiled and bowed to us both and then escorted us to the back of the restaurant where a private table awaited us. Before we even had the chance to sit down, she signaled a waiter to rush over with three Taj Mahal beers and a plate of assorted appetizers. Charlie dove into the meat samosas as Akshay talked his ear off. Meanwhile, I was wrapped up in a conversation with Akshay's mother. She spun a fascinating tale about her family's financial struggles, how they came to England with just pennies to their name, and how they spent the better part of a decade working hard to start this restaurant, which took off in popularity, much to everyone's surprise. She explained how Akshay wanted more out of life than just working in the family business. And how happy it made her that she and her husband were able to earn enough money to send him to Oxford. He had made the whole family proud when he went back to India after college and conquered the movie industry, becoming one of the biggest and brightest stars in their native country. Now she eagerly awaited his star to rise in Europe, and eventually, in America. She had always impressed upon her son that anything in life was possible, and he was now living proof that she had been right. I sat there listening, amazed over how such a beautiful, vibrant, happy woman could have given birth to such a first-rate jerk. I wasn't about to tell her that, however.

When the waiter failed to bring brown rice with our curry as I had requested, Akshay's mother was out of her seat like a shot, barreling into the kitchen to fix the situation. I turned my attention to Akshay, who now had a hand resting on Charlie's right bicep as he leaned in close to him and chattered endlessly into his ear, trying to be heard over the noisy din of the other diners.

I wanted to reach over and punch him but thought it might be perceived as inappropriate behavior given the fact we were dining for free in his family's establishment. I could only watch, seething, as Akshay doted on Charlie, laughed at his every sarcastic comment, and touched his arm as much as he could. I hadn't even realized Akshay was gay. He kept that part of himself well hidden. Until now. When he met my boyfriend. I didn't think I had any reason to be jealous. I would certainly give Charlie an earful about Akshay's true nature the minute we ditched him later. So why was this bothering me? Akshay was no threat. He wasn't even Charlie's type. At least, I thought he wasn't.

How I managed to hear my cell phone ringing through the clatter of dishes, clinking glasses, and cacophony of voices in such a small, enclosed space was a mystery. But I fished through my coat pocket and yanked out my blue-encased Nokia and pressed the Talk button.

"Hello?" I said, holding the phone to one ear as I jammed my finger into the other to block out all the commotion.

"Jarrod, it's Wallace."

I was in no mood to endure another sulk fest with our insecure, whining playwright. Especially when I saw Charlie's eyes sparkle as he spoke to Akshay. His eyes never sparkled unless he was looking at me!

"Wallace, this isn't a good time—"

"You haven't left London yet, have you?"

"No, we're having dinner in Little Bengal. Why?"

"Because they're not going to let you leave."

"Who?" I said.

"The police. They called Katrina and me just as we were heading out to see a show. They want to question everyone again. Claire's death has been reclassified as a homicide."

I fell back in my chair just as Akshay's mother delivered my brown rice.

# Chapter 9

My only thought through dinner was whisking Charlie out of the country and away from Akshay. Now, with this new bombshell, that would prove to be impossible. I wedged myself in between Charlie and Akshay as we climbed into a taxi after leaving Muhib and maneuvered my head to visually block Akshay from making any more eye contact with my boyfriend during our quick trip back to the Savoy. I had stuffed myself with so much meat and curry I was downright dizzy from the overindulgence. My eyelids drooped. All I could think about was slipping into a deep sleep with my arms around Charlie.

Charlie kept a hand over his stomach. He was miserable. We had both eaten far too much. Akshay, on the other hand, was a bundle of energy.

"I know a great pub that's open after hours on Compton. Either of you up for a nightcap?"

"I'm beyond stuffed. I think I'm going to have to call it a night, Akshay, but thank you," I said, ending the discussion.

"What about you, Charlie?"

I was floored. This bastard was making a blatant play for my boyfriend. Right in front of me. He was probably thrilled that I had declined his invitation. And he was betting Charlie would plow right over me to get some alone time with him. Well, he didn't know my Charlie. He would never abandon me for some slick Bombay boy toy.

"I'm too stuffed to go to sleep. I'll probably be up all night. Maybe a drink is just what I need to make me tired," he said.

I nearly choked on my after-dinner mint.

"Excellent," Akshay said with a gleeful smile. "We'll drop Jarrod off at the hotel, and then head on to Old Compton Road."

I spun my head around, eyes narrowing, firing laser beams of disapproval at Charlie. He didn't immediately pick up on my death-ray signals. Or was he choosing not to? This was a disaster. Our first night together after a month-long separation, and Charlie was throwing me over for Akshay. I wasn't going to have a meltdown. I was simply going to be honest and reveal my insecure feelings about this whole situation to both of them. If therapy had taught me anything, it was to be absolutely truthful in an uncomfortable situation.

"You sure you don't mind, babe?" Charlie said.

"No, not at all," I lied.

So much for therapy. No. Honesty was highly overrated. This required duplicitous countermeasures. I had no intention of getting out of that taxi without Charlie and leaving him to the flirtatious advances of a gay Indian with a startlingly sexy smile.

"You know something," I said, mustering up the performance of a lifetime. "I suddenly don't feel well. I'm a bit nauseous."

"You think it might be something you ate?" Charlie said.

I flashed an innocent smile at Akshay. "Oh, no. Everything was delicious. I'm sure Akshay's family uses only the freshest ingredients."

Okay, I was taking the low road. This was terribly unfair. But in wartime, sometimes you have to make hard choices. I grabbed my gut and moaned softly. I didn't want to overdo it. If only I could work up a little sweat on my brow. That would really help sell it. But alas, it was about forty degrees in the taxicab, so that wasn't about to happen.

"I'm so embarrassed," I said, "I never get sick. I wonder what could have caused it."

Akshay was fuming, but he covered it well. He knew exactly what I was doing. And he was going to ratchet up the stakes. He leaned forward and tapped the driver on the shoulder. "Excuse me, you better take us to the nearest hospital straight away."

Bastard! He was throwing down the gauntlet, challenging me.

"No," I whispered as if I was in some gender-bending stage production of *Camille*. "I'll be all right. Maybe if I just get some rest, the cramps will go away."

"We shouldn't take any chances," Akshay said.

The Savoy was coming up at the next block. My single-minded resolve was to just get Charlie and myself out of that cab and away from Akshay.

I reached forward and grabbed the taxi driver by the jacket collar. "Please, sir, let us off at the Savoy."

I choked the driver enough so he knew that he had better do as I requested. The cab peeled into the circular driveway that ran along the entrance to the Savoy and deposited us all at the front entrance.

Akshay made a big deal of helping me out of the cab as if he were overly concerned with my well-being. Jerk. He was just playing it up in front of Charlie. Arthur opened the front door to the hotel for us, and Charlie and Akshay ushered me inside.

"Thank you for a wonderful dinner, Akshay," I said. "I'm sorry to cut it so short."

"Not a problem. The important thing is you feel better, so get some rest," he said. Although I was certain he was secretly hoping my symptoms would get worse and I would slip into a permanent coma.

Charlie shook Akshay's hand. "Thank you, Akshay, you were a great host."

Akshay smiled, obviously smitten. "Well, it is easy to be a good host when you're blessed with such pleasurable company."

God, I hated him. What a lame-ass thing to say. I had half a mind to call him on his phony manners. But instead, I managed a weak smile and said, "Good night."

"I'm going to have a bourbon in the bar," Akshay said as we turned toward the bank of elevators. "That's where I'll be if you're feeling better later."

It was obvious that although he was including me, he was hoping that Charlie would tuck me into bed and then scurry on down to join him so they would have a little private time together. As long as I had one last breath in my body, that was never going to happen.

When Charlie and I stepped onto the elevator, I turned around in time to see Akshay waving to us as the doors closed. Finally we were rid of him.

"He seemed nice," Charlie said.

I let out a dismissive groan. Charlie knew what was coming, so he braced himself.

"He's a two-faced, nasty son of a bitch!" I spit out. "He's been mean and condescending to me ever since I arrived in London, and now all of a sudden he's trying to be best pals or something. And I know why!"

"Why?"

"He's attracted to you," I said. Now it was Charlie's turn to say I had nothing to worry about because he certainly wasn't the least bit attracted to Akshay.

"Really? You think so?"

He sounded flattered. Maybe I had overplayed my hand. That's what wild jealousy will do to a man. It causes him to let his guard down and make stupid mistakes.

"You didn't fall for that fake show of charm and good manners, did you?"

"I don't know," Charlie said with a shrug. "It didn't seem phony to *me*."

"You don't know him like I do," I said.

"Okay," Charlie said. And that was that. He had no intention of getting dragged down into a fight.

We arrived at our floor and I bounded out of the elevator and down the hall to our room, fishing for the room key in my pocket.

From behind me I heard Charlie's stern voice. "Now that's what I call a miraculous recovery."

Damn. I had forgotten I was supposed to be sick. When I reached the door to our room, I stumbled a bit, just for show, but it was a sad attempt to regain what little was left of my credibility.

I inserted the key into the lock, twisted it, and pushed open the door. I turned back to Charlie. "Maybe I had a twenty-four-minute flu."

Charlie chuckled. "Yeah. Maybe."

I was caught red-handed. Luckily, however, he was in a forgiving mood and we were up half the night celebrating our long-awaited reunion.

I had received a message to report to the theater the following morning at eight for a meeting with Detective Inspector Sally Bowles. She wanted to go over everyone's stories again given the reclassification of Claire Richards's death as a homicide. But since Charlie and I didn't get to sleep until well after four, when I pried open my eyes and saw it was twenty minutes past nine, the panic instantly started to seep through my body.

Charlie was still sound asleep as I threw on some jeans and a T-shirt and dashed out the door. It was a brisk, sunny morning as I pounded through the throng of people toward Shaftsbury Avenue. I made it to the Apollo in just under ten minutes, probably a new record. As I hurried through the rear door, I heard loud yelling. It was probably DI Sally Bowles demanding that I be arrested for my inexcusable tardiness. But as I rounded the corner and made my way past the dressing rooms and toward the auditorium, I saw DI Bowles and her gruff, doughy partner snapping handcuffs on Claire Richards's understudy, Minx.

Minx was screaming and cursing and wrenching her body in protest as Kenneth, Wallace, Liam, Akshay, Sir Anthony, and Dame Sylvia all looked on, utterly appalled. This was not the perky brunette with the electrifying smile I had met only weeks earlier. This was an explosive, unhinged woman whose wild, possessed eyes sent a chill down my spine.

I raced up to my writer, director, and fellow actors as DI Bowles and her partner hauled the screeching Minx out a side door.

Akshay, my warm and wonderful host the night before, took one look at me and turned his back. Without Charlie at my side, my stock had suddenly plunged in his eyes.

Kenneth abruptly cocked his head my way and said, "DI Bowles still wants to speak to you even though she suspects the case may already be wrapped up."

"Minx?" I said.

Wallace nodded. "The coroner found peanut oil mixed in with Claire's stage make-up. It turns out Claire was severely allergic to all nuts, and that's what caused the massive stroke."

Sir Anthony sadly shook his head. "We all heard Minx's inappropriate jokes about offing Claire so she could take over the leading role."

Liam moaned with grief, sank into a chair, and covered his face with his hands.

"But how did they connect Minx to the peanut oil?" I said.

"I saw her mixing some strange liquid in with the make-up that night," Dame Sylvia said. "I asked her what it was, and she told me it was just something to give the base more color and texture or some such nonsense."

This was unbelievable. Minx might have been a clawing, manipulative little Eve Harrington, but a murderer?

"Did anyone see Minx actually give the make-up to Claire?" I said.

Akshay finally deigned to speak to me as he raised his hand. "Not only did I see her bring the make-up directly to Claire, but I also watched as she helped her put it on."

A lethal concoction. Two separate witnesses. A clear motive. It was starting to look like curtains for Minx. But if she had planned on doing away with Claire, why would Minx bounce around the theater making jokes about it during the weeks leading up to the murder? Minx might not have been the brightest bulb in the chandelier, but she wasn't an idiot. It didn't make sense to me. Was someone lying? Dame Sylvia had the most damning testimony. She had actually seen Minx blending the oil into the make-up. Was this a part of some elaborate setup to frame Minx for her own dirty doings?

And what about the combustible Liam, whose violent temper might have driven him to the edge? Or Kenneth, who was completely belittled and humiliated by Claire, or anyone else in the company, all of whom seemed to despise Claire? Everyone, that is, except me. As my head started to flood with questions, I knew I was about to embark on yet another journey to uncover the truth. And I was going to start by finding out the identity of the mystery man who was having sex with Claire Richards in her dressing room mere minutes before her final performance.

# Chapter 10

DI Sally Bowles returned hours later from hustling Minx off to the nearest precinct for booking on suspicion of murder. She had requested I wait for her, but it was well after four in the afternoon before she decided to return and interview me again. Most of the cast had already fled by the time she charged into the theater through the front entrance. She asked that I join her in my dressing room, where she launched into a near repeat of her previous line of questioning with a heavy emphasis on the identity of the man I had supposedly heard Claire having sexual relations with minutes before the opening-night curtain.

"I've talked with every man in the company, and they all deny sleeping with Claire, with the notable exception of Liam Killoran, of course," she said.

"Someone's lying," I said.

"That someone could be you," she said.

"Why would I sleep with her? I'm gay," I said.

"You're an actor. Maybe you were acting."

"I'm not that good."

"Oh, I highly doubt that," she said.

"What motive would I have? What could I possibly gain?"

"Claire is a very successful star. People listen to her. Perhaps if you had her in your corner, she could help secure you a key role in her next film production."

If only I were that conniving. Maybe I would have more feature-film credits on my resume other than Larry Levant's disastrous low-budget slasher flick shot in south Florida last year. And a cheap *Tom Sawyer* remake in the eighties with Jason Bateman.

"Look, Detective Inspector, Claire was already in my corner. I didn't have to sleep with her. And what does this have to do with anything? You've already arrested Minx for the murder."

"There's no denying the evidence against Minx, but I just want to make sure I have covered all the bases. If you insist Claire's secret paramour isn't you, then do you have any guesses on who it might be?"

"I told you during our last interview. No, I don't."

"It's been a few days since we last spoke. I was hoping you might have remembered something."

We did this little dance for another forty-five minutes. I saw something gnawing at DI Bowles. Arresting Minx didn't feel right. Her gut told her the case wasn't closed. There was more to the story. And I had to agree.

Sally Bowles asked me to keep my eyes and ears open over the next couple of days in case I heard something unusual from one of my fellow cast members that might be of help in the case. I told her I would be happy to, if I had planned on staying in England. But right now my sole focus was boarding a plane and flying home to Los Angeles. This did nothing to dissipate any suspicions she might have harbored about my involvement with Claire's death. Fleeing the country was not the best way to illus-trate a perception of innocence. But at this point I didn't care. She had nothing on me to keep me there. In fact, she had already made an arrest. So legally I was free to go.

"Very well," Sally Bowles said, her jaws clenched from frustration. "If I need to speak to you further, I will contact you in America."

"Sounds like a plan," I said, shaking her hand and bounding for the door.

She stopped me with her stern, hardened voice. "Mr. Jarvis, I actually do have one more question for you."

I sighed and turned around.

"Do you think Minx is capable of murder?" she said, staring me dead in the eyes.

I thought for a moment before answering. "No. I really don't."

She nodded, mulling over my opinion, and then waved me away, lost in her own thoughts.

It was finally over. I was going home. Free from this loony bin of egos and ambition. As I trudged back to the Savoy, I flipped open my cell phone and called British Airways. The chipper airline representative clicked away on her computer as she tried to secure Charlie and me two coach seats on the next flight back to Los Angeles. The first available flight would be tomorrow morning. I decided to pay the one-hundred-dollar reservation change fee in order to avoid having to go through the production office. I just wanted to slip out of town unnoticed and never think of anyone connected to *Murder Can Be Civilized* ever again. Charlie had wanted to stay in town a few days, but I was through with jolly old England for now. Perhaps we could come back next year as tourists, when enough time had passed and I was no longer so close to all the emotion and tragedy of the last few weeks. I couldn't bear staying in London with the constant reminders of Claire Richards. She had been a true friend to me, and I had yet to take the time to grieve properly. Charlie would understand. He always did.

It was going on six o'clock and the cloudy gray sky was slowly giving away to nightfall. Arthur waved to me as I scurried through the door of the Savoy and raced for the elevators. I had already planned our evening out in my mind. A feast from room service. Some snuggling in our white terrycloth robes between comedies on the BBC. A little lovemaking. And then a good night's sleep before our flight back to the States. The only problem was, whenever I meticulously design the perfect evening, I allow my expectations to be raised, and when things don't work out as planned, I am resoundingly disappointed.

I jammed the key into the lock and whipped the door open. I stopped dead. My heart sank. Charlie was lying on top of the bed, his shirt discarded on the floor. Akshay stood over him, looking dashing in a blue blazer, a white shirt open enough to boast his toned, hairy chest, as he offered me his trademark sexy smile.

"Hello," I said, standing in the doorway, like a lost child on the verge of tears. They had been so engrossed in conversation they hadn't even heard the door open. Both looked up at me, startled.

"Hey, babe," Charlie said, trying to sit up but wincing from the pain of his bullet wounds. There was still a white bandage stretched across his bare torso. Akshay quickly slipped an arm around Charlie's back to assist him. I wanted to throw up.

"What's going on?" I said, trying in vain to keep my voice steady and calm.

"Akshay just dropped by to see if we had dinner plans," Charlie said.

Akshay flashed his perfect teeth at me. I wanted to punch him in the mouth and get rid of a few of them.

"I'd really rather just stay in tonight. It's been a long day," I said, watching Akshay as he finished helping Charlie sit up, but let his hands linger on his back and knee.

"I completely understand," Akshay said. "DI Bowles is like a dog with a bone. Question after question. It was exhausting. And poor Jarrod was stuck there waiting for her to speak to him all day."

There was a long, uncomfortable silence. Akshay finally got the hint. He stood upright, letting Charlie ease back against the headboard, and said, "Well, I should get going. You two have a relaxing evening."

"Good night, Akshay," Charlie said.

Akshay gave Charlie an inappropriate longing look. He didn't care that I was standing there watching. "Good night, Charlie."

It took all the self-control I could muster not to trip him as he walked out the door. He gave me a perfunctory nod as he passed me. Once he was safely in the hallway, I stepped inside and slammed the door behind him. Then I turned to Charlie.

"Look, don't wig out on me over this. When he knocked on the door, I thought it was you," Charlie said, in damage-control mode.

"I have a key," I said. "I wouldn't have knocked."

"I thought you forgot it or lost it or something."

I wanted to drop it. I really did. But I just couldn't. "Why was your shirt off?"

"He wanted to give me a massage. How could I say no?" Charlie said with a straight face.

My mouth dropped open and Charlie chuckled.

"Relax, babe," he said. "I'm joking. The bullet wound on my chest was bothering me, and I was afraid it might be bleeding so I took it off to take a look. End of story."

"I don't like him," I said.

"I know you don't. You made that abundantly clear last night. But just because you've got a problem with him doesn't mean I have to be rude to him."

Charlie watched me closely, monitoring just how close I was to a meltdown. He didn't want to risk suffering through a geyser of emotions that I could shoot off like Old Faithful.

"Nothing happened," Charlie said, slow and soft, never taking his eyes off me.

I knew I should have understood. Especially since I had my own admirer while shooting my movie in south Florida last year. A buff, handsome Navy SEAL turned private detective had been attracted to me, but from Charlie's point of view, it had seemed as if something was going on between us when in fact nothing was happening except a passing attraction. But now I was in Charlie's position of doubting and suspecting, and I knew I was not going to handle it as well as he did.

"I need some air," I said and turned around to leave.

"Oh, come on, Jarrod, don't do this," Charlie said, standing up from the bed, but still holding his bandages.

"No, I'm fine. I believe you," I said, but I was only half convincing myself. "I just want to go for a walk."

I was feeling hopelessly insecure. I knew it. And Charlie knew it.

"You're being ridiculous right now. You know that, don't you?"

"Don't talk to me like I'm a child."

"Well, you're acting like one, Jarrod. Sometimes you forget that you're no longer that cute little kid from *Go To Your Room*. You're thirty-four years old. You can't keep making a grand exit offstage whenever you get hurt. And the sooner you realize that there is no sympathetic studio audience out there that is going to go 'awwww' over your problems anymore, the better off you'll be."

I had heard enough. I turned on my heel and marched out the door. I headed out to the Strand and wandered aimlessly around the city. But it was cold, the kind of cold that cracks the bones. And I hadn't brought a jacket. I stopped in at a Starbucks in Leicester Square (Starbucks is only a few franchises away from complete world domination) and warmed myself up with a hot cup of coffee, my mind forming terribly violent thoughts about

Akshay Kapoor, my newly crowned arch nemesis. Then, I checked the movie times at several of the old palace theaters that lined the square. Nothing was starting for at least another hour. I was stuck. It was either swallow my pride and head back to the hotel room, or shuffle over to Piccadilly Circus and pass the time thumbing through CD racks at Tower Records.

Charlie was right. I was being ridiculous. I had let my absolute distrust and dislike of Akshay completely cloud my judgment. If it had been Wallace or Sir Anthony hovering over Charlie's bed and leering at him, I would not have thought twice about it. I would have laughed it off. But Akshay had been so dismissive, so disdainful of me during the entire production I had let my imagination run wild.

Whenever I feel backed into a corner, my first instinct is to run. But after a brief period of contemplating the situation, I often come to the conclusion that I might have overreacted. I smiled to myself. Charlie was probably lying in bed, watching TV and checking his watch. He knew I would be back within the hour, full of apologies for not trusting him and prepared to make up for my bad behavior with a barrage of kisses.

I trekked back to the Savoy, tail between my legs. I was as predictable as our Pekingese Snickers with a tennis ball. She would always come back with it no matter where you threw it. My mood brightened as I snatched the keys from my pocket and bounced down the hall to our room. I had debated on whether I should stop for flowers, but Charlie just isn't a flowers kind of guy. He liked chocolates but was trying to cut down on his sugar intake. I decided a full on apology from me would be enough for him tonight.

When I reached out to open the door with the key, I was surprised to find it already open a crack. I pressed my fingers against it and pushed the door open wider. Charlie wasn't in bed. The TV was on, blaring some old French and Saunders *Baywatch* sketch. I looked around the room. The bathroom door was ajar and the light turned off. Charlie was gone. Maybe he just went out to get some ice. Or ran down to pick up a newspaper in the lobby. There had to be a simple explanation. But four hours later, as I sat alone on the edge of the bed, rocking back and forth with worry, still waiting for him to return, my intuition was screaming at me that something was seriously wrong.

# Chapter 11

I briefly thought Charlie might have gone out to dinner with Akshay just to teach me a lesson, but it was going on one in the morning. He would've come back by now. Wouldn't he? This was crazy. Where was he? What was he doing? Had I gone too far this time? Had I driven him to the point of just wanting to wash his hands of me? It was possible. And absolutely horrifying to think about. Charlie and I had been together for four years now. There were challenges, just like in any relationship, but we were happy, and in love, and there wasn't any reason to think it would ever fall apart. Charlie knew I would be a high-maintenance boyfriend from the day he met me. What actor isn't? But he didn't scare easily—he was a rugged cop, after all—and he knew that in the end he could handle me.

God, this was maddening. Charlie was so predictable. I could call his every move. But this one was unexpected and worrisome. Had he gone out to a club? He didn't know anyone in London, so he would have gone alone. Correction. He did know one person. I had to know. I had to know if he was with Akshay.

I scooped up the phone and dialed Akshay's flat. I held my breath, waiting for Akshay's groggy voice to assure me that he was asleep in his bed. Alone. The phone rang ten times. Maybe he was just a heavy sleeper. Or maybe he had turned the ringer off.

I raced out of the room and down the hall to the elevator and rode down to the lobby. Arthur was off duty, so I approached the gangly, pimply-faced, twenty-year-old bellhop-in-training who stood near the concierge. He was sleepy-eyed and bored. There wasn't much to do during the graveyard shift. The lobby was now empty of guests.

"Excuse me," I said.

His eyes lit up. He recognized me instantly. Not from my life as a sitcom star, but from weeks of holding the door open for me as I returned from a series of late-night rehearsals at the Apollo.

"Yes, sir, how may I help you?" He was thrilled that someone was taking the time to talk to him.

"Slow night, I guess," I said.

"Oh, yes, sir. Very quiet," he said.

"Do you remember seeing a man, about six feet two, dark hair, nice build, leaving earlier? It was probably between eight and nine o'clock tonight."

The boy shook his head. "I'm sorry, sir, I just came on duty a half hour ago. I was at my niece's birthday party and I arrived rather late for my shift." He leaned in and smiled. "Don't tell the manager."

I promised to keep mum and crossed over to the reservations desk where a stout, curly-haired, rosy-cheeked woman in her early thirties typed on a computer. She looked up at me and smiled.

"Good evening, sir."

"Good evening. It seems I've lost someone," I said.

"Oh, dear. That's not good."

"My boyfriend."

"Oh, yes, sir. I saw the two of you leaving last night with Mr. Kapoor."

"So you remember him?"

"Oh, yes. Very tall. Quite handsome. I couldn't help but notice him, sir."

"Have you seen him tonight?"

She thought about it. She really wanted to help me. But then she shook her head. "No, sir. I can't say that I have."

"Are you sure?"

"Believe me, sir, I would've remembered."

"Have you been here at the desk all night?"

"Yes. Except for my break."

"When was that?"

"Around eight-thirty. I was gone until just before nine o'clock."

So Charlie left sometime between eight-thirty and nine. If he had actually gone out. He could still be somewhere in the hotel.

"Who covered the desk while you took your break?" I said.

"That would be Ian, sir."

"Can I talk to him?"

"Oh, he's gone home for the night."

"Do you have a number where I can reach him?"

"I'm sorry, sir, I'm not allowed to give out any personal information on the staff."

"When will he be back?"

"Tomorrow morning. His shift starts at eleven."

"Thank you."

I was lost. I had absolutely no idea what to do next. So I headed back to the room to wait some more.

Five hours later I was still waiting. And in a complete panic. Charlie hadn't come back all night. I dialed Akshay's room fifteen more times, never getting an answer. I flipped open the phone book and looked up Muhib Indian Cuisine. I didn't seriously expect Akshay's mother to pick up the phone at six in the morning, but it was worth a try. I got a machine rattling off the operating hours and location of the restaurant. I left a message asking Mrs. Kapoor to call me back at the Savoy.

By eight, I had to take action or I was going to go out of my mind. I headed back down to the lobby and out to the street, where I hailed a taxicab and instructed the driver to take me to the nearest police station.

I half expected to see DI Sally Bowles in full investigative mode when I arrived at the precinct, but since there were dozens of police stations in London, I figured that might be a long shot. The reception area was surprisingly clean and tidy considering the criminal element that was ushered through the premises all day and night. I approached a rail-thin, balding, beak-nosed man who sat behind a raised desk, clutching a cup of coffee and perusing the morning's headlines. At first he didn't notice me, so I cleared my throat. He took a long, slow sip of his coffee and then raised his eyes, settling on my face. He waited for me to speak first.

"I'd like to report a missing person," I said.

He sighed. I was asking him to do something and it annoyed him.

"He's only been gone the night, and I know in the States it has to be twenty-four hours before someone can be declared missing, but it's so unlike him to do this, especially in a foreign country," I said.

I suddenly noticed that this guy in uniform with his side patches of red hair and big nose looked just like a British version of the Beaker character from *The Muppet Show*. I almost laughed in his face.

He sighed again. He lowered his gaze back down to his newspaper in the vain hope that I would just go away. But then he saw something in the paper that caught his eye. He looked up at me and then back down at his newspaper.

Beaker shot up out of his seat, spilling coffee everywhere, and opened a door to allow me to come inside the main area housing all the officers on duty.

"Right this way, sir," Beaker said with a forced smile, his newspaper tucked underneath his arm.

He led me down a hall to an office at the end and rapped on the door. A tall Nigerian man with an angular face and wearing a tan suit stood to greet me.

"I'm Detective Colin Samms," he said in a deep, commanding voice.

"Jarrod Jarvis," I said, shaking his hand.

"He wants to report a missing person," Beaker piped in excitedly.

I saw Samms make quick eye contact with Beaker before waving him away. Beaker slapped his newspaper down on the desk in front of Samms before leaving. After we were alone, Samms casually sat back down.

"Now then, you'd like to file a report?"

"Yes. It's my boyfriend, Charlie. He vanished. Just like that. And I'm going insane with worry."

I told Detective Samms everything I could remember about the night. He listened with rapt attention, taking in every detail, jotting a few notes on a pad that rested on the desk in front of him. When I finished my story, I waited for him to respond. He consulted his notes before speaking.

"You say you left around seven-thirty and came back around nine?"

"Yes, give or take a few minutes."

"So he had to have left during that time."

"Yes."

"Why did you leave?"

"Pardon me?"

"Your boyfriend had just arrived in town. You hadn't seen him in over a month. Why did you leave?"

"Oh. We had a little spat," I said, feeling like a lonely housewife desperately trying to conceal her marital problems from the outside world. Spat. Why did I say *spat*? Why couldn't I have just said *fight*? Who says *spat* anymore?

Samms nodded. "What was this *spat* about?" Of course he emphasized the word *spat* just to make me feel even more foolish.

I explained how one of my costars was obviously attracted to Charlie and that I was threatened by it.

"So you blew up at him and then stormed out?"

"I wouldn't say blew up. And I didn't storm. I just needed some air."

"But you left angry?"

"Yes."

This was a disaster. I was coming across as some unstable, needy Twinkie. There was a long, agonizing silence before Samms lifted his head and stared at me.

"This sounds to me like a simple lovers' quarrel," he said.

"I know it does. And it was, in part. But for him to disappear like that, it just doesn't make any sense. If you knew Charlie—"

"You seem to be embroiled in a lot of those lately," Samms said.

"I'm sorry, embroiled in what?"

"Lovers' quarrels," he said, his eyes carefully weighing my reaction.

I stopped. "What do you mean?"

Samms slid the newspaper Beaker had given him over in front of me. I looked down at it, my mouth contorting into a mask of distress. It was a copy of the *Daily Mirror*, one of London's best-selling tabloids. And on the front page was a picture of Claire Richards and her young lover, Liam Killoran, their arms around each other and smiling. In a box to the lower right of the page was a picture of me. It was a recent 8 x 10 of mine that I had submitted to the producers of the play for publicity purposes.

The headline blared, "Claire Richards's Lover Claims Child

Star Killed Her in Crime of Passion!" I grabbed the paper and thumbed through it until I found the story. It was an exclusive interview with Liam, full of contemptible charges and false allegations of my romantic involvement with Claire. How she had delicately tried to extricate herself from the affair because she realized how much she loved Liam. And how I became obsessive and dangerous, and ultimately convinced Minx to administer the fatal peanut oil that caused her anaphylactic shock and subsequent stroke.

I slapped the paper back down in front of Detective Samms. "This is trash. There's not a word of truth to it."

"Yes, but you must admit to a pattern here," Samms said in a dead-serious tone.

"Pattern? What are you talking about?"

"Well, I would have thought this was rubbish too had you not come down here today with a sordid tale of a heated fight between you and your lover, and now he's vanished under mysterious circumstances. One lover dead. One lover missing. You must admit, Mr. Jarvis, it does give one pause."

If I didn't know myself, I would have suspected me of foul play too.

# Chapter 12

By the time Detective Colin Samms finished grilling me, it was almost ten-thirty in the morning. He had nothing to charge me with, but the mere fact that Charlie was missing turned up the heat on me as a suspect in Claire's murder. It didn't matter that Minx had been arrested and presumably arraigned by now. The cops were still investigating the case, trying to piece it all together, and had clearly decided I was a key piece of the puzzle. It's hard to tell exactly when the tabloids, so full of blatant lies and innuendo, had been accepted as the mainstream press. Some say it was during the OJ Simpson murder trial. The *National Enquirer* and the *Star* were unearthing evidence at a much faster rate than most legitimate news sources. Networks and cable news channels began using their stories as facts in their broadcasts. And now, the *Enquirer* seemed to enjoy the same reputation and reliability as CNN. It was a scary world. And the English tabloids were even more intense than the American trash papers. They were vicious and judgmental, printing sordid sex tapes involving the royal family without a hint of discretion or sense of responsibility. Prince Charles moaning to his long-time love Camilla Parker Bowles that his wish was to be a tampon so he could be inserted inside of her. It was a ghastly thought to begin with, but soon the revelations became part of the norm, slapped on the front page with the regularity of the daily weather forecast.

There was absolutely no evidence connecting me to Claire's murder. The cops were betting on Liam's preposterous story having a grain of truth to it. They couldn't arrest me. I was free to go. Detective Samms, however, offered vague promises that I would be watched from this point on until the investigation was concluded. It was an obvious ploy to rattle me. I left the precinct frustrated. They were less concerned with my missing boyfriend and more into somehow tying me to the crime at the Apollo. I could understand. Charlie was just a tourist. Claire was an integral part of British culture. But that didn't make it hurt less.

I grabbed a taxicab back to the Savoy and arrived a few minutes before eleven. Ian, the desk clerk who might have seen Charlie, was scheduled to work in just a few minutes. That gave me some time to run up to the room and see if Charlie had somehow miraculously returned. When I approached the room, the door was ajar and there was someone stirring inside. I held my breath and rounded the corner. But as I entered the room, I only found a smiling housekeeper fluffing a pillow. My hopes crumbled.

"Good morning, sir," she said in a working-class Liverpool accent.

"Good morning," I said, noticing the red light on my phone blinking. Someone had left a message. I pushed past her and grabbed the phone, punching the button for my messages.

The call had come in just a couple hours earlier. I silently prayed I would hear Charlie's deep, reassuring voice.

"Mr. Jarvis, this is Mrs. Kapoor, Akshay's mother, from Muhib restaurant. I received your message this morning. I have been trying to find my son all night. I called his flat. I called everywhere. No one has seen him. I'm very worried. Please call me." There was a click and then silence.

I wasn't about to jump to any conclusions. The fact that both Charlie and Akshay were missing meant nothing. It didn't mean they were together. I was just being an overly paranoid boyfriend. And even if my worst fears had a pinch of merit, there was no way I was ready to face them at this point.

I grabbed a playbill for *Murder Can Be Civilized* and raced back down to the lobby and was relieved to see a portly, smiling young man in his late twenties, with an already receding hairline and thick black glasses tipped on the bridge of his nose, behind the front desk. His gold-plated name tag said "Ian." I hurried up to him so fast the rush of air hit him in the face, immediately alerting him to my presence.

"Good morning, sir," he said. You had to love the English for their impeccable manners at all hours of the day.

"Good morning. The woman on duty last night said you relieved her during her break yesterday between eight-thirty and nine?"

He thought for a moment, and then nodded with a smile. "Yes, that's right, sir."

I reached for my wallet, pulled a small photo of Charlie on the beach during our vacation to Barbados last year out of a plastic sleeve, and placed it in front of Ian. "Do you recall seeing this man leave the hotel during that time?"

Ian picked up the photo and inspected it. "No, sir. I didn't see him leave. Sorry."

I was back to square one.

"He mostly just hung out in the lobby talking," he said.

"I'm sorry, what? You saw him?"

"Yes, sir. I saw him conversing with a man over there near the elevators. But I became distracted by a guest who arrived to check in, and when I was through he was gone," Ian said.

I slapped the playbill down in front of Ian. It was open to the page that featured a photo of the entire cast. I pointed to Akshay.

"Was he speaking with this man?" I said.

Ian shook his head. "No, sir. He was talking to *that* man."

I looked down at the photo. Ian was pointing to Sir Anthony Stiles.

I tried calling Sir Anthony's flat from my hotel room several times to no avail. I was desperate so I made an on-the-spot decision to bunk out in front of his flat until he returned. I knew his address from the cast list. He was a local, so the producers felt no need to put him up at the fancy Savoy. I jumped in a taxicab that spirited me over to Knightsbridge, the upscale neighborhood that boasted the world-famous Harrods department store, which was shopaholic Laurette's number-one destination whenever she was in London. Traffic was hopelessly congested and pedestrians clogged the street crossing over to Mohamed Al Fayed's crown jewel of consumer consumption. It took us almost twenty minutes to drive just a few blocks south to some quieter residential streets. The driver stopped at a well-kept brownstone painted brick red. I double-checked the address from the cast list, paid the driver, and stepped out onto the curb. I was about to sit down on the stoop and wait for Sir Anthony to come home, but I rang the bell just to make sure he was still out. I heard someone call from inside.

"Just a moment, please."

It sounded like Sir Anthony, and when the door was flung open, to my relief it was. He stood there, a big grin on his face, greeting me. And he was completely nude. There wasn't a stitch of clothes on him. My mouth dropped open at his flabby, powder white birthday suit, his shriveled-up private parts on full display in all their glory. Oh God. Not again.

"Jarrod, what a pleasant surprise. What brings you here to my humble abode?" he said, still not the least bit concerned that he was stark naked for everyone in his neighborhood to see.

"I . . . I . . . tried calling first, but there was no answer," I stammered, still in a complete state of shock.

"Oh no, I never pick up the phone when I am tutoring one of my students," he said with one of his conspiratorial winks.

"I don't mean to interrupt your . . . tutoring session, Sir Anthony, but I must speak to you. It's very important."

"My dear boy, you look quite frazzled. Would you care to come in? I'm sure my . . . protégé won't mind taking a short break from his . . . studies."

"No, we can talk here." The last thing I wanted was to be swept inside Sir Anthony's salacious den of iniquity.

"Very well. What is it you would like to discuss with me?" he said, not even noticing the young mother passing by pushing a stroller. The shock of seeing Sir Anthony in the buff nearly caused her to ram her baby into a street lamp.

"I heard you were at the Savoy last night," I said.

"Oh yes, I often like to drop in for a drink. They have such an elegant bar. It's a throwback to a far more raucous, festive time. Brings back many fond memories."

"Someone saw you speaking to this man," I said, flashing him the beach photo of Charlie.

"Oh, yes, I remember him. He's your boyfriend, as I recall," Sir Anthony said, leering. "Quite an impressive-looking fellow, if I do say so."

"How did you know he was my boyfriend?"

"I was just leaving the bar after a few strawberry martinis, and I saw him loitering about in the lobby. Thought he might be a rent boy, to be perfectly honest. I decided to inquire about his hourly rate. Unfortunately, he told me he was a police officer from America and was only here to see his boyfriend in a play that unfortunately just closed. Well, it only took me a few seconds to realize he was talking about our little play, and that his boyfriend was you."

"What else did you talk about?"

"We simply exchanged a few pleasantries after that. He seemed to be in a bit of a hurry. I offered to buy him a drink, but he declined. Said he was waiting for someone."

"Who?"

"I have no idea, Jarrod. I left shortly after our brief exchange. But I did see him wander into the bar after we parted. Is something wrong?"

"He's gone missing," I said.

"Oh, dear. Well, I'm sure he'll turn up. I'm sorry I cannot help you more, but I was in a bit of a hurry last night myself. You see, I was rushing off to meet one of my students. A strapping young man from the Royal Academy. Does a breathtaking Hamlet. Big star of tomorrow, if you ask me."

Down the hall from the foyer of the brownstone I heard a toilet flush. Sir Anthony blushed. "He's still here cramming for his exams. You know how devoted students like to pull all-nighters."

"Yes. Well, thank you, Sir Anthony," I said.

"Cheers!" Sir Anthony waved good-bye to me, as did his nether regions. He shut the door and I was left alone to fret and worry and fear the worst.

# Chapter 13

When I returned to the Savoy, it was already midafternoon, and I was hoping the bartender from last night had begun his shift. The bar, exquisitely appointed with antiques and plush chairs, was relatively quiet, with just a few patrons talking in hushed tones as orchestral music wafted in the background. I spotted one elderly woman clutching a bourbon straight up with one hand while grasping the side of the bar for support with the other as she teetered on top of an unwieldy stool. It was Dame Sylvia Horner. Claire was a teetotaler compared to this boozy broad. The bartender was nowhere in sight.

I ambled over to Dame Sylvia and slid onto a stool next to her.

"How are you, Sylvia?" I said.

She slowly turned, huffing and puffing, making a Herculean effort to maintain her balance. Her face was overly done with powder, and her lipstick was smeared and running over the borders of her lips. Her hair was hastily pulled up in a gaudy pink headband. And she wore a fur coat over a white and pink pantsuit. She looked more like a haggard drag queen after an all-night binge than a theatrical legend. Someone needed to delicately advise Dame Sylvia not to dress herself when she'd been drinking.

Her eyes squinted to focus on my face. She still wasn't sure who was talking to her. Who could blame her? It was already three o'clock in the afternoon. Her happy hour had started at nine this morning.

"Jarrod, I thought you'd gone home," she slurred, not the least bit happy to see me.

"Not yet. I'm trying, though."

"Would you like a drink?" She looked around for the bartender, but the sudden movement caused her to sway and nearly topple over. I quickly leaned in, grabbing her by the elbow to help keep her upright.

"No, thank you. It's a little early for me," I said.

She gripped the bar with both hands and stared at me as if I were an alien from another planet who had come down to observe local custom. Not drink? It was an entirely foreign concept to her.

She shrugged. "Suit yourself."

"Actually, I'm having a bit of a problem locating my boyfriend."

"Did you try that fruitcake Anthony? You want to find a boy, he's got them in all shapes and sizes," she cackled.

"I just came from his flat. No luck there," I said, suddenly realizing I never did get a look at the young buck he had hidden in the back of his flat. But the thought of Charlie and Sir Anthony together was just too fantastic, too ridiculous to even consider.

"He'll turn up," Sylvia spat out between gulps of her drink. "They always do. Whether you want them to or not. And believe me, I've had several husbands who would have made me much happier if they had stayed missing."

"It's just so strange. I mean, he's never done this before . . ."

"Give him some time," Sylvia said, not really concerned with my problem but content knowing I was there to keep her from falling to the floor.

"Time is one thing I've got," I said. "The police would prefer I stay in town until they're done with their investigation of Claire's murder."

Sylvia put her drink down and turned to me. This was a momentous occasion. She had actually let a glass of bourbon out of her sight for a split second.

"Why? You had nothing to do with it. It was Minx," she said.

"The police just want to make sure they have it right," I said.

Dame Sylvia's mouth dropped open, appalled. "Why, that's insane! I saw her mixing that concoction that killed Claire with my own two eyes! How dare they doubt me? Are they implying that I am an unreliable witness?"

"Oh no, not at all," I said, trying to calm the old bat down. "They couldn't ask for a more upstanding and—"

Dame Sylvia slammed down the remainder of her drink and banged the empty glass on the bar several times in an effort to find the bartender.

"And . . . lucid witness," I said, trying hard to sell it.

"Any prosecutor would be proud to have me, a respected member of the artistic community, sitting in that witness box and pointing the finger at that manipulative little trollop Minx," Sylvia said. "Or whoever it was."

I raised an eyebrow. "What do you mean?"

Sylvia was confused and her throat was parched. She was in need of more liquor, and the bartender was MIA.

I gently placed a hand on Sylvia's fur coat sleeve. "Sylvia, what did you mean when you said whoever it was?"

Sylvia grumbled something to herself about the Savoy's bad service, and then her glazed-over, dull eyes tried hard to keep me in focus.

"Jarrod, I saw Minx pouring some kind of liquid into the make-up. That fact is indisputable. But . . ."

"But what?"

"Well, to be perfectly honest, one of my many adoring fans had delivered a gorgeous bottle of scotch to my dressing room earlier in the day. And you see, even at this advanced stage of my career, I get terrible butterflies in my stomach on opening night."

I suddenly knew where this was going. "So you had a shot?"

"Yes. Several, actually. I lost count after seven."

The big reveal that Dame Sylvia was drunk on opening night was about as big a shock as finding out Joan Rivers had a face job.

"Dame Sylvia, are you saying you're not absolutely sure it was Minx you saw mixing the peanut oil into Claire's make-up?"

"Of course I'm sure. Why would I ever inform Detective Inspector Bowles it was Minx if I was not 100 percent positive of the fact?"

"But if you had been drinking—"

"I can hold my liquor, young man," Dame Sylvia said, leaning forward, waving her finger, and completely sloshed. "And I am telling you right now, I am positive it was a woman."

"You mean Minx," I said.

"Yes, Minx is a woman. It could have been her," Sylvia said.

"You're not sure, are you?"

Dame Sylvia gazed around the room for the bartender. "I should slap your face for questioning my judgment, young man, but I won't if you find the damn bartender and get him to pour me another drink."

"Your vision was blurry from the booze. You saw a woman tampering with the make-up and you just assumed it was Minx because of all the jokes she had made about offing Claire so she could assume the starring role."

Dame Sylvia was now embarrassed for divulging so much to me. "It had to be her. That hateful little bitch. Who else *could* it have been?"

She had a point. And even if Sylvia's hazy recollections couldn't be counted on in a court of law, Akshay did see Minx not only bring Claire the make-up but assist her in applying it. She was still the number-one suspect.

The bartender finally returned, much to Dame Sylvia's relief. He was a small man, East Indian, wearing a red vest, white button-up shirt, and black pants. He had a tiny nose, but monstrous-sized teeth that threatened to swallow his face when he smiled.

"Young man, where the hell have you been?" Dame Sylvia barked.

"The bathroom, ma'am. Sorry," he said, bowing to her great presence as he refilled her glass with another generous shot of bourbon.

"Where's that?" Dame Sylvia snickered. "New Delhi?"

The bartender laughed, but his smile was tight enough to suggest he would have preferred knocking her bony, drunken ass off the bar stool.

"Excuse me," I said, as sweet as I could be. "I hate to bother you, but I'm looking for someone who was in here last night."

"I was here. Who are you looking for?"

I slid the picture of Charlie in front of him.

The bartender's eyes lit up. "Yes, yes, of course I remember him. How could I forget him?"

"Why? What did he do?" I said.

"It's not what he did. It's whom he was with. Akshay Kapoor. He may not be that famous here, but back home he's like a hero. I've seen all his movies. I own every one on DVD."

I tapped the photo with my forefinger. "So this man met Akshay? Were they here long?"

"About twenty minutes. That is how long it took me to work up the courage to ask Mr. Kapoor for an autograph." The bartender pulled a napkin out of his breast pocket and waved it proudly in front of my face. "See? He signed it. Do you know how much I could get for this back in India?"

I was trying to stay calm. "Did they leave together?"

"Oh yes. They seemed quite tight," the bartender said.

Dame Sylvia took a big gulp of her drink and slapped the glass down in front of the bartender again. "I always knew that towel-head was a fag."

I stood up from the bar and wandered aimlessly away, my whole world slowly falling apart.

# Chapter 14

As I left the bar, I felt as woozy and disoriented as Dame Sylvia did but I was, in fact, stone-cold sober. This was a nightmare. Charlie and I had been together for four glorious years. Were they glorious to both of us or just me? Was I one of those ignorant spouses who ignored the warning signs and blindly skipped along, oblivious to my spouse's unhappiness and discontent? Was he sticking it out just to appease me, waiting for some smooth-talking Bollywood heartthrob to sweep him off his feet so he could finally be rid of me? My insecurities bubbled brightly to the surface, making me question every self-absorbed action or comment I had made during our entire relationship. Two years ago I had forgotten his birthday while shooting an intensely dramatic episode of *Joan of Arcadia*. I was so wrapped up in my role as a kindly minister who counsels Joan on how to deal with hearing God through the voice of a school crossing guard that I stood up Charlie, who was waiting for me at one of our favorite neighborhood haunts, Off Vine. And on his birthday! Was that the moment he decided he had enough of me? Or was it this play? He had been wounded in the line of duty, and instead of staying by his side, I shot off to London in a desperate attempt to reignite my career. But he had encouraged me to go, insisted I go. So how could I have said no? Should I have more thoroughly examined his desire to be rid of me? I questioned everything. But I still lacked a sufficient number of facts. So Charlie met Akshay in the bar, and they were seen leaving together. Did that necessarily mean they were having an affair or that they were hatching plans to run away together?

I glanced over to Ian, the lanky, young desk clerk, who caught my eye and sadly shook his head. Still no messages from Charlie. I saw Arthur looming by the door, a thin, pitying smile on his face. Word had spread fast throughout the hotel. I had been dumped. I hadn't slept in almost two days. My eyes were heavy, my body slow and lumbering. I had to rest. And taking a nap would at least be a temporary escape from this hellish turn of events.

While I waited for the elevator, I fumbled for my cell phone and speed dialed Laurette. She was still with Larry in Maui, no doubt soaking up the sun and plenty of mai tais. I had received word early on during my stay in London that they were renting a condo on the beach for six weeks because his Disney film had been pushed back a few months after his rising tween star got busted for DUI. Larry was using the free time to work on a new romantic comedy script, which Laurette promised would blow the lid off the Internet dating scene. I got her voice mail, which was no surprise. Why answer your phone if you're in Hawaii? I waited for the beep.

"Laurette, it's me. Please call me when you get this. I don't want to alarm you or anything, but things aren't going well. And I just need to hear your voice. I'll fill you in when you call. But please call back soon. I love you," I said.

I clicked off the phone and tried to keep it together until I was safely hidden back inside my hotel room.

A bell rang, and the gold elevator doors opened to reveal Wallace Goodwin's wife, Katrina. She wore a gray turtleneck sweater and black pants with a charcoal overcoat. She gripped the handle of a Pierre Cardin carry-on suitcase that rolled behind her. A pair of oversized dark sunglasses nearly covered her whole face. She didn't even acknowledge me as she brushed past, heading straight for the checkout desk.

"Katrina?" I said.

She stopped and pivoted on her heel. The Savoy was dimly lit during all hours of the day, so Katrina had to lower her gigantic glasses in order to make sure it was me. Her eyes were red and puffy. She had been crying.

"Jarrod, I'm sorry, I didn't see you . . ." Her voice cracked and trailed off.

"Is everything okay?" I said.

She nodded, but her eyes welled up with tears and she pushed her sunglasses back up over her face to hide them.

"Are you leaving?"

"Yes."

"Where's Wallace? Isn't he going with you?"

She stood there, not sure what to do or say. Her whole body started to shake, and I thought for a moment she might collapse to the floor. She was a far cry from the chatty woman I had encountered in Starbucks with her husband just five weeks earlier. I bounded over and gave her a hug.

"What is it? What's wrong?" I said.

"Nothing, Jarrod. I'm fine. Please, I need to hurry. I have to get to Heathrow. I don't want to miss my flight home."

"Did you and Wallace have a fight?" I said.

Katrina's greatest fear was showing any cracks in her picture-perfect life. That was completely unacceptable. She didn't want anyone looking down on her, or judging her, or feeling sorry for her. It was important to present a strong, united front even if things were crashing down behind the scenes. Despite the teardrops streaming down her face behind her huge sunglasses, she tried valiantly to keep a smile on for appearance sake.

"Everything's fine, Jarrod, but thank you for your concern. Are you and Charlie staying in town for a while longer to enjoy the sights?" she said, finally getting a hold of her emotions.

"Charlie's not here. I don't know where he is," I said. "I haven't said this out loud to anybody, but . . . but I think he may be having an affair . . . with Akshay."

Katrina burst into tears. I had no idea she was so invested in my relationship with Charlie.

"I don't really have concrete proof or anything," I said, taking her hand and trying to calm her down. "But there does seem to be a disturbing amount of circumstantial evidence."

Katrina sat down in one of the big white and pink striped plush chairs in the lobby. I kneeled down next to her, still gripping her hand. She was sobbing now, gasping for breath, losing her composure completely.

"I'm sorry, Jarrod, I'm sorry, I'm never like this . . ." she wailed.

This was not news to me. Usually she was so tightly wound she could be used as a ball of yarn for a cat to playfully swat around.

"I know, Katrina, I know, but maybe you'd feel better if you just let it all out. Tell me what's wrong," I said.

She finally removed her sunglasses to reveal a hollow-eyed, pale, exhausted face. Katrina had gotten about as much sleep recently as I had.

"I understand your fears about Charlie," she said, still crying. "More than you know."

"Wallace?"

She nodded. I was stunned. Wallace just never seemed the type to cheat. He was so devoted to his hot little number of a wife. I used to see him gaze at her with a look of utter disbelief as if it were inconceivable to him that he was able to snare such a remarkable catch for himself. He was devoted to her and would do just about anything to preserve their relationship and protect her from any harm. Which left the million-dollar question.

"Who?"

Katrina took a long, sharp intake of breath before she reached into her coat pocket, pulled out a tissue, and began systematically dabbing away the dreaded tears that had so maliciously smudged her face. "Claire."

I nearly fell out of my chair. Wallace and Claire? Impossible. They were so different. Claire was so vibrant and sexual, and a real live wire. She was like a rich chocolate confection in an expensive stainless-steel dessert cup. And Wallace, well, he was just so Jell-O pudding. Of course, I couldn't exactly share these feelings with Katrina since, after all, she was married to the guy.

"Katrina, are you sure?"

"I found this," she said, pulling an aqua blue crystal earring out of her pocket and dangling it in front of my face. "It belongs to Claire. I saw her wearing them after the tech rehearsal when we all went out for drinks. I even commented on how beautiful they were. I just found it in our room."

"But that doesn't mean she and Wallace . . ." I said. It was still such a fantastic concept to consider. Claire sleeping with Wallace.

"I confronted him with the earring, and he caved faster than a child caught with candy before dinnertime."

So Wallace was the one I heard with Claire in her dressing room when I delivered her opening-night gift. He would have been the last man in the theater that I would have guessed. I might have even put the flamboyant Sir Anthony ahead of Wallace on the list. Just goes to show you I'm not the crack detective I sometimes like to think I am.

"The sad thing is, Jarrod, he almost sounded proud. Like it was some big accomplishment that he actually got the great Claire Richards to go to bed with him." Katrina sat up in her chair and sniffed back her flood of emotions, trying desperately to regain some kind of stoic resolve. "At first he was terrified I might find out the truth. He didn't know why Claire had singled him out, but he decided to go with it. She was probably just using him for sex."

Highly unlikely, if you asked me, especially given the strapping physical attributes of her Irish lover, Liam.

"Or possibly she was trying to get her role expanded in the play, or Dame Sylvia's part cut down," she said.

Now that was a much more likely scenario.

"Whatever the case, I noticed him acting nervous and jumpy, but I assumed he was just jittery over his first play opening. I never dreamed he was hiding something from me," she said. "When Claire died, I noticed that Wallace seemed almost relieved. No one would ever have to know what had happened between the two of them. But when I confronted him with the earring, he knew the jig was up."

With all the backstabbing and bed hopping going on at the Apollo Theatre, perhaps if we had mounted a production about the backstage story of *Murder Can Be Civilized*, it might have been more widely accepted than the far less exciting script written by Wallace.

"So you've left him?" I said, resting a comforting hand on Katrina's arm.

"Yes. I'm going home to Los Angeles," she said, rising suddenly. "I don't know if Charlie has been unfaithful to you or not, Jarrod, but let me tell you this. Before today, I would have told you point-blank you were being paranoid. But now, I have to say anything is possible."

She grabbed her Pierre Cardin carry-on handle and rolled it behind her toward Ian, who waited with a bright smile behind the reservations desk.

I watched her go for a moment before calling out. "Katrina?"

She placed her room key in front of Ian and circled around to face me.

"Were you anywhere near the make-up station at the theater on opening night?" I said. If Dame Sylvia had been telling the truth, that a woman tampered with the make-up, the only other woman even remotely connected to the company besides Minx was the playwright's wife.

"I wasn't even at the theater until ten minutes before curtain. I was shopping on Regent Street," she said.

I didn't know whether to believe her or not. But if she was telling the truth about just finding out that her husband was sleeping with his leading lady, then she would have had absolutely no motive to mix the peanut oil into Claire's make-up.

"Have a safe flight home," I said.

"Thank you, Jarrod," she said as Arthur hustled over to help her with her bags.

"Excuse me," a deep voice said from behind me.

I turned around to find Detective Colin Samms and his chubby-faced, bearish partner hovering over me.

"Yes?"

"We need you to come with us," he said in a grave tone.

This was serious. Something was wrong. My mind instantly went to Charlie. Had they found him? Was he alive? Or . . . The alternative was too grim to even think about.

# Chapter 15

"**D**o you have any news on my boyfriend, Charlie?" I said. Detective Samms stared at me glumly, his mind working to make sense of what I had just asked him. Obviously he hadn't given much thought to Charlie's mysterious disappearance.

"Oh, right," he said. "No, I'm afraid not. I'll assign a detective to the case tomorrow if he hasn't turned up."

He still believed Charlie had just taken off. And I was starting to suspect the same thing. But if Charlie had indeed ditched me, he would have at least had the good manners to take the time to write me a Dear John letter. That's what was so frustrating. Not knowing.

Detective Samms and his partner escorted me to a black sedan and whisked me away from the Savoy. I asked why they needed me for follow-up questioning, but they didn't answer me. After that, we rode in silence. Within minutes, we pulled up to the police station of our first encounter.

As we entered the lobby area, I saw Minx gathering up her belongings from the desk sergeant. Her hair was mussed, her mascara smeared from crying. She was slumped over, humiliated.

She had probably never before been seen in public looking like such a mess, and it was killing her.

"You're letting her go?" I said to Detective Samms.

"Yes," he said as he gripped my arm tight and steered me down the hall toward his office.

When we were behind closed doors, Samms gestured for me to take a seat. He circled his desk and sat down to face me while his imposing partner remained standing so close behind me I felt his gut pressing into my back as he breathed in and out heavily.

"So Minx didn't do it?"

"She's still a suspect," Samms said. "But we're putting *everyone* under a microscope to see what we can find."

"Let me be the first to tell you that Dame Sylvia's story is a bit wobbly," I said. "She's certain she saw a woman mixing the peanut oil into Claire's make-up, but she's not 100 percent convinced it was Minx. She had been drinking and her eyesight may have been a bit, shall we say, compromised," I said, choosing to be cooperative and hopefully helpful.

Samms nodded. He wasn't surprised.

"The peanut oil didn't kill her," he said.

"What?" I sat up in my chair so fast Samms's chubby-faced partner clamped his hands down on my shoulders to fasten me back into my seat. He was afraid I was about to lunge at his partner or try to make a run for it.

Samms slid a manila folder across his desk towards me. I picked it up and flipped it open. It was Claire Richards's medical records.

"Read what's highlighted at the bottom of the page," Samms said.

I scanned down to find a doctor's scribbling that was highlighted with a yellow marker. I had trouble reading it at first, as all doctors have a tendency to write illegibly. But the facts were clear. Claire Richards had only a mild case of peanut allergy. She didn't even carry an autoinjector that administers epinephrine, which is the leading antidote for a severe reaction. In fact, her case was so mild it would take nearly six ounces of peanuts to cause any swelling or rashes on the skin.

I glanced up at Samms. "So if she didn't have a massive immune response to the peanut oil, how did she die?"

Samms shrugged. "The medical examiner so far has found no traces of poison in her body but is going back to redo the autopsy. When he found traces of peanut oil on her face and learned of her allergy, he focused mostly on that. He's afraid he might have missed something."

"What does any of this have to do with me?" I said.

Samms unfolded the tabloid that featured Liam Killoran's exclusive interview emblazoned across the front page. "He's got a lot of interesting things to say about you in here."

I sighed. "You know, it's a bit disturbing that the police pay attention to this trash. In case no one has bothered to tell you, they make 99 percent of this stuff up."

"It's the 1 percent of truth we're concerned about," he countered.

"You actually believe the tabloids?" I said.

"Not necessarily. But Killoran is a very convincing witness."

"Witness to what? He didn't see anything. He's just making all of this up because he hates me," I said, my face reddening.

The chubby-faced partner finally spoke up. "Is he lying about how you were the one who stole Claire Richards's Oscar?"

"Yes! I was the one who caught the thief in Claire's dressing room! He knocked me over as he ran out with it," I said.

"So what did this thief look like?" Samms said.

"I don't know. He was wearing a mask. And it all happened so fast," I said.

Samms drummed his fingers on the desk as he stared me down. "You were the only one out of the entire cast and crew of the play who saw this mysterious intruder?"

"I was early for a meeting and the only one around at the time. Look, what does this have to do with Claire's death?"

"We're simply trying to connect all the pieces, Jarrod," Samms said, never taking his eyes off me. "We just want to talk to everyone who might have had some deeper connection to Ms. Richards."

"Well, I've already told you, I was not sleeping with her. The man you *should* be talking to is Wallace Goodwin," I said.

Samms raised an eyebrow, surprised. "The playwright?"

"He was the one who was having an affair with Claire, not me. He was terrified that Claire was going to spill the beans to his wife. And as I've already told DI Bowles, I heard someone having sex with Claire in her dressing room minutes before the curtain on opening night. I can only assume it was Wallace. That's means and a motive."

Samms jotted a note down on a yellow pad. "You have proof of this?"

"His wife told me," I said.

"Where can we find her?" Samms said.

My heart sank. "She's gone."

Samms eyed me suspiciously. "Gone?"

"She left the country this morning."

"How convenient," the partner piped in, a spray of his spittle landing on the back of my neck. I casually reached behind my head and wiped it away with the palm of my hand.

"Okay, assuming Mr. Goodwin was having relations with Ms. Richards in her dressing room on the night she died," Samms said, "what were you doing lurking outside?"

"I wasn't lurking!"

"You were obviously eavesdropping."

"I was delivering a gift," I said.

"A gift?" Samms flashed his partner a knowing smile.

"Flowers," I said, instantly regretting it.

"How romantic. You're a regular Romeo. For someone who was not at all involved with his leading lady."

"I gave everybody a gift! It's kind of an opening-night tradition!" I was on the defensive now.

"Did you ever consider the fact that your close relationship with Claire might have something to do with your boyfriend's disappearance?" Samms said.

"What are you talking about?" I said.

"It's all over the papers. Your boyfriend might have picked up a copy, read all about your escapades, and just decided he'd had enough."

"That's not possible," I said.

They were convinced I was hiding something. Liam had managed to twist their minds around enough so that they actually believed I was Claire's murderer. But I had to remain steadfast and true and know deep in my heart that eventually the true killer would be revealed. That is, if it was a murder now that the peanut oil had been ruled out as the cause of the death. I had to believe that. Just as I had to trust that Charlie would return to me safe and unharmed from wherever he was and still be in love with me. I just had to have faith. For the sake of my own sanity.

# Chapter 16

I knew I had to keep my cool in front of Detective Samms, or I was going to completely unravel. Laurette. I needed Laurette. She was a master at calming me down, putting things into perspective. But ever since she had met Larry, she had been less and less available, and I would be lying if I didn't admit that her budding new relationship was stirring up more than just a little bit of jealousy.

After another hour of intense grilling, Samms ordered his chubby-faced partner to drive me back to the Savoy. And as we pulled up to the luxurious front entrance, the squinty-eyed lackey barely slowed the car down enough for me to jump out. The London police were obviously not big fans of my eighties TV show.

As I swept through the lobby towards the bank of elevators, Ian, the young, towering desk clerk, worked hard to avoid eye contact. He just didn't have the heart to break the news that there had still been no word from Charlie. When I reached my room, I quickly entered, shut and bolted the door behind me, and then sank to the floor and lost it. I cried. Hard. This entire ordeal had taken such a toll on me, and I was tired of burying my emotions and trying to keep a level head. I sat up against the door, my knees to my face, and sobbed uncontrollably for what felt like hours. Finally, as the sun outside slowly slipped away and the room darkened, I crawled to my feet, brushed myself off, and wiped the last tear from my cheek. I had to stay strong. I had to be proactive. I had been trying to keep everybody back home out of this drama—except Laurette, of course, who was my rock—but I was way beyond the point of protecting people anymore. Besides, someone might have some information I did not have. I was going to reach out to everybody for some help, and the best person to start with was my psychic/house sitter, Isis. I scooped up the phone and punched in an overseas call to Los Angeles. It rang a few times before a harried, distracted voice picked up.

"Yes? What?"

"Isis, it's me, Jarrod."

"I knew you were going to call me today," she said, a smugness in her voice. She loved boasting about her premonitions.

"Listen, Isis, this is very important. Have you heard from Charlie?"

"No. Why? Is something the matter?"

Of course I should have asked her if she knew I was going to call, why didn't she already know Charlie was missing? But I needed her support desperately, and if I called into question her talents as a psychic, she might turn on me.

"He's vanished. We had a fight." I said.

"Oh, Jarrod, what did you do now?"

She always sided with Charlie. In fact, everyone in our circle always sided with Charlie. Perhaps it had something to do with me being a high-maintenance actor. The fact is, most times even I sided with Charlie once I thought about it.

"Nothing. It wasn't a bad fight. But I stormed out and wandered around for a bit like I always do, and once I cooled off and came back to apologize, he was gone. And that was two days ago."

There was a pause. Isis expected me to tell her Charlie had

been missing for only a few hours. Not a couple of days. This was serious.

"Isis?"

"Just a minute," she said in a grave tone. She was trying to get a visual lock on Charlie's location. I didn't say another word. The last thing I wanted was to interrupt her if she was coming up with something useful for me.

"I see soft, sandy beaches and a crystal blue ocean," she said.

"But we're in London," I said.

"No. Charlie's not in London. It looks like he's on vacation somewhere."

This was ludicrous. I couldn't believe that Charlie had suddenly gotten the urge to go lie around on a beach somewhere and not bothered to tell me.

"Anything else?" I said.

Another long pause. "No, honey, I'm sorry, that's all I see." She was disappointed that she couldn't give me more. "What are you going to do now?"

"I don't know. There's so much going on. The police think I had something to do with Claire Richards's murder, and this Charlie thing, it's just so weird. Why would he just take off like that and not even bother to leave me a note?"

I heard a bark in the background and I got a lump in my throat.

"Give Snickers a kiss for me," I said.

"I will, sweetie," Isis said. "She misses you both desperately."

I wanted to ask Isis if she had seen more and just wasn't telling me. Was she hiding something? Isis could sometimes be selective about her visions in order to protect my feelings.

"Bye," I said, my voice cracking as I hung up the phone. I just wanted to be home. With Charlie and our dog, all curled up on the couch watching a DVD and eating Indian food. Scratch that. I was done with Indian food. I wanted no more reminders of Akshay Kapoor.

Next on my call list was Susie Chan, Charlie's ex-wife and a rising medical examiner in Los Angeles. Susie was plugged into the LA crime scene and proved to be an invaluable resource from time to time whenever I got the urge to insert myself into a local murder case. Even though she was thousands of miles away, I was sure she was following the Claire Richards case intently, and she might have some additional insight. But more importantly, she was still on friendly terms with Charlie, and they chatted regularly. There was a slim chance he might have been in contact with her. I called her cell and found her at home. She had been up all night conducting an autopsy and was taking a few hours off to recharge her batteries. But she was in the middle of watching *The View*, a show she loathed because all of the women, especially that wedding-obsessed Star Jones, bugged the hell out of her. Still, she was drawn to it like a passing motorist glued to a car wreck. She was a bit distant until the show went to a commercial, and then she finally focused on our conversation. My hunch was right. She had been devouring all the details related to the Claire Richards case, especially all the tabloid fodder and insinuations of my involvement.

Susie and I had always had a strained relationship, but we did share a love of gossip and scandal, and she did know me enough to assume I wasn't the vicious monster the papers seemed to be making me out to be.

"I knew it was all a bunch of crap the minute they tried to make you out to be bisexual and sleeping with Claire," Susie said. "I mean, come on, we all know you've got everything but a rainbow flag tattooed to your ass."

I asked if Susie had heard from Charlie, and she said no. She dropped by the house to check on him a few weeks ago, but that was the last time they had spoken. She quickly jumped back onto the topic that interested her more. Claire's murder.

"What do the police think?"

"They think I did it."

"No, really."

"I'm serious."

Susie laughed. She had seen me use a newspaper to usher a spider out the front door as opposed to just squashing it with the heel of my shoe.

"That's preposterous," she said.

"Susie, I'm really worried."

"Oh, don't be. They'll wisen up soon enough. Tell you what. I had this fling with a studly British doctor at a medical convention in Paris last year. He's well connected in London. Let me call him up and see if he'll e-mail me a copy of Claire's medical report. If there's anything they're missing, I'll be sure to spot it," she said.

"Thank you, Susie, but I meant I'm worried about Charlie."

"Oh, just give him some time. He's probably off sulking somewhere. He'll be back."

I hadn't told her he'd been gone for two days and that Isis saw him on a beach somewhere. I just thanked her and hung up. These calls weren't helping one bit. They were just making me even more distressed. But Susie had given me an idea. I hadn't checked my e-mail in days.

I fired up the laptop that I had brought with me and waited for it to boot up. After quickly typing in my screen name and password, which was *Snickers* in a fitting tribute to my adoring pet (plus it was easy to remember), I logged on and downloaded my mail.

I scanned the long list and was disheartened to see it was mostly spam mail promising nude photos of Britney Spears and life-changing penis enlargements. I began deleting them and had almost cleaned out the entire box when my finger stopped just short of erasing an e-mail from a Hotmail account called Bollywood Bad Boy. Under the subject line was typed "From Charlie." What was this? I took a deep breath and then opened up the file and read it.

*Jarrod, this is very hard for me to say because I care about you and I don't want to see you hurt, but I've fallen in love with Akshay. There's no other way to say it except to come right out with it. I know this must be a shock to you. I certainly know it is to me. I don't know how this happened but it did, and though I care for you, I can't deny myself this chance at happiness. I hope you understand and I'm sorry if this causes you some pain. Love, Charlie.*

I sat there in a state of shock, nauseous, my entire body shaking. I just kept replaying the imagined scene of Charlie lying next to Akshay on a beach somewhere, feeling guilty about ditching me without explanation, and Akshay graciously offering to let him send me a Dear John letter from his e-mail account. This wasn't happening. It couldn't be.

The phone jarred me out of my trance and I picked it up, hoping to hear Charlie's deep, comforting voice chuckle and say "April Fool's" even though it was June.

"Jarrod, I'm so sorry I haven't returned your call until now, but Larry and I chartered a boat and went scuba diving for a couple of days and I left my cell phone behind at the hotel. Can you believe I got certified to go deep-sea diving? I get nervous when the water in my bathtub gets too close to those tiny chrome drainage holes."

Laurette. Thank God. It was Laurette. I had waited so long for her to call me back, and I was frozen, not saying a word, too consumed by trauma and despair to even speak. She immediately picked up on it.

"Honey, what's wrong? What happened?"

And I let loose with everything, blabbering on and on, filling her in on the most minute details. And as a dutiful best friend, she listened to every word, patiently interjecting only once at the point where I told her Charlie had sent me a breakup letter from Akshay's e-mail address. "Bastard!"

When I was finished, she said the words I had been waiting to hear.

"Just hold on, sweetie. I'll be there tomorrow."

She was half a world away spending time with a man she cared deeply for but was willing to drop everything and rush to my side. I loved her so much. When we hung up, I knew she was already on the Orbitz travel Web site checking fares from Hawaii to the United Kingdom.

I hated ruining her long-overdue vacation. But my life had suddenly veered off into a surreal and unfathomable direction, and I needed moral support from the strongest, most loyal person I knew. Because deep down in my gut, I knew things were only going to get worse.

# Chapter 17

Less than twenty-four hours later, Laurette was on the ground and calling me from a taxicab on her way into the city from Heathrow Airport. She instructed me to leave the hotel immediately and walk to Kettner's in the West End, an upscale eatery in the heart of the theater district where the creative crowd swarms after a show to unwind and deconstruct that evening's performance. Laurette and I had much bigger topics to analyze and discuss, and she knew that feeding our stress was the key to dealing with all of these incomprehensible events. I did as I was told.

While at a small corner table waiting for her to arrive, I ordered a Vanilla Absolut and Diet Coke, my new cocktail of choice because of its low caloric content. It tastes like a flavored soda and has the remarkable ability to sneak up on you and knock you on your ass. If ever I needed to dull my senses, today was the perfect day to do it.

It was still early and the restaurant was fairly empty except for a few stragglers who had been wandering about buying up last-minute tickets for tonight's shows. The main dining room was spacious and bright, and the immaculate waiters stood off to the side, waiting to jump in and serve your every need. I kept my own waiter hopping by slamming down the drinks he brought me at an alarming rate. We had developed an unspoken agreement that once the glass was empty, he would return with another. I wasn't a big drinker, but I suspected all that was about to change. I was starting to take my cue from my beloved Claire and her rival, Dame Sylvia. As I plucked the cherry from my fourth cocktail and popped it into my mouth, I heard a commotion at the front door. I turned to see Laurette, wearing a stylish black coat and matching floppy hat, lipstick and make-up perfect, plowing her way past the host and scanning the room for me. Once her eyes settled on my broken, slumped-over self, she almost broke into a run to reach me.

I stood up and she threw her arms around me, squeezing me tightly to her ample bosom, and held me there. The Kettner's wait staff watched with rapt attention, though they were used to such drama since their establishment played host to a batch of overly dramatic actors every night of the week. We must have stood there hugging for a full five minutes before she gripped my shoulders, pushed me back for inspection, and stared at me, her eyes brimming with tears.

"Oh God," she said. "You look like hell!"

"It's been one of those weeks," I said.

"Sit down. We have so much to talk about," Laurette said before dropping her butt down on one of the plush, cushioned chairs and flipping open a menu. As important as my life was to her, she needed the appropriate entrée to accompany the discussion. And with the big bombshell of Charlie leaving me heading our list of topics, this was no time to even consider a low-carb, low-fat, or sugar-free option.

She motioned for the waiter, who scampered over with an expectant smile on his face. "We'll both have the Prince Edward casserole," she said, closing the menu and handing it to him. A perfect choice. The Prince Edward was a rich, delectable comfort-food dish loaded with potatoes, cheese, and meat. Just what the doctor ordered. Maybe not Dr. Atkins. But he'd never know. He died a long time ago.

"Very good, ma'am. Anything to drink?" he said.

"I'll have whatever he's having, but double it. I could only get a coach seat, and I wound up next to a screaming baby for eleven hours," she said. Despite Laurette's desire to be a mother someday, she really despised being anywhere near children. She just assumed that her child would not pick up any nasty habits such as crying and pooping in its pants that plague other babies.

"All right, I'm just going to come out and say this, put it right out on the table," Laurette said, clutching my hand.

"Okay," I said, a little hesitant.

"I refuse to believe Charlie has left you," she said. "Something else is going on here."

I handed her a printout of the Dear John letter, and she read it quickly. "This doesn't sound like him at all. Charlie's a hell of a lot more direct than this. Maybe this Akshay guy sent this just to screw with you."

"Maybe," I said, fighting back the urge to cry again. "But the evidence isn't exactly reassuring. We fought, people saw him leave the hotel with Akshay, and whether he sent this e-mail or not, it did confirm what I was already thinking."

Laurette saw a lone tear glide down my cheek and her face morphed into a mask of pity. She knew I hated when she felt sorry for me. I had always had a problem with people pitying me. It dated back to when my sitcom *Go to Your Room* was cancelled. I couldn't escape the dozens of sympathetic looks from all the adults around me, who assumed this marked the end for me and that I would never work again and wind up a drug-addled, emotionally crippled has-been. In spite of her attempts to hide it, Laurette couldn't help herself.

"Laurette . . ." I said.

"I know, I know, I'm not supposed to feel bad for you, and I don't. I swear—"

"No," I said, lifting her hand to my mouth and kissing it softly. "I just want to say I'm so glad you're here."

"Me too," she said, her eyes disappearing behind a fountain of tears.

We then commenced with our night of gluttony, gobbling up heaping spoonfuls of the hot, steaming Prince Edward casserole and gulping down cocktails numbering in the double digits until we were sufficiently stuffed and plastered.

And though we never reached any formal conclusions or solutions to the Charlie problem, I took solace knowing I was no longer going to have to deal with this on my own. Laurette would stick by my side for however long it took.

After paying the bill and struggling to put her chic black coat back on, Laurette stumbled as she focused on a young, thin blond man with an electric smile and a tiny waist slipping on a coat to leave.

"That's not . . . It can't be," Laurette slurred.

It was. It was the noted English actor Jude Law, who made a splash as the snooty, manipulative gay lover in the Oscar Wilde biopic with Stephen Fry. Then he went on to earn Oscar nods for his memorable roles as a rich playboy in *The Talented Mr. Ripley* and as a romantic Civil War hero in *Cold Mountain*. He was barely thirty and already on a par with some of the true greats such as Anthony Hopkins and Peter O'Toole. Of course, that was before *Alfie*.

Jude was alone and trying to maintain a low profile. But now that he was on Laurette's radar, that would ultimately prove to be an impossibility. Laurette was loud and pushy enough sober, but when she was flying high from overindulgent liquor consumption, she was a walking storm warning.

I reached out to grab Laurette's arm, but she was already halfway across the restaurant.

"Jude! Jude!" she screamed, waving her floppy hat in the air to get his attention. She didn't need the hat.

Laurette knocked aside chairs and fellow patrons to get to him. Jude looked up, startled to see this large woman with glassy eyes bearing down on him. He nodded to her and made a dash out the door.

Laurette swiveled back and gestured for me to follow her. "I heard he's looking for new management. I want to make a pitch to get him into my stable," she said, brushing aside a pair of horrified waiters and following Jude Law out the door. I suspected that Jude would not leap at the chance to join Laurette's firm. After all, her last client of note had been one of the kids from *Full House*, and it wasn't those teenage billionaires the Olsen twins. But you never know. Laurette was a master at working miracles, and I never doubted her uncanny ability to focus and achieve her goals. Jude Law had no idea what he was up against.

I slapped some money on the table to cover our bill and hustled out the door after Laurette. Outside, it was complete pandemonium. Laurette was struggling in a crush of photographers and reporters. Jude Law was long gone. At first I was confused. Were the paparazzi this intense that they would chase Jude Law all over his hometown just to get a shot of him leaving Kettner's?

No. I was suddenly hit with the startling realization that they were not interested in Jude Law at all. They were after me. Laurette was trying to grab my hand as the mob of twenty reporters and photographers blinded me with their flashbulbs and deafened me with their endless stream of shouting. Did I steal Claire Richards's Oscar? Was I sleeping with both Claire and Liam? Did I really frame Minx for Claire's murder? The British tabloids were never going to stop hounding me until their questions about Claire's death were answered. This was the juiciest scandal to hit London since young Prince Harry wore a Nazi armband to a Halloween party.

Laurette finally managed to get a hold of me and yanked me out of the flock of press. We bolted down the street, clutching hands, still swerving a bit from all of our alcohol consumption.

Passing an unmarked car parked on the curb down the block, I caught a glimpse of two men inside. One was Detective Samms's chubby-faced underling. He ducked down in the front seat to avoid being seen, but it was too late. I knew they had put a tail on me. I was under a microscope. The press, the police, they were all keeping an eye on me. The whole world had a front-row seat to watch me slowly self-destruct.

# Chapter 18

Laurette and I beat a hasty retreat back to the safety of the Savoy. She had tipped her taxi driver an extra twenty-five pounds to deliver her luggage to the hotel ahead of her after dropping her off at Kettner's to meet me. When we arrived, the lobby was unusually quiet. Arthur the doorman was nowhere to be seen, and Ian, my favorite desk clerk, was off duty. I sat down on a classic print ornate couch to regroup as Laurette checked in. I closed my eyes and attempted a little meditation to get centered and said to myself over and over, "All will be fine. All will be fine." I tried very hard to believe it.

"Jarrod?" a man said as I popped my eyes back open.

Wallace Goodwin stood before me. His suit was rumpled, his hair mussed up, his eyes bloodshot with worry and fatigue. I barely recognized him. When he spoke, his voice was scratched and weary.

"I've been ringing your room trying to reach you. How are you feeling?" he said in a rare moment of compassion.

"It hasn't been easy. Not only have I had no time to grieve for Claire, my boyfriend is AWOL and the entire city is calling for my beheading!"

"I've been reading about you in the papers. They're even talking about you on TV. Maybe you should just get the hell out of Dodge," he said, trying to be helpful.

"The police are tailing me, Wallace, they're not going to let me go anywhere. This is an absolute nightmare."

"I'm so sorry," he said, reaching down and resting a hand on my shoulder. "I feel as if this is somehow my fault. If I hadn't talked you into doing this play, you never would have come here and gotten mixed up in all of this."

"I wanted to do the play, Wallace," I said. "I *needed* to do the play."

"Well, if there's anything I can do . . ." he said absently, his voice trailing off.

"Actually, there is," I said.

He jolted upright, surprised. He hadn't really counted on me taking him up on his offer.

"What?" he said, clasping his hands together and clearing his throat.

"You can come clean about your affair with Claire Richards."

His face went pale.

Out of the corner of my eye I saw Laurette pick up her room key and turn around from the front desk. Her eyes settled on Wallace Goodwin and she frowned. Laurette wasn't one of Wallace's biggest fans. In fact, she despised him. She always said he was one of those writers with no spine. Never standing up for someone else's joke. Always the last to compliment somebody on their script because he had to make sure everyone higher up than him liked it too. She was right. He was a wuss. But I had enthusiastically brushed all those qualities I hated about him aside when he offered me the chance for a comeback. In some ways, I was no better than he was.

Laurette marched over to us, but stopped short just out of Wallace's eye line to eavesdrop on our conversation.

"I don't know what you mean, Jarrod." Wallace said in a sad attempt at denial.

"Come on, Wallace, I ran into Katrina in the lobby when she was leaving. She told me everything."

"She got it all wrong. There has been a big misunderstanding."

"You offered to help me. If you tell the police the truth, maybe they'll ease up on me," I said.

"And start accusing me!"

"Well?" I said, staring dead center into Wallace's scared, beady eyes.

"I didn't kill her! I swear it!"

"But you did sleep with her. Come on, Wallace, you can admit it. On some level you must be very proud of yourself."

Laurette's jaw dropped almost to the floor. She couldn't believe what she was hearing.

Wallace began to fidget. He always did this when he was about to cough up something he had been trying to keep down. "Okay, yes. Yes. We hooked up a couple of times. It was very short-lived. And it was a huge mistake. We never should have done it," he said. "I love my wife, and I can't believe I jeopardized everything for a brief fling."

"Then why did you do it?"

"I don't know. She was so complimentary of my writing. I've been considered a lame comedy writer for decades, worked on some of the worst shows in TV history. Up until a few months ago, I was a washed-up has-been."

I couldn't possibly imagine how that felt. A lame comedy writer, I mean. Working on some of the worst shows in TV history and being a washed-up has-been was second nature to me.

"I was on the D-list in Hollywood, with no prospects to speak of. And with nothing but time on my hands, I banged out this silly little play. I almost tossed it in the garbage after reading it. I thought it was a piece of shit. But on a lark, I mailed it unsolicited to a couple of theatrical producers. I had zero expectations. And then, all of a sudden, this woman, this major star I watched accept an Academy Award on TV got a hold of it and started talking about my talent, my gift," he said, shaking his head slowly. "And I got swept away by it all."

"Claire wooed you?" I said, trying hard to cover my incredulity.

"Yes. I knew what I was doing was wrong. But I figured Katrina would never have to know. Then she found that earring . . . I was so stupid. I was so damn scared to lose her, I lied at first, which just made it worse."

"Was that you in Claire's dressing room the night of the opening?"

Wallace nodded, ashamed.

"Wallace, please, you have to tell the police. If you try to hide the truth, it'll only come back to bite you in the ass later."

"No!"

Laurette stomped over and whacked Wallace in the back of the head with her big, black floppy hat. "You pathetic little rat! How dare you not speak up when you know it's hurting Jarrod!"

"I know Jarrod didn't kill Claire. In fact, according to the police, Claire might not even have been murdered. She might have died of natural causes."

"Then what's stopping you from admitting the truth?" I said. "Your wife already knows. And your stock in Hollywood will probably skyrocket once your affair hits the papers. You'll be hot again."

"It's that psycho boyfriend of Claire's, the Irish thug. He's nuts. He'll come after me," Wallace whined.

"He's going to find out eventually, Wallace, and the longer you wait, the worse it's going to be," I said.

"I'll be out of the country by then, back home in LA," he said.

"He can always track you down," Laurette offered. "And I hope to God he does."

Wallace flashed her a wounded look. He hadn't been aware of Laurette's complete and utter contempt of him. He then whipped his head back around to face me.

"I'm sorry, Jarrod, but I can't. Maybe I will get some kind of notoriety if this gets out, but then I'll never get Katrina back. It will be too humiliating for her."

"I'll tell the police," Laurette said. "And it'll be out anyway."

"I'll deny it. You're his best friend. You'd probably say anything to help him out."

Laurette lunged at Wallace, her fingers reaching out to wrap tightly around his scrawny little chicken neck. He quickly sidestepped her and circled around the couch to keep her at a distance.

Wallace lowered his head and said softly. "I'm sorry. I'm really, really sorry." And then, before Laurette could dive over the couch and beat the crap out of him, Wallace raced for the bank of elevators.

Laurette dropped down on the couch next to me and I threw my arm around her. It was clear that if I was going to go down for Claire's murder, Wallace the Weasel would simply watch in silence. And do nothing. That's what you call a show-business friendship.

# Chapter 19

It was tough getting to sleep that night. I spent hours tossing and turning, watching the clock, replaying the events of the last month over and over in my head. I'm amazed by how your life can change in an instant. One minute you're happily partnered and begging your manager to get you a reading for a small lab assistant role on the Jill Hennessy coroner crime drama *Crossing Jordan*. The next moment you're in a foreign country, suddenly alone and single and accused of murdering one of the shining stars of the West End theater scene. Finally I tired of staring at the ceiling and flipped on the television. I watched a four-hour late-night marathon of one of the more recent classic English sitcoms, *Keeping Up Appearances*, about a snooty woman overly concerned with taste, style, and etiquette. She tortured her mild-mannered husband and meek neighbors on her never-ending quest to improve her social standing and worked overtime to downplay her trashy, low-rent relatives. The hilarious adventures of the stuffy Hyacinth Bucket made me howl. And laughing helped wash away some of the tension that was keeping me awake, and I was grateful to the incomparable timing of Patricia Routledge, who played the lead role.

After I watched four straight episodes, my eyelids grew heavy and I was hopeful that I was about to drop off to sleep. I drew the covers up and settled into my mountain of pillows when the phone rang suddenly.

I was fully awake again. Sighing, I reached out and answered the phone. It was just after five in the morning.

"Hello?" I said into the phone.

"Jarrod, honey, it's me, Mom. Am I calling too late? I get so mixed up with the time difference. It must be almost midnight over there."

It was my mother, Priscilla Jarvis. When I thought about it, Mom was the American version of Hyacinth Bucket, especially when it came to torturing my mild-mannered father.

"Clyde, I've got Jarrod on the phone! Pick up the other line! I said pick up the other line! Oh, for heaven's sake, his hearing aid battery must be low. Jarrod, are you still there?"

"Right here, Mom."

"How early is it in Scotland?"

"I'm not in Scotland. I'm in England."

"England. Ireland. Scotland. All the same to me. Doesn't the queen own all of them anyway? So did I wake you?"

"Actually it's not late anymore. It's early. Just after five A.M."

"Oh, I'm sorry. I knew I shouldn't have asked Clyde to figure out the time difference. He's terrible at math. Clyde!"

I heard a click and the voice of my beleaguered father, Clyde Jarvis. "Hello? Hello?"

"Hi, Dad."

"Son, how the hell are you? Are we calling too late?"

"It's five in the morning there, Clyde!" my mother yelled in both our ears. "You added up the time difference wrong!"

"It's okay," I said. "I was up anyway."

"Damn. It's after eleven at night here . . . and oh, I see what I did. I forgot to factor in daylight savings, and let's see, do you add six hours for eastern time or central time?"

"Doesn't matter. No worries. I'm up and about."

"We have to be up early tomorrow. We're driving to Orlando for a golf tournament," my mother said. Both of my parents became avid golfers once they retired to Florida. Dad spent months teaching my reluctant mother how to play, and now she had a better handicap than he did. It was a major sore spot, and one we tended to brush aside to avoid raising his blood pressure.

"Son, we've been reading about you in the papers," Dad said.

"Don't worry, Jarrod, we don't believe a word of what they're writing about you. I think you should sue them for libel, don't you, Clyde?"

"Who do you think did it, son?" Dad said. He was even a bigger conspiracy enthusiast and armchair detective than I was. It drove my mother crazy. When they would watch the old *Murder, She Wrote* reruns on A&E every night, during the course of the episode he would identify every major guest star as the culprit. First it was Lyle Waggoner. Then Jamie Farr. No, it had to be Shirley Jones. At the end of the show when the true killer's identity was revealed, he would smugly turn to his wife and say, "See, I told you." It bugged her so much she stopped watching the show with him and just focused on her *TV Guide* crossword puzzles.

"The police are not even 100 percent certain yet that Claire Richards was murdered," I said.

"Oh, I think she was. And I think it was the boyfriend. Why else would he be so intent on bad-mouthing you in the press? He's trying to cover his tracks by throwing the scent onto someone else," Dad said.

"Clyde, just twenty minutes ago you were saying it was Minx the understudy," Mom said with an aggravated tone in her voice.

"Too obvious. Hey, son, how well do you know the playwright? No one's talking about him."

"You remember Wallace Goodwin, Clyde. He wrote for Jarrod's show. We had him over for dinner once. Nice man, with the pretty wife," Mom said.

"I just found out he was sleeping with Claire," I said.

There was a pause before my mother practically spit through the phone, "I never liked him, never trusted him. I can't say I'm surprised."

"He did it!" my father bellowed. "Case closed. Unless it was the director. I read an interview with him. Sounded pompous and full of himself to me. Wouldn't trust him as far as I could throw him. He could have done it."

"Maybe," I said.

"Son, we could skip the golf tournament at Disney and come over there to help you solve this mess."

"No, I'll be fine. They haven't arrested me or anything, and I'm sure they'll figure it out soon enough."

"Besides, Charlie's there for moral support, right?" Mom said.

I was hoping the subject of Charlie wouldn't come up. But I had sent an e-mail to my parents in Florida just after Charlie arrived to tell them he had surprised me by showing up un-announced in London, so they knew he should be with me at this very moment.

"No, Mom, he's not."

"But you wrote and told us—"

"I know, Mom. He was here. But he left."

"Where did he go?" Dad asked.

"He broke up with me."

There was a long silence as my parents slowly took in this news. My mother had never been fully comfortable with me being gay. My father was much more willing to accept it. But Mom adored Charlie, and if I had to be with someone of the same sex, in her mind I couldn't have picked a better man.

"He went back to his wife, didn't he?" Mom said. "I knew it. I always thought he was too manly to be gay."

"Priscilla, that's got to be the dumbest thing I've ever heard!" Dad said. He rarely raised his voice to my mother, except when it came to protecting my feelings. "I have two words for you. Rock Hudson!"

My mother worshipped Rock Hudson during her youth, and when he died of AIDS in 1985, after years of covering up his homosexuality, my mother took it hard. It was right before her own son landed on the front pages of the tabloids kissing another boy at the LA Gay Rodeo. That definitely was not one of her banner years.

"I'm sorry, Jarrod, I didn't mean to say—"

"It's okay, Mom. He didn't go back to Susie. He left me for another man. One of the actors in the play. Akshay Kapoor."

"He did it! I bet he's the one who killed Claire Richards!" my father said.

"Oh, Clyde, Charlie didn't kill anyone," Mom said.

"Not Charlie! This Kapoor guy," Dad said.

"What kind of name is Kapoor?" Mom said.

"East Indian," I said.

"Oh, I hate curry. Upsets my stomach," Mom said.

"Does he have one of those red dots on his forehead, son?" Dad asked.

I suddenly noticed a red light on my phone flashing. It was my second line. Someone was trying to call the room.

"Mom, Dad, I have another call."

"Who would be so rude as to call you this early in the morning?" Mom said.

"We did," Dad said.

"Only because you can't add," Mom said.

"Can I put you guys on hold?"

"Are you kidding? Do you know how much this call is costing us?" Mom said. "Take your call, and we'll talk later."

"Love you, son," Dad said.

"I love you too," I said and they hung up. I switched over to the new call on line two.

"Hello?" I said.

At first there was nothing but dead air. And then I heard his voice.

"Jarrod, it's me."

Charlie. It was Charlie. I could barely speak.

"Are you there?" he said.

"Yes."

"Jarrod, I didn't mean for this to happen."

"I know."

"I handled it badly. I was completely unfair to you."

"I've been out of my mind, Charlie. You just disappeared. I thought something bad had happened to you."

"I'm still trying to figure everything out," he said.

"Are you really in love with Akshay?" I said, my mind reeling from finally having some kind of contact with my boyfriend.

The silence was interminable. And then, in a soft, pained voice, he said, "I think so, yes."

"And you're not going to tell me where you are so I can come to you and we can talk this out?"

"No, I can't do that. Not yet anyway."

"Charlie, this is crazy. Please, just tell me where you are!"

"I have to go now," Charlie said.

"No, please, don't hang up!"

"It's probably best if you just fly home to LA. Make sure you give Snickers a big kiss for me. I miss him so much."

"But not me," I said.

"Good-bye, Jarrod," Charlie said and there was a deafening click.

I sat on the edge of the bed and stared at the now-mute TV screen as Hyacinth Bucket passed a junk heap of a car. A dog sprang out from the smashed window and barked at her, and the shock of it sent her hurling into the bushes. Normally I would be doubled over with laughter. But not today.

And then it hit me. Charlie had asked me to give Snickers a kiss for him. He said he missed him very much. There was only one problem. Snickers was a female Pekingese. Charlie of all people knew that. He was the one who took her into the vet to get her spayed per Bob Barker's explicit instructions on *The Price Is Right*. He never would have made that kind of mistake. Who would get their own dog's sex wrong? Was this some kind of tip-off? Was he trying to tell me something? I was only sure of one thing at this point. Something was seriously wrong with this whole scenario.

# Chapter 20

Laurette had traveled halfway around the world to be with me during my time of need. She was exhausted when we parted, and the last thing I wanted to do was bang on her door at five-thirty in the morning. But after pacing back and forth in my room, my brain bubbling over with conspiracy theories, I had to wake her. Racing down the hall and pounding on the door, I silently prayed she would be up, battling jet lag and unable to adjust to the time difference.

"Who the hell is it?" barked a groggy, raspy voice. It was the monstrous, moody Laurette only a select few of us ever saw, and only after a night full of too many apple martinis. Or perhaps at the gym when I dragged her out for an early Sunday morning spinning class.

"It's me," I said. "I heard from Charlie."

There was some faint rustling from inside, and after a few seconds the door flew open. I jumped back a bit, startled by a face caked in dried-up beauty cream, a black sleep mask flattened against her forehead and wild, unruly hair that I initially mistook for a fright wig.

Laurette caught the horror in my face before I had a chance to cover it up. "Give me a break. I wasn't expecting company."

She glanced down the hall to make sure a wandering guest wasn't going to catch sight of her, and then she used one hand to fasten shut the blue Japanese kimono with gold dragons that she picked up on a two-day shopping spree in Hong Kong. With her other hand, she grabbed my shirtsleeve and yanked me inside the room, shutting the door behind us.

"What did he say? Did he admit he was with Akshay?"

I nodded, and Laurette fell back on the bed, still clutching the front of her robe, the air escaping her. She couldn't believe it. Finally, when she spoke, she could barely raise her voice above an anguished whisper.

"This doesn't make any sense," she said. "Charlie would never—"

"I don't think he did," I said before relaying the part of our conversation where Charlie got the sex of Snickers wrong.

Laurette took this in, her eyes widening. "Do you think he was trying to give you some kind of secret message?"

"Yes. I think someone was forcing him to make the call."

"Akshay?"

"Who else?"

"But why would Akshay hold Charlie against his will?"

"Maybe Akshay is some kind of obsessed East Indian version of Glenn Close from *Fatal Attraction* who got it into his head that he and Charlie are meant to be together and will go to any lengths to make that happen."

But why hadn't I seen those signs before? I knew he was besotted by Charlie, but would he go so far as to kidnap him?

I scooped up the phone on Laurette's bedside table, cradled the receiver between my ear and left shoulder, and flipped through my miniature telephone book, which I had stuffed in my breast pocket before coming to Laurette's room. As I started punching in some numbers, Laurette stared at me, aghast.

"Who are you calling this early in the morning?"

"Sir Anthony Stiles. Don't worry. He'll be up. Probably tutoring one of his young male protégés on the art of fondling your scene partner."

After a few rings, a rather chipper Sir Anthony answered the phone. "Are you calling from outside? Is the bell not working again?"

"Excuse me?"

There was a pause. "Who is this?"

"Sir Anthony, it's Jarrod Jarvis. I'm sorry to be calling you so early."

"My dear boy, what is it? What's happened?"

"I'm afraid my boyfriend might be in some kind of trouble."

"What kind of trouble?"

"I'm not sure. But Akshay Kapoor may have some information on his whereabouts."

"I never trusted that Bollywood brute."

"I really don't have any further details, but I would like to pay a visit to Akshay's flat, and I knew if anyone kept that cast contact list for the play, it would be you." Definitely, since my understudy's phone number was on that list and he was a shaggy-haired, droopy-eyed, adventurous young buck who played for both teams.

"Why, yes, I'm sure I have it here somewhere."

I heard some rustling in the background, and then a bell ringing.

"Be right there," Sir Anthony called out, suddenly a slight tension in his voice.

"I'd normally comment on how rude it is that someone is calling on you at this obscene hour, but here I am hounding you over the phone."

"Oh, don't be silly, Jarrod. I was up. And I'm expecting him.

Nice young chap from a Dutch acting school in Amsterdam. Here as an exchange student. We met on a train earlier today. I promised to share a few pointers."

"I see," I said, refraining from making any kind of perceived sarcastic remarks for fear Sir Anthony might withhold Akshay's flat address.

"I realize my tutoring time is a bit unusual, but the poor boy just got off work. He's a dancer at one of those cocktail bars on Charing Cross Road."

The bell rang again. "Yes, yes, I'll be there in a minute," Sir Anthony shouted as he flipped through more papers. "Persistent young lad, isn't he?"

I was afraid Sir Anthony might give me the brush-off if he got worried his young, hard-bodied new boy toy might flee out of exasperation, but luckily he located the cast list, and I jotted down Akshay's flat address in South Kensington.

After hanging up, I turned to find Laurette already half dressed. She was applying some eyeliner and combing out her tangled hair at the same time. "I'll be ready in two minutes."

She wasn't about to allow me to go break into an apartment on my own, especially in a foreign country.

Within ten minutes we were in the back of a cab for the short drive over to Akshay's London flat. The sun was just coming up, and a few joggers huffed and puffed up and down the dampened streets on this cold, foggy morning typical of old Mother England. We rolled past the Victoria and Albert museums and turned onto a narrow side street, stopping in front of a three-story brownstone situated on a well-kept corner. We paid the driver, and as he sped away, Laurette and I stood there staring at the old building with absolutely no clue as to how we were going to get inside.

"Sir Anthony said Akshay lives on the first floor. Maybe he left a window open," I said.

We hurried up the four steps to the front door. I jiggled the knob. It was locked. No surprise there. I leaned over the railing to get a good look inside the flat. It was dark, but I could make out the distinctive décor inspired by his home country. Lots of Indian Thakat wood furniture, the doorway to the kitchen adorned with a metal valance with wispy, billowing, multicolored curtains evocative of the region, and hardwood floors softened by an area rug with an intricately woven pattern.

I pushed up on the windowpane, but it wouldn't budge. It was locked from the inside.

"What do you see?" Laurette said.

"It's a beautiful apartment," I said.

"Oh, let me see. I love the Home and Garden channel," she said, leaning over the railing, squeezing past me to gawk in the window. Her left hip pressed against the doorbell, and we heard it ring inside.

"What is that?" Laurette said.

"You. Stop leaning against the bell."

Laurette repositioned herself just as a light in the living room snapped on and someone walked through the gauzy curtains separating the living room from the kitchen. I gasped as Akshay's mother stared at our surprised faces pressed up against the window. I didn't know what to do, so I waved.

Mrs. Kapoor quickly unlocked the front door and welcomed us inside. She was almost relieved to see us. This certainly put a crimp in the covert activities we had planned, but it saved us from possible arrest for breaking and entering.

Ever the consummate hostess, Mrs. Kapoor immediately prepared some herbal tea and a plateful of biscuits, and the three of us sat at the kitchen table. I felt as if some kind of explanation was in order.

"I've been trying to reach Akshay for the last couple of days, but he doesn't seem to be answering his home phone or his cell," I said. "I didn't want to leave for the States without saying goodbye." I was trying to give the impression that her son and I had grown fond of each other during my time in London. I felt no need to tell her I detested her pompous, arrogant, boyfriend-stealing spawn.

Mrs. Kapoor nodded somberly. "Well, like I said on your voice mail, I have been trying to reach him myself. He never goes this long without calling." She was fighting to remain calm. Her mother's intuition was telling her something was perilously wrong. "Sometimes he will send my husband and me e-mails, but we know nothing about computers."

"Do you have any idea where he might have gone?" Laurette said.

"I've thought about it. Akshay loves to travel, but he never leaves without telling us where he's going. I thought perhaps he was cast in a movie back home at the last minute, but I called our relatives in Mumbai, and they say no one's heard from him."

I didn't want to further complicate matters by explaining to Mrs. Kapoor that my boyfriend Charlie was also missing and might be with Akshay, so I decided not to mention it.

"Mrs. Kapoor, would you mind if I looked around with my friend here?"

She threw up her hands. "I don't see what good it will do. I have searched every inch of this flat and found nothing that tells me where I can find Akshay."

"Maybe a fresh pair of eyes could make the difference. Please."

"Of course. Be my guest. But I must go home. My husband believes I am overreacting, so I came over here while he was still sleeping. I have to get back before he awakens and notices I'm gone."

"We'll leave everything as we found it. I promise."

"Just find my son. Please." The worried lines in Mrs. Kapoor's face deepened. She set her cup of tea down, straightened her beautiful red print wrap, gave us each a peck on the cheek, and then left.

Laurette and I wasted no time searching the flat, rifling through papers, opening desk drawers, playing all of Akshay's answering-machine messages. There were at least four messages from his mother, her concern growing with each one. I wandered into the back bedroom, where a stack of head shots and books on acting cluttered a small desk next to an old, oversized, outdated computer. Akshay had been so busy clawing his way to the top he hadn't had time to upgrade his system. It suddenly struck me what Mrs. Kapoor had said in the kitchen. She knew nothing about computers, which meant she probably hadn't even bothered to turn this one on. There might be a clue on his hard drive. I flipped on the power switch and waited a full three minutes before the clunky old machine was up and running. I went into his e-mail account and scanned the long list of messages, mostly porn ads and get-rich-quick scheme offers. There were a couple of notes from fellow actors who updated him on the state of their own careers. That's what we actors do in e-mails. We start out by asking how you are in one brief sentence to be polite, and then we launch into a detailed dissertation of our own self-involved lives that could last pages. I finished perusing the messages and nearly clicked out of the message box before my eye caught it.

"Laurette! Come in here!" I hollered.

Laurette wandered in with a wooden spoon and a carton of strawberry yogurt. I gave her a withering look.

"Is that a clue you found in the refrigerator?"

"What?" she said. "It was already open. I was afraid it would go bad."

I spun around and pointed at the screen. "Look at this e-mail. I almost missed it."

Laurette leaned down over my shoulder to read the message. It was a confirmation notice from an on-line British travel agency called UK-away.com. It included an itinerary on Olympic Airways detailing a flight two days ago from London to Athens and connecting to a commuter flight to the Greek island of Mykonos as well as a confirmed reservation for a one-bedroom apartment at the Andromeda Residence in Mykonos town.

"They went to Greece?" Laurette said.

"No. Akshay booked a single ticket. Charlie didn't go with him."

"Well, maybe they didn't travel together. Maybe Charlie met him there."

Was Charlie in Greece? Or was he still here in London? Or somewhere else? Something about Greece kept bothering me. I had been there before. Years before I met Charlie. It was undeniably one of the most beautiful places I had ever visited. I was struck by the stunning white structures with blue shutters and trim that melted into the peaceful landscape. I spent hours on the soft sands of the beaches staring out at the endless, bright blue crystal ocean . . . Wait a minute. Soft sands and crystal ocean. My God! Isis's prediction. She was insistent that Charlie was somewhere with soft sand and a crystal ocean. Greece! It had to be Greece!

I leapt up from the chair, banging into Laurette and almost knocking her over. "Charlie's in Greece! Come on!"

"We're going to Greece?" Laurette said, a hint of excitement in her voice.

"Yes." I quickly shut down the computer. We were heading back out to the living room when we heard the front door open. Laurette and I exchanged quizzical looks.

"Do you think Mrs. Kapoor came back?" Laurette said.

I put my hand up to silence her, crept a few feet to the curtain separating the bedroom from the hallway, and lifted it back just a bit. Two men with dark features, both hulking and intimidating in stature, began ransacking the flat.

Laurette and I stood in the bedroom, paralyzed by fear, with no idea how we were going to get the hell out of there.

# Chapter 21

As the two brutes rifled through drawers and sliced open the upholstery on a few chairs, Laurette began hyperventilating. I grabbed her hands and squeezed tightly, silently taking quick breaths in and out with her as if we were practicing for a Lamaze class. I knew if she panicked, we were dead. Whoever these thugs were, they had no qualms about breaking the law, so they probably wouldn't mind breaking a few of our bones as well.

There was no way for us to escape out the front door without them seeing us, so our only chance was slipping out the window in Akshay's bedroom. Luckily, he was on the bottom floor of the building, and if we could maneuver around a clunky old window air-conditioning unit, we had a good shot of climbing down into a back alley and slipping away undetected.

I guided Laurette to the bed and sat her down, keeping a firm grasp on her hands and locking eyes with her. I whispered, "Don't worry. I'll get us out of here."

I tiptoed over to the window and unlocked the latch, carefully and quietly lifting up on the pane. It rose effortlessly, and a quick smile formed on my lips. This was going to be easier than I thought.

But that was before the air-conditioning unit wobbled free and pitched forward, crashing to the floor and crushing my right toe. I screamed in agony, not only alerting the two goons in the living room but half the neighborhood as well. Akshay had never bothered to fasten the unit. He had just stuffed it in the window and used the pane to hold it in place. Why on earth would an Indian actor who was used to the sweltering temperatures of Bombay need air-conditioning in one of the coldest, grayest countries in the world anyway? Of course, the answer to this burning question would have to wait. Pounding footsteps were fast approaching the bedroom.

I dashed across to the door, my toe throbbing with pain, and tried to slide the bolt into place just as two bodies slammed against it, cracking the thick wood. The two slabs of beef on the other side reared back and hurled themselves into it again. The door threatened to fall apart as I pressed my right shoulder up against it in a futile attempt to keep them out.

Laurette yelped and scurried over to the window, managing to slip one leg out into the alley. She ducked her head to cram herself through just as the window slid back down, wedging against the back of her neck and trapping her.

She strained to push up on the pane, but it wouldn't budge. "Jarrod, I'm stuck!"

I knew I was not going to be able to hold the door in place much longer, but if I left my position for even a second, the two monsters outside would instantly be in the bedroom with us. I had to make a choice. It was going to be painful, especially for Laurette, but it was our only hope.

The two apes rammed the door with their bodies one more time. I could hear them step back for a final assault that would unquestionably smash the already damaged door to bits. I grabbed my opportunity to desert my post, leapt over the bed, and with a running start, my hands outstretched, I collided with Laurette, snapping the window pane in half and sending her hurtling out the window. I saw her crash to the cobblestone street in a shocked and breathless heap. Out of the corner of my eye, I glimpsed the dark-skinned bodybuilders smashing through the door like a team-up between the Incredible Hulk and the Thing.

Without waiting for introductions, I dove out the window after Laurette just as the Hulk took a swipe at me, barely missing locking one of his ham fists around my ankle. Laurette had just sat up to catch her breath and survey the damage when I landed face first in her crotch. She screamed again. I don't know if it was out of the pain from the impact or the surprise of my out-of-character landing position. I wasn't going to take the time to find out. Jumping to my feet and wincing from the intense aching in my toe, I grabbed Laurette's hand and we hauled ass out of the alley. Hulk and Thing were grunting as they attempted to squeeze through the small window frame to get to us.

Harried, sweating, and panicked, we staggered into the middle of the street, where we were nearly run down by a bottled-water truck with its horn blasting. It missed us by inches as we raced to put some distance between our pursuers and us. Laurette lagged behind because of some unwieldy shoes she had bought in Maui a few weeks ago. Who wears high heels to a break-in?

After flagging down a taxicab, I opened the door for Laurette. She was still disoriented and out of breath and took too much time climbing in the back. So when I saw the Hulk and Thing emerge from the alleyway and scan up and down the streets in search of us, I grabbed her butt with both hands and lifted her up off the ground. She let out a muffled squeak as her body flopped down on the leather-cushioned backseat. She was used to Larry pawing her, but not me. I jumped in after her, keeping my head down so as not to be spotted. The fiftysomething, fleshy, watery-eyed, red-nosed driver looked us up and down through his rearview mirror.

"Where to?" he asked in a thick Irish brogue.

Laurette and I had absolutely no idea. I turned my head and peered out the back to see the Hulk and Thing still looking for us. Luckily they hadn't spotted us yet. Thing became frustrated and angrily kicked over a trash can with his foot.

Laurette sat up and confidently said to the driver, "Heathrow Airport, please."

The driver leered at her in his mirror and didn't make any attempt to turn on his meter or drive away.

Laurette leaned forward. "Did you hear what I said? Heathrow Airport."

The driver snickered and kept his bloodshot eyes firmly focused on her.

"What's so funny?" Laurette demanded.

"Um, honey," I said, pointing to her blouse.

In all the commotion, Laurette had not noticed that the buttons on her blouse had popped off and her bra was askew. Her breasts were flopping free from any restraints, and the driver was simply enjoying the show.

"Omigod!" Laurette wailed as she grabbed her breasts and stuffed them back inside her bra. Then she slapped the driver upside the head. "Pervert!"

The driver cackled, turned on the meter, and we sped off, leaving the Hulk and Thing in the dust.

I turned to Laurette. "You know, if the police find out that I've left the country, I'll be in big trouble. I'm their number-one suspect in Claire Richards's murder."

"If we don't go, then we may never find out what's going on with Charlie," she said, flashing the still-grinning driver a put-out glare. "Besides, you're not officially under arrest. You're just under surveillance."

That didn't make me feel any better about blowing town. But I had to get to the bottom of Charlie's disappearance, and Greece was my best bet. Laurette was already on her cell/picture phone booking us a flight to Athens as I sat back and wondered how we had suddenly been caught up in our very own episode of *The Amazing Race*.

# Chapter 22

Ifeared Inspector Bowles or Detective Samms might have flagged my passport at the airport in the event that I tried to flee the country, and as Laurette and I made our way through passport control, a stern-faced official held up a hand as I tried to pass through. There was an agonizing moment of sheer tension before the official broke into a wide grin and said, "Baby, don't even go there!" Thank God. A fan. After I signed an autograph, he happily waved us on, and Laurette and I boarded our flight without further incident.

When our Olympic flight from London to Athens landed at six o'clock that evening, Laurette was back on her phone trying to book us a flight to Mykonos. But as the summer season was fast upon us, it was virtually impossible. All the commuter flights were jam-packed with European and American tourists, and our only option was a five-thirty A.M. flight four days from now. Laurette wasn't used to not getting her way and tried threatening, cajoling, bribing, and begging the Olympic Airways representative, all to no avail. We were going to be stuck in Athens. Normally this would not be a problem. We would simply check into Laurette's favorite five-star Hotel Grande Bretagne, which was within walking distance of the world-famous Plaka district, an exotic labyrinth of alleys, streets, and stairs lined with neoclassical houses and mansions, all gorgeously decorated with tiled roofs depicting various Greek gods and goddesses. It's also chock full of shops, restaurants, a famous flea market around Monastiraki Square, and a few small museums. But there was no time for any indulgent meals or shopping excursions on this trip. And our tour of the Acropolis, the Benaki Museum, and the Olympic Village from the Athens 2004 games would have to wait. My instincts were screaming that Charlie was in some kind of trouble, and we had to get to Mykonos fast to find him.

Laurette rang Dimetrius, a travel agent she used to represent in Hollywood who had recently moved back home to Greece. He had traveled to America to become the Greek Tom Cruise, but Laurette was only able to secure him one nonspeaking role as a Middle Eastern terrorist in a TV movie depicting the hijacking of a TWA flight in the eighties and starring Lindsay Wagner. He stayed in town another ten years holding out hope his fortunes might change before finally returning to Athens with his tail between his legs. Luckily he and Laurette had stayed in touch.

Dimetrius worked his magic and secured us two tickets for a hydrofoil departing Piraeus, the main port of Athens, to all the Cyclades islands (including Mykonos) through their domestic Minoan Lines. The ferry was scheduled to depart at nine o'clock, which was cutting it close since we were still maneuvering our way through customs at the Athens airport and it was already approaching seven.

Neither of us spoke Greek, nor understood a word of it other than "ouzo," which is a famous Greek drink made of a precise combination of pressed grapes, herbs, and berries. Two shots of it and you're on top of a rickety bar stool doing a striptease to Gloria Gaynor's "I Will Survive" in the divey but welcoming Alekos Island Bar in Kolonaki, Athens's first gay bar. But enough about my past indiscretions. Because of our lack of local language skills, the alert driver pegged Laurette and me as suckers right away, and the taxi ride to the port of Piraeus wound up costing us over a hundred dollars in U.S. coin. Neither of us had the energy to fight the driver, so we cut our losses and headed on to the ferry.

Laurette was already feeling grungy and ragged and in desperate need of a shower. Neither of us had any luggage, since we had fled Akshay's apartment and headed straight for the airport. I promised to buy us both some new threads the minute we arrived in Mykonos. The boarding passes were waiting for us at the Minoan ticket office per Dimetrius's instructions, and soon Laurette and I were seated at the below-deck bar, sipping ouzo and splitting a bag of potato chips. They didn't sell the Greek liquor onboard the ferry, but there was a gaggle of college-age Australian backpackers who had come well stocked and were more than happy to share their booty.

The ferry chortled and coughed to life and then slowly made its way out of the harbor toward the open sea before picking up speed and jetting across the Aegean Sea toward our destination of Mykonos.

I downed my second shot of ouzo. Luckily, there was neither a rickety bar stool within my reach nor any hint of Gloria Gaynor on a neighboring tourist's boom box. My head was already spinning, and I had to grip the ugly orange Formica table I sat at with Laurette. She was already eyeing a plate of plastic-wrapped brownies on the snack bar counter after we made short work of our one measly bag of potato chips.

Laurette spun back around. "Got any euros? I have to have one of those brownies."

I reached into my back pocket but lost my balance. I nearly toppled over to the floor before a hefty, bald German tourist passing by caught my arm and held me steady.

I offered the sturdy German a weak smile. "Thank you. I'm all right."

He nodded, not quite believing me, and moved on. I handed what was left of my money to Laurette.

She leaned in to me. "Are you okay?"

I wanted to say no. I wanted her to know the devastating toll all of this drama was having on me. First my Oscar-winning costar in my first play keels over dead on opening night. Then my boyfriend vanishes without a trace. Then the police suspect me of murder. Then I get a phone call from Charlie informing me our long-term relationship is kaput. Now I'm on a boat, drunk on ouzo, heading to a Greek party island on the flimsiest of clues, hoping to find out how my life fell apart so fast and on such a grand scale. I wanted to scream, "No! No, I'm not okay!" But instead, I simply clasped Laurette's hand and quietly whispered, "I'm fine."

"You look pale. Maybe you should go up top and get some air. I'm going to buy one of those brownies."

She was focused like a laser beam on that plate of brownies and shot out of her chair in an instant, barreling over to the snack bar with a fistful of my remaining euros.

She was right. I needed fresh air. I was choking from claustrophobia and too much liquor. Too many crying babies and too much wafting smoke surrounded me. I needed vast, open space. I stood up carefully, gripping the edge of the table, and made my way to the stairs. I climbed up to the top deck, my head still spinning faster than Jeff Gordon speeding around a NASCAR racetrack. I thankfully sucked in a deep breath of the cool, misty ocean night breeze.

The deck was deserted, lit only by the glistening half-moon. I swayed to the railing, my arms outstretched to maintain balance, and grabbed the metal handrail. Behind me I heard someone cough. I turned around, but no one was there.

"Hello?" I said.

No answer. Just the roar of the ferry's engine and a splashing sound as the bow of the boat cut through the waves.

I turned back and stared up at the moon. Charlie and I had spent many evenings over the course of our four years together gazing at the moon, from the sandy beaches of Rio de Janeiro to our own backyard in the Hollywood Hills. I had to wonder if we would ever have that opportunity again.

By the time I noticed a body coming up fast behind me, it was too late. I didn't even have the chance to turn my head an inch to see my assailant before a strong arm hooked around my neck and squeezed the last gasps of air out of my throat. He yanked hard with his forearm, and I felt my windpipe about to crack. Was it one of the goons from Akshay's apartment? Had they managed to follow us to Greece? I rocked back, trying to throw my attacker off balance, but he was like a pit bull and not about to let go.

I tugged violently at the gray wool sweater that covered his arm, but it was no use. His grip was too tight, and I was going to black out within seconds. I could only imagine what would happen if I passed out. He would probably lift my still form up over the rail and drop me into the deep, dark sea. I'd be left to the mercy of some taunting sharks that would circle around me for hours, nipping at my arm, my leg, until blood filled the water and the feeding frenzy began. I couldn't let that happen. I was terrified of all water-related deaths like drowning and shark attacks. I couldn't let my life end this way.

My only hope was a long-cancelled private eye show called *Jake and the Fatman* starring William Conrad (famously cast as TV's *Cannon* in the seventies) and a hunky mid-eighties piece of beefcake called Joe Penny. I guest-starred in one episode as the Fatman's inquisitive nephew, who ran afoul of some counterfeiters led by former *M\*A\*S\*H* icon Wayne Rogers. At the show's climax, an exchange was arranged. My precocious thirteen-year-old life for a couple of million in fake bills. We shot the scene at the Santa Monica pier on the famous indoor carousel. Rogers had me clasped to his chest, a thick forearm around my neck as we circled around on a brown plastic horse. William Conrad had the bag of money and a revolver pointed at Rogers's head. It was a Mexican standoff. But in an earlier scene, Jake (Joe Penny) had taught me a few self-defense moves, much to the chagrin of my sweaty, overweight uncle. At just the appropriate moment, I threw up my hands, bending my fingers back, and gouged the eyes of my captor. During the second take I got a little too carried away and poked Wayne Rogers for real. He was rushed to the emergency room and never forgave me. The next day they used a short stunt double to stand in for me while they finished Rogers's pick-ups because he refused to work with me anymore.

But all these years later, that nifty trick came back to help me. I threw up my hands, bent the fingers, and scored a direct hit. I felt the nooselike grip of my attacker loosen just a bit, allowing me the chance to nail his foot with the heel of my shoe and push away from him.

The man covered his face with his hands, howling in pain. He was big and muscular and I wasn't about to wait for him to regain his composure. I bent over and plowed right into his stomach headfirst, knocking the wind out of him. He fell to the ground, and I leapt on top of him, straddling his chest, grasping his wrists and forcing them down to the deck floor of the ferry.

I stared into the wild, enraged green eyes of Liam Killoran.

"What the—?"

The momentary shock bought him some precious seconds, and he took full advantage of it. He kneed me in the groin. The air escaped me with a whoosh, and before I knew it he was up on his knees and clocked me square across the chin. I felt a bottom tooth loosen from the impact and grabbed my face. He was on me like a flash and wrapped both of his big, callused hands around my throat.

"You thought you were going to get away with it, didn't you?" he snarled.

"Liam . . . I . . ." My voice was gone, cut off by the strength of his squeezing hands. I couldn't reason with him.

"You thought you could run off and disappear. That I'd never find you."

I felt my knees give out. I was like a rag doll as the life slipped out of me.

And then, the Australian backpackers who had so generously shared their bottle of ouzo with Laurette and me wandered onto the deck to smoke some weed.

"Hey, what are you doing?" a cute, curvy blond girl yelled as she and her friends rushed Liam.

Liam knew he was outnumbered and didn't stand a chance against the young hard bodies who were racing to my rescue. He jumped to his feet and scampered off into the darkness.

The Australians knelt down beside me. One of the strikingly handsome young men lifted my head in the crux of his arm and whispered in my ear that everything was going to be okay while another sandy-haired muscle boy gently held my hand. The perky blond girl poured me another shot of ouzo. Maybe Liam had succeeded. Maybe he had choked the life out of me and this was the gateway to heaven. It sure as hell felt like it. I could have lain there for hours being attended to by these magnificent angels from down under. But as the cold night air slapped my face awake and Laurette's high-pitched, drunken scream at my condition snapped me back to reality, I knew that Liam Killoran was somewhere loose aboard this ferry with the single-minded mission to avenge the death of his true love by slaughtering me.

# Chapter 23

The Australians wasted no time in alerting the captain of the ship about the attack, and he immediately dispatched his crew to search the entire ferry. Liam was nowhere to be found. He was either hiding someplace they had overlooked or had jumped overboard. I knew he wouldn't try to assault me again since I was now surrounded and protected by the Australian backpacker brigade. They were pumped up and overflowing with machismo from heroically saving my life and were itching to flex their muscles again if need be.

The stress of the situation forced Laurette to buy the entire plate of brownies from the snack bar and we sat at our favorite orange Formica table and devoured them with the gusto of two castaways rescued from a deserted island after two weeks without food.

"Do you think this Irish guy is somehow connected to the two guys we saw ransacking Akshay's apartment?" Laurette said as she carefully picked the walnuts out of her brownie due to her own nut allergy, much like Claire's.

"Beats me." I shrugged. "There's so much weird stuff going

on, I don't know what's what. There seems to be a lot of people looking for something."

"Like what?"

"Well, right after Claire died, I caught a guy in a red ski mask searching her dressing room. Liam noticed that her Academy Award was missing and of course accused me of taking it. But anybody could have made off with it, even before she collapsed on stage."

"Maybe somebody else did steal it before the guy in the ski mask had a chance to break in and snatch it for himself. Maybe it was Akshay. He could have swiped it while Claire was onstage, and that's what those two guys were looking for at his apartment."

I rolled this theory over in my mind. It was possible. But who were all these thieves? Where did they come from? And why was one best actress Oscar from a tepid, overrated farm film of the eighties worth so much effort to get? And was it even related to Claire's mysterious death?

However, the fact remained I was less concerned with clearing my name and solving Claire's murder than I was with finding Charlie.

As dawn broke, the Minoan ferry moved toward the sandy shores and chalk white beauty of one of the most vibrant Greek islands, Mykonos. Once we docked, the passengers filed off to explore the breathtaking vistas, to stroll up and down the white-washed streets of the town center, or to browse the glorious golden and diamond-studded rings, bracelets, and necklaces displayed in the windows of the jewelry artists of Mykonos. The island has always been a striking dichotomy. On the one hand, there are the street peddlers selling from their donkey stands, women sweeping the streets in traditional Greek black dresses and head scarves, church bells tolling all over the island. It's from another time. But contrasting that traditional image is a far more hedonistic aspect of Mykonos. There is the fashionable jet set that dines at the opulent gourmet restaurants. Then there are the wild, partying tourists who dance at the trendy clubs until the wee hours of the morning, when they sneak away with their designated paramours back to the privacy of their hotels for a little passionate lovemaking before the inevitable hangover starts its reign of terror. There is no other place in the world that comes close to the originality and escapism of Mykonos.

Laurette whipped out a scrap of paper from her purse and studied it. Back in London she had quickly jotted down the address of the Andromeda Residence where Akshay had made a reservation.

"Lakka Square Rohari. It's somewhere in the town center," she said, looking around, confused and lost.

After asking an elderly Greek woman with silver hair and a black scarf tied around her head for directions, we were promptly sent up a steep incline of cobblestone steps toward a row of hotels and condos. It would be impossible to work with a physical description of the property, since almost all of the structures on the entire island were painted white and adorned with blue trim and shutters.

The sun was blazing and both Laurette and I were sweating as we reached a wrought-iron gate. The entrance was unassuming, and we would have missed it if I hadn't asked a Japanese woman in a thong who was passing by if she knew where we could find the Andromeda Residence. She pointed at the gate to our right. We had no idea we were standing right outside the entrance.

As we entered the hotel grounds, I was struck by the beauty of the multicolored gardens of red and yellow flowers, the glistening, gorgeous blue swimming pool, and the immaculately kept, freshly painted condos.

Laurette, the consummate hotel queen, was duly impressed. She charged toward the registration office, and I followed closely on her heels. A lovely young woman with jet-black hair, clear, perfect olive skin, and kind brown eyes greeted us. She wore a red print wrap over a blue bathing suit and reached out to shake our hands.

"Welcome to Mykonos," she said with a big, electric smile. "I'm Delphina."

After introducing ourselves, Laurette handed Delphina a confirmation number for the reservation she had made while we were waiting for our Athens flight to leave from Heathrow. Delphina smiled, took our credit card information, and within seconds, handed us over the keys to a two-bedroom suite. She offered to help us with our bags, but we told her we didn't have any with us and would be buying clothes here on the island.

She lit up and laughed. "Now that's the way to travel," she said in perfect English with a flavorful Greek accent that bespoke her heritage.

As we turned to go, I thanked her, and then said, "Oh, by the way, one of the reasons we chose this hotel—besides its obvious beauty—is because we heard through the grapevine that one of our favorite actors in the world is staying here. Akshay Kapoor. We're huge Bollywood fans!"

Laurette, quick to join in, added, "If I could get his autograph, I could die happy."

Delphina smiled and then leaned in conspiratorially. "Yes. He is indeed staying here."

Laurette squealed with delight.

"Don't worry," I said, "We won't bother him . . . too much."

Delphina laughed heartily. "He's a very nice man. But keeps to himself. He's spent most of his stay here in his room. It's such a shame. We've had such lovely weather."

"Is he in his room now?" I said.

"No. Today was the first day he's actually gone out."

"Do you know where?" Laurette said.

Delphina nodded. "Super Paradise Beach. He asked me to write directions on how to get there. He took a bus and then a taxi boat."

"What's so super about Paradise Beach?" Laurette said.

"It's the gay nudist beach," I said, having been there one or two times myself.

"I'm not taking my top off. I'll tell you that right now," Laurette said.

"What's the big deal? You already flashed the taxi driver in London," I said, smiling.

Once Laurette and I checked out our nicely appointed, spacious room, we dashed to a nearby clothing shop for some beach wear and then hustled down to the town center to grab a taxicab to Super Paradise Beach. We didn't want to risk missing Akshay, so we ruled out the bus ride and taxi boat, which would eat up far too much time.

The ride to the other side of the island was harrowing and nail-biting. Our driver swerved around lumbering donkeys and reckless tourists on mopeds before whipping along a steep, narrow cliffside access road with nary a guardrail before skidding to a stop at a rocky cove. Laurette, her eyes bugged out in a state of shock from the death-defying journey, hurled some euros at the driver and climbed out of the car. I offered a weak thank-you before I followed her out, resisting the urge to drop to my knees and kiss the ground.

As the driver peeled away, his rear tires kicked up enough dust to cause both Laurette and me to cough and sputter. We walked to the edge and looked down, taking in the lush expanse of beach that made up Super Paradise. Unfortunately, the golden sand was barely visible due to the endless sea of umbrellas that did little to hide the hundreds of nude sunbathers from all over the world flashing their private parts. Some were stretched out on blankets, others frolicked in the aqua blue Aegean surf, still more gyrated and clapped to a blasting hot dance remix of the Mamas and the Papas' "California Dreamin' " on the far left side of the beach.

Laurette and I trudged down the access road to another perch overlooking the beach that housed the Coco Club, an upscale outdoor café that provided a relaxed ambiance for its chic clientele. We ordered a couple of Coca-Cola Lights (the European version of Diet Coke) and took a seat at a small table overlooking the beach. We both scanned the crowd, but it was pointless.

"We're never going to find Akshay down there. It's too packed with people," Laurette said.

Not about to give up, I searched up and down the rows of topless, bronzed bodies for any sign of him. But Laurette was right. It was an impossible task. Even if he was down there somewhere, it would take us hours to locate him, and at any time he could leave by taxi boat and head back to Mykonos town without us ever seeing him.

"Maybe we should just go back and wait for him at the hotel," Laurette offered, already hot and tired, her skin burning from lack of a proper sunscreen.

My gut was telling me he was here. I wasn't ready to give up yet.

"Omigod," Laurette said under her breath.

"What? Did you spot him?"

"No, look at those two. Absolutely stunning."

I followed Laurette's gaze away from the beach to the rocky cove adjacent to the Coco Club. She was watching two men in their mid-twenties, both hard-bodied, Greek, and gorgeous, emerge from the surf. As they gripped the jagged rocks and pulled themselves out of the water, we both gasped. Both were over six feet tall, one smooth and lanky like an Olympian swimmer, the other broader and muscled with a mat of dark, wet, curly hair across his chest. They were like two Greek gods, Apollo and Neptune, suddenly brought to life. Except instead of togas they were decorated with tight red Speedos.

"Be still my heart," Laurette sighed.

Both of us watched them, our tongues practically hanging out of our mouths, as they climbed up the rocks to a hidden alcove to meet someone. As the two gods began talking, I was able to make out a man who had his back to us. He was in white slacks and a white T-shirt and wore a pair of sandals. His skin was dark enough to be East Indian or just really browned from the sun. Could it be? He never turned to face us, but I was able to discern from the gestures, the swagger, the attitude that it was him. It was Akshay.

I jumped to my feet and bolted for the dirt path leading toward the cove.

"Now, don't be a stalker," Laurette said. "We can admire from afar."

"It's him," I called back. "Let's go."

Laurette grabbed her bag and ran to catch up with me as I scurried down the path toward Akshay and the gods. From what I could see, Akshay clutched a burlap sack that Apollo and Neptune kept reaching for, but Akshay gripped it tightly and was talking a mile a minute. Was it some kind of exchange? What was going on?

Laurette scrambled to keep up with me, and just as we got within a few hundred feet of Akshay, we heard a loud popping sound. I stopped in my tracks and watched in horror as Akshay grabbed his chest. Blood began seeping out onto his white T-shirt and he grabbed the muscular forearm of one of the gods to steady himself. There was another pop. Akshay reared back and fell against the rocks. Both Apollo and Neptune were unarmed (there was absolutely no way they could be concealing guns in those Speedos). Their eyes widened at the realization that someone was shooting at them, and they quickly backed away from Akshay.

One of them looked up to see me and for a split second believed I was the shooter. I shook my head and mouthed, "No!" Then I ducked down behind a large boulder, yanking Laurette down with me. There was an agonizing silence.

I peeked above the top of the large orange-colored rock and saw Apollo and Neptune dashing down to the water's edge and diving into the surf below. They never resurfaced.

I glanced down at the beach to see several nude sunbathers chattering on their cell phones. They had undoubtedly witnessed the shooting and were now presumably calling the police.

I scanned the entire area but didn't see any shooter. He had probably already made his escape.

Before Laurette could stop me, I came out from behind the rock and raced down to where Akshay's body rested against a patch of grass just next to a rock on the dirt trail.

I knelt down beside him. His eyes were wet, he clutched his bloody chest, and he was desperately trying to take in quick, short breaths. He was still alive.

"Akshay . . ." I said, gingerly taking his hand.

He looked up at me and tried to register surprise but was too weak.

"Jarrod . . . ?" His voice trailed off.

"Where's Charlie?" I said.

Akshay opened his cracked, parched lips, but no words came out. All he could do was point to the burlap sack that he had dropped a few feet away when he fell. I reached over and scooped it up, loosened the string tying it together, and peered inside. I already knew what I would find inside. It was Claire Richards's Academy Award.

"Did you take this from Claire's dressing room?" I said.

Akshay attempted a nod and then slowly reached out, his

hand shaking, and encircled my wrist with his fingers with all the strength he had left in him.

"Ulysses . . . Karydes . . ." he said in a pained whisper.

"Who's that?"

"A famous Greek shipping tycoon," Laurette offered. "He owns half of Greece. Makes Aristotle Onassis look like a welfare mother."

I shot Laurette a questioning look.

"I tend to read a lot of articles on the world's wealthiest bachelors, you know, in case some day I need a sugar daddy," she said.

I turned back to Akshay. "What about Karydes? Does he know where Charlie is?"

Akshay let go of my wrist. His eyes glazed over and his body went limp as he quietly succumbed to the bullet lodged in his chest.

I began shaking him, futilely hoping he might wake up to supply me with just a little more information. How was Charlie connected to Claire's Oscar? How would a powerful multimillionaire Greek shipping tycoon know where Charlie was? Unlike me, Charlie had never even been to Greece before.

Laurette gently touched my shoulder. "Jarrod, the police just arrived. We're going to have some explaining to do. Why don't you let me handle it?"

I nodded, staring at Akshay's corpse, suddenly realizing that someone was going to have to tell his mother that her adored son was dead. It would devastate her.

Laurette was a master at bulldozing over authority figures. It was a finely tuned talent that served her well in show business. We both knew that if we came clean with the cops about following Akshay here, we would be hounded and questioned for hours, possibly days, thereby reducing our chances of finding Charlie. Besides, if this powerful and almighty Ulysses Karydes was the key to locating Charlie, then he no doubt had the local police in his back pocket, and they would never allow us to get anywhere near him.

The only two people who had even seen us near Akshay were the stunningly beautiful Greek studs Apollo and Neptune, and they had hightailed it out of there at the first sign of trouble. No, it was best to allow Laurette to work her magic.

She spun a fanciful yarn about how we were married and worked in Los Angeles as talent manager and actor (Laurette never thought it wise to stray too far from the truth) and how I had lost out on a big feature-film role to the much younger Tobey Maguire. She decided to spirit me away to Greece to help me forget about my career troubles. We only arrived just a few hours ago and were now traumatized by witnessing a man being gunned down on the hiking path. She adamantly insisted that she did not know the murder victim. She neglected to mention that I, on the other hand, did, but the police assumed that since we were together she was speaking for both of us. Damn, she was good.

The officers looked me up and down as Laurette prattled on with her story. I offered a tight smile as I clutched the burlap sack containing Claire Richards's Oscar to my side, hoping they would think it was just a picnic lunch we had brought along.

The police took copious notes, and Laurette offered the address to the Andromeda if they needed to contact us for any reason. The police made it clear they were in no way through with us, but Laurette miraculously managed to browbeat them into allowing us to go so we could try to salvage what was left of our much-needed vacation.

Thanks to Laurette's performance, the officers believed we were innocent tourists who just happened to be in the wrong place at the wrong time. They even offered to drive us back to our hotel, but Laurette insisted we return by taxi so as not to inconvenience their investigation. Her real agenda was to get away from the cops as soon as possible, before either of us said something that might trip up our official story.

I felt guilty about feigning ignorance and lying to the police. But the stakes were too high at this point. I could feel it. Charlie was on this island. I was so close to getting him back. I couldn't jeopardize losing track of him again by playing my cards too soon and confessing everything to the police.

On the taxi ride back to the Andromeda, Laurette and I discussed our next course of action as we fondled the priceless Academy Award that was now in our possession. We hatched a plan that began with making contact with the wildly rich and probably dangerous Ulysses Karydes. I had a sick feeling in the pit of my stomach that we were about to dive into the deep end of some very scary shark-infested waters.

# Chapter 24

"If you want to find Ulysses Karydes," Delphina said as she sipped her cosmopolitan, "you can find him at the Music Café down at Mykonos port. He has lunch there with his bodyguards every day."

By the time Laurette and I made it back to the Andromeda Residence, Delphina and a handful of guests were already aware of Akshay Kapoor's death and were gathered around the pool for the hotel's nightly sunset cocktail hour and buzzing about the news. Mykonos saw little crime, least of all murder, so by now it was already the talk of the island. Delphina offered us a couple of her famous cosmos, and we gratefully accepted. We were somewhat worried that Delphina might report to the police that we had been inquiring about Akshay upon our arrival, but she gave no hint of turning us over to the local authorities. In fact, she simply said she was sorry for the loss of our treasured acting hero and left it at that. Laurette and I knew that the police would be showing up soon to canvass Akshay's room for any clues to the identity of his murderer and didn't want to be around for a reunion.

Delphina never asked why we needed to locate him or why we weren't more shaken up by the death of our favorite actor. She probably figured that if we were somehow mixed up in it all, it was the police's business, not hers.

After downing our cosmos, thanking Delphina for her hospitality, and nodding good night to the other guests, Laurette and I retreated to our room with the intention of keeping a much-needed low profile.

The police did show up at the Residence to question a few guests. Laurette peeked through the blinds to see several officers trudging toward Akshay's room, but after a couple of hours, they vacated the premises and all was quiet again.

"Do you think the police already know it was Ulysses Karydes who had Akshay killed and are just going through the motions so no one can accuse them of being in his pocket?" I said, allowing my conspiracy-theorist tendencies to once again fight their way to the surface.

Laurette shrugged. "Beats me. I just hope we're not getting in over our heads."

"Well, we have no choice but to keep plowing ahead if we ever want to find Charlie."

Laurette nodded. She knew I was right even if she didn't like it. She opened the burlap sack we had taken from the murder scene and pulled out Claire Richards's Academy Award. "What do we do with this?"

"I'll have Delphina keep it for us in the hotel safe until we figure out how it fits in to all of this. And tomorrow, we'll have lunch at the Music Café."

Now that we had witnessed a murder, the reality of what we were involved in was dawning on Laurette, and she was scared. I'd be lying if I said I wasn't. But I am an actor and better at hiding my abject fear. At least if we were going to go down (either tossed in jail for Akshay's murder or drowned at sea by a corrupt

Greek shipping tycoon) we would be together, best friends to the end.

Although word of Akshay's murder spread fast across the island, the startling news did nothing to dissuade vacationers from hitting the shops and beaches on the gloriously sunny day that followed. When Laurette and I had showered and dressed and made our way down the cobblestone steps into Mykonos town, two cruise ships had already docked in the harbor. Hundreds of passengers had disembarked to soak up the ambiance of the picturesque port and slap their credit cards down at all the quaint shops along the winding, narrow streets.

When we reached the port and located the Music Café, there was a rush of activity in the far left corner. Several waiters, all in white, hovered over a table shaded from the sun by a white and red umbrella. They were doting on someone, and we instantly knew who it was. Laurette and I sat down at a table across from an overweight American couple talking in a twangy, thick Southern accent. They were trying to decipher the menu.

"It's all Greek to me," the man chortled as his wife dutifully giggled at his lame joke. Laurette offered them a polite smile, and that was all they needed to strike up a conversation.

"Are you American?" the wife said.

"Yes," Laurette answered, already regretting ever making eye contact.

"We're from outside Little Rock, Arkansas. What about you two?" the husband said.

"Los Angeles." Laurette smiled.

There was a slight pause from the couple, and their plastered-on smiles melted just a tiny bit, but they quickly recovered.

I kept my eyes trained on the corner table. The waiters finally dispersed to fetch some food and drink, and I saw Ulysses

Karydes for the first time. He was a bear of a man, with a barrel chest and thick, tree-trunk legs. He wore a yellow short-sleeve shirt that clung to his dark, olive skin and tight white slacks that looked as if they were going to rip apart at any moment. His face was round, but hard, and he had a big, fleshy, pockmarked nose. Three muscular young men sat at the table with him. Two of them were Apollo and Neptune from the day before. The third was even younger, with shoulder-length dark hair and a beautiful, angular face with thick, enviable eyelashes and a soft mouth. In ancient times, he might have been a model for one of the famous Greek statues.

"LA, huh?" the husband at the next table said. "We don't have occasion to meet people from the land of fruits and nuts."

He meant it just as he said it. In his small mind, we were all gays and crazy. And maybe there was a grain of truth to that. At least in my world.

I didn't mind them insulting us as long as they didn't draw attention to us. The last thing Laurette and I needed was for Ulysses Karydes to be aware of our presence. My current plan was to let Karydes finish lunch and then follow him home so we could scout out his property and hopefully unearth more clues that might point us in the direction of Charlie.

"Baby, don't even go there!" the wife suddenly squealed, loud enough for everyone wandering along Mykonos port to hear.

It was my damn catchphrase again. The one that made me famous. The one printed on T-shirts in the eighties. And the one that has hounded me for almost twenty years. My sitcom, *Go to Your Room*, was a big deal at one time. And apparently it was well known in the outlying communities around Little Rock, Arkansas. At Heathrow Airport, the phrase had helped Laurette and me get through security in a timely fashion. Here it was about to blow our whole plan.

"I thought that was you!" the wife chirped before fishing in her purse for a pen. "I kept saying to myself, 'It can't be him.

He's way too old,' but then I thought, hell, Virginia, the show's been over for years. People lose hair and get wrinkles. They don't stay a cute little boy forever."

I wanted to kill myself.

She slapped her fountain pen down on the table and then picked up the napkin underneath her bottled water. "Could I get your autograph? My kids will never believe I ran into you. In Greece, of all places!"

I snatched the pen and the napkin and quickly scribbled my name. Mr. Arkansas was still in a state of confusion. He undoubtedly never watched situation-comedy repeats. I pegged him for an NFL and Fox News kind of guy. I wasn't being traded to the Dolphins, nor was I right-wing commentator Sean Hannity, so he had no reference for my celebrity.

I forced a smile as I handed the napkin back to her. I glanced over to see Ulysses Karydes staring over at us. Our little eruption had caught his interest. This was not good. So much for incognito.

Laurette leaned over and whispered in my ear, "Should we just make a run for it?"

I sat frozen in place, not really knowing what to do. Ulysses spoke to the young, waiflike man with the long hair, and he was up on his feet in an instant and marching over to us. Laurette and I held our breath, half expecting him to pull a gun out of his back pocket and shoot us dead on the spot.

Instead he offered us a sweet smile and said in a sexy Greek accent, "My name is Philander. I work for Mr. Karydes, who is over there. He lives on the island and is—"

"Oh, we know who he is," Laurette said.

Philander nodded. His warm smile was intoxicating. "Of course. Well, Mr. Karydes wanted me to ask you if you would care to join him for lunch."

Lunch? This was not the plan. Our mission was to be covert. Not to break bread and share stories with the guy we were supposedly staking out. But Laurette was already pushing her chair back, looking for any excuse to ditch the chatty tourists from outside Little Rock.

"We'd love to," she said, before turning back to the Arkansas couple. "Enjoy the rest of your vacation." The husband was just as glad to be rid of two West Coast show-business radicals as we were to be rid of him. His wife had already secured an autographed napkin to show off back home, so she didn't care one way or the other. They offered us polite nods and went back to trying to figure out the Greek equivalent of hamburger on their menus.

Laurette and I cautiously followed Philander over to Mr. Karydes's table. Apollo and Neptune stood as we approached. Each one pulled out a chair for us. I glanced at both of them, wondering if they recognized either of us from the incident at Super Paradise beach the day before, but if they did, neither one was giving anything away.

Philander took a seat next to me. Apollo and Neptune remained standing.

"Thank you for agreeing to join me," Ulysses Karydes said in a deep, commanding voice. "I'm Ulysses. You have already met Philander, my assistant. These are my bodyguards, Leandro and Khristos."

The muscle boys nodded to us, but never cracked a smile.

Ulysses then turned to me. "I am a huge admirer of your work."

This took me by complete surprise. A billionaire Greek shipping tycoon spent his time watching a forgettable sitcom about a precocious kid who was forever trying to pull the wool over the eyes of his parents? Come on. This had to be some kind of a joke.

Laurette raised an eyebrow. She was thinking the same thing as me.

"You must understand," Ulysses said. "I am a businessman through and through, but I have an insatiable appetite for popular American culture. I see every TV show, read every book, buy every movie on DVD. I have an enormous collection of memorabilia. In fact, I own an original shooting script of your show from 1985, signed by you."

"How on earth did you get that?" I said.

"Ebay. Where else?"

Laurette and I sat there, our mouths opened, still stunned by this disconcerting revelation.

"I also own a 'Baby, don't even go there' T-shirt, the actual pup tent used in the classic two-part camping episode, and the limited-edition *Go to Your Room* board game by Mattel."

Ulysses smiled proudly.

"You're that big a fan of my show?"

Philander touched my arm with his hand and added, "Not just your show. Mr. Karydes has devoted an entire wing of his home to film and television memorabilia. He has JR Ewing's Stetson, the Terminator's sunglasses, and his most prized possession, the original ruby slippers from *The Wizard of Oz*."

"You've got to be kidding me," Laurette said, letting it just slip out without thinking.

There was an awkward moment. I gently kicked Laurette under the table. This man may have been a loon, but he was a rich and powerful loon who could probably do with us what he wished.

As outlandish as this all sounded, pieces of the puzzle were slowly starting to fall into place. If Karydes was such a huge collector of TV and movie artifacts, then it made total sense that he would want to get his hands on Claire Richards's Oscar.

"I'd love to know what other famous pieces of history you have or would like to get," I said.

"It's like an obsession. Once you start, you can never stop," he said. "There is always something else I want to get my hands on, some valuable prop or piece of clothing. It never ends."

"What about an Academy Award?"

Karydes sat back and gave me a considered look. But he wasn't about to play his hand just yet. "I suppose it depends on who it once belonged to. Katharine Hepburn? Yes. Meryl Streep? Yes. Tatum O'Neal? Not a big priority." He laughed heartily.

"What about Claire Richards?" I said, going for it.

I could feel the tension fill the air. Leandro and Khristos bristled. Philander froze in place. Laurette gasped.

Ulysses remained calm and unshaken. "That would be a great acquisition. But how would I ever come to possess such a rare piece of history?"

"I might know of someone who may know how to get it," I said.

"Akshay Kapoor?" Ulysses said, his steely eyes locking onto mine.

"Akshay died yesterday. He was shot." I wasn't telling him anything he didn't already know. "Did you know him?"

"As a matter of fact, I did," Ulysses said.

Philander made a move to interject, to stop his boss before he said too much, but Karydes waved him away.

Laurette watched the scene as if caught up in the latest episode of her favorite soap opera, *One Life to Live*.

"He was a liar and a cheat and the world is a better place without him," Ulysses said, almost spitting out the words.

"Come on, Mr. Karydes, what did you *really* think of him?" I said.

Karydes laughed. "You must not have been that big of an admirer of Kapoor's if you're willing to make jokes so soon after his unfortunate demise."

"We weren't exactly close," I said.

"Mr. Kapoor owed me a lot of money. Tens of thousands, in

fact. He knew I loved the world of show business and suckered me into investing in a wide range of ill-fated film projects."

"You didn't have to bankroll him."

"No. I knew the risks. But he never used the money to make movies. He gambled it away recklessly. And our agreement firmly stated that if he used the funds for any endeavor outside of making films, then he would have to pay it back with interest. Which he never did."

"Sure sounds like a motive to knock him off," I said.

Laurette's eyes bulged. She didn't like me confronting Karydes because both of us could wind up just like Akshay, plugged with a couple of bullets.

"I may not be mourning his death. But I didn't kill him."

"Then why were your guys Leandro and Khristos meeting him at Super Paradise Beach yesterday just before he was killed?"

Philander gently placed a hand on my knee and squeezed it as a warning to stop while I was ahead. But I had gone too far down the road to turn back. I had a lot of questions that needed to be answered. And the first one was why was Philander leaving his hand on my knee?

Karydes chuckled. I was more of a sparring partner than he expected, and he was rather enjoying our exchange. He had no idea I was scared out of my mind but channeling a brash, young, reckless private eye I played in a *Rockford Files* reunion movie.

"Akshay came to Mykonos to pay back what he owed me," Karydes said. "I sent my boys to meet him. Before they even had a chance to retrieve what was rightfully mine, someone shot him."

"Was he paying you back in cash or something else?"

Karydes studied me. He turned to Laurette, whose eyes screamed, "It's him! Not me! He's the one pissing you off! Don't look at me!" But she kept her mouth shut and stayed by my side.

Philander, meanwhile, finally removed his hand.

Karydes' eyes shifted back to mine. "You were obviously there watching. You tell me. Did Akshay have anything of interest on him? And the bigger question is do *you* now have it?"

"Maybe. But I didn't come here to steal off a dead man. I came here looking for someone," I said.

"And who might that be?"

"A man."

"We have many men on Mykonos, all of them able and willing. Feel free to indulge all you want."

"I'm looking for a specific man. His name is Charlie. He might have been here with Akshay."

"Why would I know anything about one of Akshay's tricks?" Ulysses scoffed.

"He's not a trick," I said, anger rising in my voice. "He's special. And I need to find him."

Ulysses appeared to be debating with himself. There was no formal offer of a trade on the table. If he did indeed know where Charlie was, he wasn't going to tell me just yet.

He casually shook his head. "I'm sorry. I can't help you. I don't know who this Charlie is."

"Then I guess we're done here," I said, standing up. Leandro and Khristos made a move to block my exit, but Ulysses waved them off.

"Are you sure you won't stay and have some lunch?" Ulysses said, ever the consummate host.

"I'm afraid we're just not hungry," I said, glancing at Philander, who surreptitiously eyed me up and down.

I took Laurette's hand and led her away. She reached down and scooped up a piece of bread from the basket as we walked away.

"Speak for yourself," she growled. She popped the bread into her mouth and through her chewing said, "What do we do now?"

"We have to find out if Karydes has Charlie stashed away somewhere."

"And what if he does? How are we going to get him back?"

"Karydes obviously is drooling over Claire's Oscar. He's dying to get his hands on it. So we offer a trade."

"God, I hope you know what you're doing."

I didn't have the heart to tell her that I had absolutely *no* idea what I was doing.

# Chapter 25

I figured the only shot I had at uncovering some vital informa-tion was to somehow charm it out of someone. And my best chance of success was to target Ulysses Karydes's handsome young assistant, Philander. After all, he was sending me clear signals during my visit with his boss. My challenge was isolating him from Karydes and his two ripped goons, Leandro and Khristos.

When Laurette and I strolled past the pool inside the Andromeda Residence, I saw Delphina stretched out on a chaise lounge and wearing a bright lime green bikini that accentuated the curvy contours of her supple body. She was a knockout. Laurette took one look at her and sighed, defeated. She was al-ways comparing her own body to other women and was con-stantly in a state of hopelessness. I had long given up that practice, especially after filming a TV movie with a young, shaggy-haired buck named Brad Pitt. I played his younger brother in the film about a group of teenagers exacting revenge on the town bully, which we shot a few years before Brad's breakthrough role in *Thelma and Louise*. I worked out at the gym for three hours every day, hoping to develop at least a fraction of Brad's sculpted abs.

But it was an exercise in futility. You can't fight what nature gave you. Laurette, however, never learned that lesson.

"I'll be in the room sulking," she said to me and then shuffled off, rifling through her bag for our room key.

I watched her go, and then turned to Delphina. Her eyes were closed as the sun's warm rays washed over her lean, deeply tanned form.

"Delphina?" I said, leaning down. My body cast a shadow over hers, and she opened her eyes, surprised. She shielded her eyes with her hand, and then smiled.

"Jarrod, did you find Mr. Karydes?"

"Yes, he was exactly where you said he would be. Turns out he saw the show I was on when I was a kid. He asked us to join him."

"That's wonderful. You're very lucky to have Mr. Karydes for a friend. He's a very powerful man. He can give you anything you want."

"Well, there's one thing I want that I'm not sure he's willing to give me."

"What is that?"

"His assistant."

She gave me a knowing wink. "Philander. Isn't he adorable?"

"Oh, yes. I think we really hit it off."

"Well, I would tread very carefully. He used to be Mr. Karydes's lover."

"Used to be?"

"Mr. Karydes has what you might call a short attention span. He goes through boyfriends faster than J Lo goes through husbands."

We both laughed.

Delphina reached down, picked up a green-tinted martini glass, and took a sip of her happy hour cosmo. "But Philander was special and Mr. Karydes knew it, so he kept him on as his assistant."

"Do you think they still sleep together?" I asked.

"Maybe every now and then, but like I said, whenever Mr. Karydes is around beautiful boys, his head is like an oscillating fan. Back and forth. Back and forth. Always cruising for his next conquest."

"Well, I have it on good authority that Philander might be interested in me."

"What good authority?"

"His hand on my knee."

"That's a very reliable source," Delphina said with a chuckle.

"You seem to know a lot about what goes on around here."

"You live on Mykonos your whole life, you get plugged into all the gossip."

"Tell me, is there a place where I might find Philander when he's not tending to Mr. Karydes's every whim?"

Delphina thought for a moment. "Montparnasse."

"What's that?"

"A piano bar. About a ten-minute walk from here. Philander goes there every night around eight when Mr. Karydes is having dinner. He has a few cocktails, silently curses his boss, and then scurries back to the compound by eleven to tuck him in for the night."

I gave Delphina a peck on the cheek. "Thank you."

She gently took my wrist in her hand and squeezed. "Be careful, Jarrod. Mr. Karydes is a very jealous man. It doesn't matter that he and Philander are no longer involved. Once you belong to Mr. Karydes, you belong to him for life."

"I'll bear that in mind."

I hurried back to the room. Laurette was curled up in bed underneath the comforter and sleeping soundly. We were both exhausted from our travel adventures, but after taking a long nap myself that stretched into the early evening hours, I had to shower and change and slap on some sweet-smelling cologne if I was going to try and seduce my prey.

After slipping on some white pants and a beige silk shirt, I kissed the still-slumbering Laurette on the forehead and quietly left the suite. Delphina, the doll she was, had dropped off some written directions to the Montparnasse Piano Bar on her way to dinner. I followed them to the letter up a steep incline to a row of bars and shops facing the vast expanse of the Aegean, which glittered and danced under the bright, blinding moonlight. When I reached the Montparnasse, I unbuttoned the top two buttons of my silk shirt to show off some skin, hoping Philander might be impressed, before opening the door and entering.

Inside, the festive atmosphere startled me. All the tables were filled with straight couples, gay couples, groups of friends. Everyone sang along as the three-hundred-pound, bitchy English queen at the piano banged out a medley from *Hello, Dolly*. I felt awkward and self-conscious and didn't know where to turn. There was an open stool at the bar, so I made a beeline for it. I hopped up on it, ordered a Coca-Cola Light and Vanilla Absolut, and then scanned the room for Philander. There was no sign of him. I checked my watch. 8:10 P.M. If Delphina was right, he should have been here by now. Maybe he was running late. Maybe Ulysses insisted he stay on the grounds tonight.

I joined the crowd in a rousing rendition of "When the Parade Passes By." A drunken, red-faced Scot from Edinburgh sidled up and asked me if I was interested in taking a walk along the rocky beach outside, which was code for a sloppy quickie, but I politely declined.

Out of the corner of my eye, I saw the men's room door swing open and Philander glide out. He wore a tight-fitting T-shirt and blue jeans. His long, thick hair was matted down by gel and his eyes were downcast. He was walking straight toward me. I suddenly realized his stool was right next to mine. I picked up his half-empty bottle of Amstel Light from the bar and held it out to him as he approached.

When he looked up to see me grinning at him with his beer in my hand, he stopped in his tracks. His mind worked quickly to process my presence, but I could tell he decided to chalk it up to coincidence, and only then did he offer me a smile.

"Where's your girlfriend?" he asked before taking a long sip of his beer.

"Back at the hotel. Sleeping. And she's not my girlfriend."

"How fortunate."

"For whom?"

"For both of us."

Philander leaned up against the bar and kept stealing glances at me. The piano player had segued into *A Chorus Line* and most of the crowd had draped their arms around each other to sway in unison to his dramatic rendition of "What I Did for Love."

I turned to the bartender and ordered us another round.

"Are you trying to get me drunk?" Philander asked, caressing my shoulder with the back of his hand.

"You have a problem with that?"

"No. But if I have too much, I'm not responsible for my actions."

"That's the plan," I said, reaching around behind him and squeezing his right butt cheek.

From the bulge in Philander's pants, I knew my little seduction dance was working. He spun my stool around so I was facing him and cupped my face in his hands.

"Do you know what 'Philander' means in Greek?"

I shrugged, not having the faintest idea.

"Lover of man."

Perfect.

He guzzled his Amstel Light within two minutes, and I signaled the bartender to bring him another one. Meanwhile, I excused myself three times to go to the bathroom, taking my drink with me and pouring it down the sink each time.

After two hours of flirting and touching and singing, Philander was slurring his words, swaying back and forth, and raising his voice well into the red zone on the obnoxious meter. I had to work fast.

"Want to get out of here?" I said, slipping my arm around his waist.

"Yes. But where can we go? Your hotel?"

"Can't. My friend is there. Where do you live?"

"In a guesthouse on the Karydes compound." He laughed. "Forget going there."

"Why not? You live alone in the guesthouse, don't you?"

"Yes, but there are cameras everywhere. Uli watches my every move."

I remembered the friendly, red-faced Scot from earlier in the night who had his own suggestion. "How about we take a stroll along the rocky beach outside. Plenty of little hiding places there, I bet."

Philander lit up. "Sounds good."

I tipped the bartender twenty euros for indulging our raucous behavior and nodded to the bitchy English queen at the piano as we passed. He sniffed at me derisively, and I concluded that he had probably been trying to score with Philander for months and resented me for succeeding during his opening set.

I wrapped my arm around Philander's waist and led him off the cobblestone path onto the slippery rocks of the shore. I spotted a few pairs of men, their eyes darting about as they disappeared behind the jagged rocks to fool around in the darkness. Philander was already rubbing his hands over my chest as we walked, but his shaky attempt at a pass only caused him to lose his balance. I gripped him tighter to keep him from falling.

When we were a safe distance from the horny tourists and the sounds of show tunes from the Montparnasse evaporated in the night winds, I sat Philander down on a flat rock. He fumbled for the zipper on my pants, but I managed to pull away without completely discouraging him. He sighed and was under the impression that it was his own inebriation that was preventing him from successfully getting inside my pants.

"Come here," he slurred, reaching out for me.

I let him pull me toward him, and he awkwardly planted a few wet kisses on my mouth. I kept my lips sealed, hoping to avoid him driving his tongue down my throat. I had to keep him going, though, at least until I found out what I needed to know.

"You are so cute," I said as I playfully ran my hand through his hair. The gel was so greasy I had to wipe it off on my white pants, leaving an unsettling stain. "I can't imagine why Ulysses would throw you away."

Philander frowned, stung by the words. "He didn't throw me away. I'm still there, aren't I?"

"Well, I heard he's got a new boyfriend."

This was news to Philander. "Who?"

"An American."

"Uli would never date an American. They're too loud and crass."

"Well, someone saw an American on his property. Tall guy, black hair, well built."

"Oh, him," Philander said, relieved. "He's not his boyfriend. He's . . ."

"What?"

Philander sat back. His head was spinning. I was on the clock, because he was going to pass out at any time. "I can't really talk about it."

"Mr. Karydes is obviously just sparing your feelings. He doesn't want you to know what's really going on between them."

"No!" Philander said, shifting his weight in a desperate attempt to stop the spinning. "That American wouldn't even be there if it weren't for that good-for-nothing Indian."

"You mean Akshay?"

"Yes, he betrayed Mr. Karydes. Tried passing off..."
Philander was confused. He knew he shouldn't be talking about
any of this, but he was drunk and his guard was down.

"The Oscar," I said. "Akshay stole it. He owed Ulysses a lot of
money, and offered to give him Claire Richards's Academy Award
if he would erase the debt."

"Yeah, but the stupid ass tried passing off..."

A fake. Akshay tried fooling Uli with a counterfeit statue. He
planned to keep the real one and sell it for a lot of money. Dumb
move, considering Uli was a connoisseur of memorabilia. The
pieces were coming together. Philander's eyes were half opened.
He was struggling to stay awake. I only had seconds left.

"When Karydes realized he was being conned by Akshay, he
decided he needed some bargaining leverage to show him he was
serious?" I said.

Philander half nodded, his eyes getting heavier every moment.

"Why did he kidnap the American?"

"He sent two of his men to London to go rough up Akshay,
who was there doing a play. They saw him with the American
and assumed the two of them were a couple..." Philander said,
his head drooping.

So Uli gave the order to kidnap Charlie, who he thought was
Akshay's lover. They spirited him here to Mykonos, probably on
Karydes's private jet, and stashed him somewhere until Akshay
turned up with the real Oscar. It all made sense. But where was
Charlie? He could be anywhere. Mykonos wasn't a huge island,
but there were a lot of discreet hiding places.

"Where is your boss keeping the American?"

Philander's head swayed to one side and his eyes were clamped
shut. I shook him, but he was out. I carefully lowered his head
until it rested against a rock. I didn't need anything more from
him. I knew the whole story. It was all about an exchange. Charlie

for the Oscar. Akshay was the thief in the red ski mask. He stole the award from Claire's dressing room. But he got greedy. And it led to Charlie's abduction. Akshay might have been a cad and a cheat, but he couldn't just let Charlie die. So he booked a flight to Mykonos to hand over the real thing and get him back. Akshay had proven so untrustworthy, however, Uli wasn't taking any chances and dispatched a couple more of his henchmen, the Hulk and Thing, over to London to ransack Akshay's apartment for the statue in case of another double cross. That's where Laurette and I came in.

But now, I was in the power position. I had the coveted Academy Award that Ulysses Karydes wanted so badly. All I had to do was contact him and arrange my own exchange. That still left some troubling questions. Why would Karydes kill Akshay before he got his hands on the Oscar? Or was it someone else? And was the person who shot Akshay dead at Super Paradise Beach the same person who somehow murdered Claire Richards on the opening night of Wallace Goodwin's play? And if she didn't die from the peanut oil, then what killed her? I had to find out the truth before the British police tossed me in prison for the crime. But first, I had to get Charlie back.

# Chapter 26

Icould only imagine Ulysses Karydes's rage when he discovered his ex–boy toy Philander was not accounted for after curfew. Philander was out for the night and would probably not open a bloodshot eye until well after dawn. The panic would quickly seep in, and he would stumble back to the property to take his licks from his blustery boss.

It was only a little after one in the morning and the clubs were still hopping with activity as I raced back to the Andromeda to shake Laurette awake and fill her in on my recent discoveries. A group of strapping young Swedes, blonde, blue eyed, and rip-roaring drunk, waved for me to join them at an outdoor table at Pierro's, Mykonos's most famous gay bar. I smiled but didn't slow down. There was much to do if I was going to bargain for Charlie's freedom.

I hurried up the cobblestone steps and was only a few hundred feet from the Andromeda when I barreled around a dark corner that was hidden from the bright street lamps. My stomach suddenly twisted into a knot. It was dark and ominous, and my gut was telling me I had just made a giant mistake. Two men jumped out of the bushes and grabbed me. One came at me from behind, wrapping a thick arm around my chest while the other lifted my legs off the ground. I twisted my head around to call out to the drunk Swedes just around the bend, but the man behind me anticipated it and clamped a giant paw over my face. I struggled violently, kicking my legs, nailing the one holding my feet across the jaw. He angrily pinned my feet under his arms, holding tight, and the two men carried me off the path, through the brush, and into a deserted alley across from a row of houses with chipped paint and weathered shutters, a far cry from the more opulent hotels.

As the guy in front of me grunted and cursed in Greek, his face fell into the light from the nearly full moon. It was Leandro. I could only guess Khristos was behind me, silencing my cries for help with his massive hand.

I was a lot more of a fighter than either anticipated, and after I clocked Leandro in the head with the heel of my shoe, he angrily dropped my legs, leaving his partner to hold me down all alone. Leandro whipped out a switchblade from his shorts and cackled as he flipped it open. He then swiftly marched up and pressed the tip of the sharp blade against the skin just underneath my left eye.

"Quiet," he hissed. "Or I pop it out with one flick of my wrist."

I wasn't about to accessorize with an eye patch for the rest of my life, so I immediately stopped fighting. I went limp, and after a few moments, Khristos took his hand away and stepped back. Leandro held the knife tip to my face just long enough for me to know he meant business, then lowered the blade. He kept it gripped in his hand, leveled at me, in case I tried anything stupid.

"If you're looking for Philander, he's back that way taking a snooze," I said, pointing toward Mykonos town.

"We want the Oscar," Leandro said, his brown eyes narrowing.

"Oscar who?"

Leandro lifted the knife back up in front of my face, turning it so the reflection from the blade caused my eyes to squint. "Get cute again," he growled, "and I *will* cut you."

"We know you have it," Khristos said.

So much for the exchange. I was no use to Charlie dead. If I didn't hand over Claire's Academy Award, I had no doubt they would stab me to death and stuff my corpse into a trash bin. If I handed over the statue, I would be left with no bargaining chip. Charlie's fate would be left in the hands of a corrupt gay Greek shipping tycoon. Maybe he would let him go. That was a stretch. If released, Charlie could someday come back to haunt him. So could I, for that matter. We were both probably marked men once Ulysses got his hands on the Oscar. I had about five minutes to come up with a plan before we were back at the Andromeda and I was waking Delphina up to open the hotel safe that housed the little piece of movie history that had caused so many problems.

"Okay," I said. "I'll get it for you. I have it safely stashed away back at the hotel."

Leandro and Khristos exchanged looks, silently consulting with one another, before Leandro motioned with the knife for me to start walking. I raised my hands in the air as I passed them, but Khristos slapped them back down to my sides.

"Act natural," he said. "And no tricks."

We emerged from the bushes and shuffled up the steps toward the Andromeda Residence. When we reached the gate, I pulled out the key to unlock it and was surprised to find it already open.

I passed through first and out of the corner of my eye saw a man pressed up against the white stone wall to the right of the gate. He was tucked back in the shadows, but I saw his hand and it clutched a big rock. He didn't move, so I kept walking. When Khristos swept in behind me, the man leapt from his hiding place and cracked the rock across Khristos's skull. The Greek

217

stud never knew what hit him. He dropped to the ground in an instant.

I spun around to see Liam Killoran, his eyes wild with fury and his body crouched for an attack. By the time Leandro realized something was seriously wrong, Liam was on him like a jungle cat, yanking him to the ground, straddling his chest, and punching his face over and over again with his big-knuckled fist.

I saw the glint of Leandro's blade shimmer as he slowly brought his arm to drive it into Liam's chest.

"Watch out!" I yelled, sprinting forward and stepping on Leandro's forearm, driving it back to the cement that surrounded the hotel's glistening aquamarine swimming pool. I pushed all of my weight down on Leandro's arm, and his fingers splayed from the pain, the knife clattering free. With my other foot, I kicked the knife across the ground, where it teetered at the edge of the pool but didn't fall in.

Liam stopped his relentless pounding for a split second, a bit taken aback by just how close he had come to having a knife plunged through his heart. Leandro seized the opportunity to drive the palm of his hand into Liam's nose. Blood spurted everywhere as Liam instinctively covered his face. Leandro knocked him aside and ran back out through the gate, disappearing into the night.

I stripped off my shirt and handed it to Liam, who was trying to stop the bleeding. "Here, pinch your nose with this."

Liam complied, a little dazed but otherwise unhurt.

"Is it broken?" I asked.

Liam shrugged. "Might be. Doesn't matter. Been broken lots of times before."

You have to love the brawling Irish.

"What are you doing here, Liam?"

"I've been following you."

"That much I know. Our little reunion aboard the ferry is still very fresh in my mind."

"I was hoping that if I stuck close to you, you'd eventually slip up and give me some kind of evidence I could use to tie you to Claire's murder."

"I didn't kill her," I said with a sigh, tired of constantly having to proclaim my innocence.

Liam nodded as the gushing blood from his nose hopelessly stained my shirt. "I know. I saw you in the bar with that guy. You really are gay. You were telling the truth. You were never even romantically involved with Claire."

Finally. The big lug found a light bulb that wasn't burnt out from too many all-night benders at his local Dublin pub.

I explained to Liam why I was in Greece, who was holding my boyfriend captive, and how I intended to use Claire's Academy Award to get him back. Liam, who felt bad for giving me such a hard time and who was probably the first straight man ever to be thrilled to learn I was gay, was now my staunch ally. He also figured that it was in his best interest to help me. Because in the end, the trail we were down just might lead to the true identity of his beloved Claire's killer.

Liam retrieved the discarded knife before hauling Khristos's unconscious body up off the ground. He roughly grabbed the man's arm and threw it around his neck. I got on the other side, and we dragged him toward the suite I was sharing with Laurette.

Suddenly a light flipped on and a door opened. Delphina stuck her head out. "Is everything all right?"

We both froze. And then I smiled. "A little too much to drink. I have no idea where he lives, so I'm going to let him sleep it off in my room."

"You naughty boys," she said, giving us a wink. She stopped long enough to gaze longingly at Liam. "Sure is a shame *you're* gay. Just my luck."

Liam so wanted to correct her impression. She was a lively, sumptuous young woman, but now was not the time to indulge his libido. I threw him a look of warning, and he kept his mouth shut. Delphina disappeared back inside her room, and after a moment, her light went out.

Liam and I carried Khristos's dead weight toward the door of the hotel suite as I fished for the key in my pocket. We hadn't a moment to waste, because I had a sickening feeling that time was rapidly running out.

# Chapter 27

When Liam and I burst through the door of the suite carrying Khristos's limp body, the door to Laurette's room was open. She shot up in bed with a start and yanked the covers up to her neck.

"Jarrod, what's happening? Who is that?"

"Liam Killoran. He was Claire Richards's boyfriend."

Laurette's stunned look gave way to a more admiring gaze. She wasted no time in jumping out of bed and throwing on a see-through nylon robe over her silk teddy. She sashayed out into the living area like Kate Moss in Versace on a Paris runway. She was clearly out to impress.

"Is this some kind of after-hours party? What's everybody drinking?" she said with an inviting smile.

Liam and I gently lowered Khristos onto a floral print couch. He slumped down, his head falling forward.

Laurette crinkled her nose with disdain at the unconscious body in our room. "He obviously needs to be cut off."

Liam marched into the bathroom, picked up a glass, and filled it with water. As he came back, Laurette fell in behind him.

"I'm Laurette, by the way," she said, trying to ignore the bloodstains on his face and shirt.

"Nice to meet you," he said before splashing the water on Khristos's face. Uli Karydes's henchman coughed and sputtered. Liam then grabbed him by the hair, pulled his head back, and slapped him hard across the face with the back of his hand.

Laurette raised an eyebrow at me. I shrugged. This was Liam's show. I was just a spectator at this point.

Khristos moaned, slowly coming around. Liam grabbed him by the shoulders and shook him. His eyes opened. He was disoriented at first, trying to piece together the events that had gotten him here. When he turned to see me and Laurette, and the hulking Irishman hovering over him, he fell into a panic and made a move to stand up. Liam was ready for him. With a big, calloused hand, he shoved him back down.

Liam reached into his pocket and pulled out Leandro's knife. He played with it a little to build up the tension in the room. "Relax. Get comfortable. You may be here awhile," Liam said, staring down at the now-nervous Khristos.

"Mr. Karydes won't like you taking one of his employees hostage," Khristos said, keeping his eyes trained on Liam, whose nose was now caked with dried blood.

"Well, the police here may turn the other cheek on some of your boss's illicit activities, but I sure as hell bet the cops in London aren't going to let him weasel out of a murder," I said.

"Murder? Mr. Karydes already told you. He had nothing to do with the Indian actor's death," Khristos said, his eyes darting around in search of some means of escape.

"I'm not talking about Akshay. I'm talking about Claire Richards."

The mere mention of her name hit Liam hard. He fought back tears, trying with all his might to maintain his tough-guy act to keep Khristos in line.

Khristos stared at me. "I don't know who that is."

"Sure you do," I said. "Your boss and I talked about her earlier today."

"I do not make a habit of eavesdropping on Mr. Karydes's private conversations."

"You were standing right there. How could you not hear? Claire Richards is an Oscar-winning actress."

"Yes, yes, okay, maybe I have seen one or two of her movies," he said.

"Your boss is a big collector of movie memorabilia. Maybe he wanted to add an authentic Academy Award to his museum. Maybe he sent you to get one by any means necessary. Maybe you broke into her dressing room and things went sour. You accidentally killed her."

Khristos's eyes widened. "That's ridiculous! Claire Richards was on the stage in front of hundreds of people when she died. Someone put peanut oil in her make-up and she died of an allergic reaction."

"Guess you know more about Claire Richards than you've let on," I said with a smile. "What else are you hiding?"

Khristos leapt to his feet, pushing me out of the way and making a break for the door. Liam was on him with the swiftness of a cheetah, bringing him down and pinning his arms to the floor. Riled with fury, Khristos picked his head up and spit in Liam's face. Liam reeled back and clocked him across the jaw with his fist.

Laurette and I both sprang forward.

"Don't knock him out," I yelled. "We need to find out about Charlie."

"I hate to see you boys fighting," Laurette cooed. "You're both just so darn cute." She regretted saying it the minute it flew out of her lips.

"Why don't you call Larry, you remember Larry, your boyfriend?" I said.

"You're one to talk. I didn't bring an Irish hunk and a Greek stud back to the room. It's a gay three-way just waiting to happen."

Not wanting to argue, I stepped around Laurette and walked up behind Liam, who still straddled the Greek. Staring down at Khristos, I said, "You know who poisoned her, don't you?"

"No!" he cried.

"And you know who shot Akshay!"

"No!"

"And you know where the American is being held, don't you?"

He hesitated for a split second before sighing, "No."

I grabbed the knife out of Liam's hand, pushed him off Khristos, and knelt down in front of the Greek. I drove the tip of the blade up against his throat just as his partner had done to me. "Talk to me, Khristos, and you may just walk out of here alive."

"It had to be Akshay," Khristos wailed. "He knew the Richards woman would never just hand over her Oscar. And that statue was his only way out of a massive debt. He was desperate. He probably killed her, poisoned her somehow. Then, with her out of the way, he had the opportunity to steal that award."

Khristos eyed the knife at his throat. He was terrified.

I had to admit it made perfect sense. But why go through the trouble of murdering Claire? After all, he had backstage access. He was in the cast of the play. He could have waited until Claire was onstage and Liam was occupied, and then all he had to do was just break into her dressing room and snatch the statue. No. He didn't have a strong enough motive to kill her. And if he did do it, then we would never really know the truth, because he was dead. Which led to the next big question. Who killed Akshay? I believed what Ulysses Karydes and his henchmen were claiming. Akshay had the Oscar on him when he died. Why would they kill him? They were so close to getting what they wanted. They might have roughed him up a bit for trying to double-cross them with a fake, but he had made good on his promise to deliver the genuine artifact. Why risk scrutiny from the authorities for no reason? Someone else was behind these killings. Someone not connected to Akshay and not connected to Karydes. Which put me back to square one.

But there was still the pressing matter of Charlie. I pressed the knife deeper into Khristos's skin, just enough to draw a trickle of blood.

He screamed. "I told you, we didn't kill anybody!"

"But you did kidnap someone, and I want to know where he is," I growled.

"I don't know what you're talking about!" Khristos was weeping.

"The American. I want to know where he is."

I twisted the knife a bit, making the cut wider. Khristos screamed. Liam watched me in the moment, a little concerned about just how far I was willing to take this. Even Laurette had her doubts. She had never seen me like this before. But I had never lost my boyfriend before to a gang of Greek thugs. And I surprised even myself with the sheer focus of my rainbow-colored vigilantism.

Tears ran down Khristos's face. He was stuck. Either betray his boss or get his throat cut. He looked up at me, his eyes pleading. They were met by a grave, determined stare. And it was at that moment that Khristos finally believed I was dead serious.

"The compound. Your American friend is being held on Mr. Karydes's compound."

# Chapter 28

Grabbing a fistful of Khristos's hair and yanking his head back until it pounded against the floor, I leaned over his face and waved my knife menacingly.

"Okay, here is what you're going to do," I said. "You're going to hightail it back to your boss and tell him to meet us today at noon at Agios Sostis Beach."

The last time I had traveled to Mykonos, I met a local while skin diving who invited me there for lunch. It was a very isolated strip of beach, quiet, with low dunes that could conceal quite a lot of secret activity. It was about as far outside of Mykonos town as you could get and still be on the island. The only house in the vicinity was a tiny shack owned by a kindly Dutch woman and her Greek husband who operated a homey tavern. I remembered they had to close when it got dark because they had no electricity. It was the perfect locale for an exchange. Out of the way. But with a pair of witnesses if anything went wrong.

"You tell Uli to bring Charlie unharmed and we'll give him his damn Oscar," I said.

Khristos was on his back, sprawled out on the floor, frozen.

Sitting on top of him, I tapped the tip of the blade against the bridge of his nose.

"Are you hearing me, Khristos?" I said.

He quickly nodded.

"If your boss tries anything stupid, or if Charlie has so much as a bruise on him, not only will I make it my personal mission to skewer him like a souvlaki, I'll personally come back for you too."

Why couldn't I ever be this good in an audition? I could be raking in a fortune playing a variety of badasses on all those franchise cop shows like *Law and Order* and *CSI*.

Laurette, who was never without a biting and sarcastic comment, was utterly speechless. This was indeed a first. She simply stared at me, part of her impressed and another part of her scared silly by my forceful display of brutish bravado.

I slowly stood up and stepped over Khristos's prone body. Liam watched him like a hawk as he scrambled to his feet, ready to pounce on the Greek henchman if he made any kind of unexpected move. But my tough-guy act had worked. He backed slowly toward the door.

"I'll tell him," he said. He stumbled into the door, felt for the knob with his left hand, and swung it open. When he was reasonably confident that I wasn't going to jam the knife into his back when he turned around, he made a break for it and disappeared into the darkness.

Laurette dropped to the couch and exhaled loudly. "I didn't sign up for this."

Liam grinned at me. "That was fucking incredible! You were so awesome, so believable, that piece of shit nearly wet his pants!"

"We've only got a few hours until we have to grab a cab over to the beach. It's clear across the island. At least a half-hour drive."

"Shouldn't we call someone for backup?"

"Who? Karydes owns the local cops. And if we call the authorities in Athens, they'll never get here in time. Besides, if we bring an army, Uli could panic and kill Charlie," I said. "We're on our own."

"Don't worry, Jarrod. I'll have your back," Liam said. This was quickly turning into one of those low-budget action movies with Casper Van Dien that Showtime aired in the wee hours of the morning.

"We better wake Delphina up and get the Oscar out of the hotel safe," I said, heading for the door.

Laurette followed me, turning her head and smiling at Liam. "We'll be right back."

As I marched across the yard toward the office, Laurette shuffled along in her slippers, trying to catch up.

"Jarrod, wait, this is insane," she said, reaching out to pull at my arm. "You can't be doing this. First of all, as cute as the Irishman is, he strikes me as a tiny bit unstable. Look up 'loose cannon' in the dictionary, and you'll probably see his picture."

"I'm going to need a crazy man on my side if I'm going to pull this off."

"Please, let's call someone, anyone, before we rush into this. Honestly, Jarrod, wake up. Think about what you're doing."

"I'm only thinking of Charlie right now," I said.

"And if you screw this up, Charlie is the one who is going to pay the biggest price."

I had already been obsessing about that very fact, and when she said it out loud, it all came crashing down on me. But failure was not an option at this point. And I couldn't let my best friend in the world chip away at my resolve.

"I can only go by what my gut is telling me, Laurette."

I spun away from her and rang the bell outside the office door. I waited another few seconds and rang it again. A light popped on inside and someone fumbled to unlock the door.

Delphina, her eyes heavy, her hair tangled, yawned as she opened the door to find us. "Yes?"

"We're sorry to wake you, Delphina, but it's an emergency. We need to get something out of the safe."

She was annoyed, but her desire to be a good hostess over-whelmed her irritation, and she waved us inside.

Delphina asked no questions. She just wrapped her powder blue robe tightly around her and led us behind the desk to the safe. She spun the dial a few times, and after a click, she turned the lever and the stainless steel door opened. She reached inside, pulled out the sack, and handed it to Laurette.

"Is there anything else?"

"No, that's all," I said. "I'm truly sorry to be bothering you so late."

She forced a smile. "No trouble. Enjoy the rest of your night. Or the start of your morning."

"Thank you," I said and we headed for the door.

"Oh, Mr. Jarvis, Ms. Taylor," she said. "If you find yourselves in any kind of trouble, please don't hesitate to come to me. I may be able to help you."

"That's very kind of you," Laurette said.

"I'm very serious," she said, folding her arms. "You know where to find me."

We thanked her again and left the office. As we crossed back to our room, Laurette clutched the top of the sack in her fist, swinging it by her side.

"What do you suppose that was all about?" Laurette asked.

"Well, she obviously knows we're up to something. We haven't exactly been acting like your typical American tour-ists."

"She was so ominous. It was kind of creepy. You think she peeked inside the sack and saw what was in it?"

I shrugged.

"We better make sure she didn't swipe the Oscar and replace

it with a candlestick or something," Laurette said, opening the sack and fishing inside for Claire's Academy Award.

She wrenched the statue out of the confines of the sack and held it up in the air. "Looks like the real thing to me."

At that moment, just as I opened my mouth to warn her, Laurette crashed her knee into a chaise lounge by the pool. The shock caught her off guard, and she lost her balance. I reached out to grab her, but it was too late. She toppled over, and in a desperate bid to steady herself, threw the Oscar into the air. She landed on the cement with a thud.

Just as my eyes shifted upward in search of the flying Oscar, I saw it plummet back to earth and land a few feet from Laurette. Oscar hit the cement headfirst. There was a sickening crack, and the little man's gold head separated from his body and rolled over the side of the pool, where it splashed into the aquamarine chlorinated water and sank to the bottom.

"Damn it, my knee is bleeding!" Laurette wailed.

I stared at the decapitated Oscar.

"Jarrod, did you hear me? Can you run back to the room and get a wet towel and a Band-Aid?"

I glanced over the side of the pool, and made out the stoic tiny face of the poor, unlucky, beheaded Oscar. Laurette had no idea yet that her clumsiness might have just cost Charlie his life.

# Chapter 29

"How are you ever going to take care of a child you adopt from China if you can't even look after an inanimate object?" I said, jumping into the pool to retrieve Oscar's head. I knew I was wrong to say it, but I was distressed about Charlie and my emotions were getting the best of me.

"How could you attack me like that? After all we've been through together!" Laurette bellowed. "I know you're upset, I know the statue is our best chance of getting Charlie back, but to question my mothering skills . . ."

I didn't hear any more. I took a big gulp of air and swam down to the bottom of the pool and scooped up Oscar's head in my fist. When I shot back up to the surface, I saw Liam lumbering over to Laurette.

"What happened?" he said.

Laurette raised the headless statue up in the air for him to see.

"Christ, we're dead," he whispered.

"No, Charlie's dead if we don't figure something out," I said, lifting myself out of the pool and handing Liam the little gold head. I twisted my shirt in my hands, wringing the water from it.

"Jarrod, I'm sorry . . ." Laurette had calmed down from the

shock of her fall and decided after years of friendship, she might as well cut me some slack for my harsh words. She plopped down on the chaise lounge that had caused her unfortunate tumble and carefully examined her wounded knee.

I marched over, leaned down, and kissed her lightly on the forehead. She looked up at me and gave me a gentle nod. Both of us knew our blowup was a result of the agonizing pressure we were under. There was no need to discuss it any further.

"What now?" Liam said. It was clear he was now our partner in all of this, because he was so close to avenging his beloved Claire's death he could taste it.

"Maybe we can call Mr. Karydes and just explain what happened. He might understand. He might even still want the Oscar, head or no head," Laurette said hopefully.

"No," I said. "I'm not going to risk making him mad."

"Maybe we can fix it," Liam said.

Laurette's eyes widened. "We can use Krazy Glue!"

"There's no guarantee we can repair it, and we'll be losing valuable time. Looks like we're just going to have to rescue Charlie before we're supposed to meet Karydes."

"How do you propose we do that?" Laurette asked, her eyes wide with curiosity.

I took a deep breath. "Raid the compound."

A nervous giggle escaped Laurette before it slowly dawned on her that I was completely serious.


Laurette and Liam accompanied me down the stone sidewalk to Mykonos town, still unsure whether I was crazy enough to go through with this off-the-cuff plan. I approached a snoozing cab driver slumped down in the front seat of his taxi, parked off to the side of a tiny traffic circle surrounded by shops and cafés.

I shook the sleeping driver awake. "I need you to take us to the Karydes estate."

The driver just sat there like he didn't hear me.

"Do you know where it is?"

"Everybody knows where it is," he said. "But you don't want to go there unless you're invited."

"I'll give you a hundred euros if you take us at least within a half a mile of the place. We'll continue on foot from there."

A hundred euros perked up the driver's ears. He shifted around to see if I was serious. I was already waving the bills in my hand.

"Half now, the other half when we get there."

He snatched the money out of my hand, spun around, and fired up his beat-up, dented taxicab.

Laurette's head was spinning from my macho posturing. "How do you know Charlie's still there?"

"Khristos said he was there. Why would they move him? Besides, the last thing they'll expect us to do is show up now, before the scheduled exchange. Who is going to be stupid enough to break into the place in the predawn hours?"

"This is a suicide mission!" Laurette wailed.

"That's why you're not going. There's no way I'm going to be responsible for my best friend getting shot."

"What about Liam?" Laurette said.

"He can tag along or not. That's his choice. All I know is, if Charlie's going down, I'm not letting him go down alone."

Liam stared at me, trying to figure out if I had gone off the deep end. Was I so out of touch with the reality of the situation that I was going to get him killed?

I got in the back of the cab.

Liam put up his hand. "I'm in." He turned and gave me a slight smile as he followed me into the backseat. "Are all actors this crazy?"

"You of all people should know. You're an actor too."

"No, I'm not," Liam said with a smile. "That was all Claire's idea. She just wanted to fuck with the director."

"Well, you're still an expert on crazy actors. You were sleeping with the spokeswoman for crazy actors."

Liam couldn't argue after two roller-coaster years with the mercurial Claire. I just hoped that Charlie would have the opportunity in the near future to commiserate with Liam about living with self-involved, daft actors.

# Chapter 30

After Laurette waved us off, it was a short ride to Psarou Beach, a remote yet dramatic enclave surrounded by high, majestic mountains populated with lush, vast villas nestled comfortably into the landscape. Below, a smattering of luxurious yachts rocked gently in the water surrounding the beach. This was undoubtedly Eurotrash central.

"Which one is Karydes's place?" I asked as I pulled the other fifty euros out of my wallet and handed it to the driver.

"The biggest one, of course," he said, as if I had just asked the stupidest question he had ever heard. He pointed toward the top of the highest mountain.

The villa dwarfed the properties below it and stretched halfway across the peak. It was white with blue shutters, like almost every other property on the island, but stood out simply because of its expansive size. It was going to be a long hike to get up there.

Liam and I barely had time to get out of the cab before it sped away. The driver had no intention of allowing anyone to see him dropping us off and thereby connecting him to us.

"So we're going to have to search that whole place for your boyfriend? This is fucking nuts," Liam said, shaking his head.

"It's not too late to pull out."

"Forget it. I'm pumped now. Let's just do it."

Liam led the way, and it was slow going for a while as we navigated our way through a thicket of trees and brush, hugging the side of the access roads up the hill so we could jump into the bushes if a car passed by. It was a quiet morning. We only had to duck out of sight once, when an elderly man in shorts and no shirt sauntered by carrying a basket of black olives he intended to sell by the roadside to the wealthy residents.

When we finally had the Karydes compound in our sights, Liam shifted gears and suddenly transformed into Joe Action Hero. He crouched down to get a good look at the compound.

"No guards outside. Shouldn't be too hard to get up to the house. Once we're in, though, I'm betting it'll be a whole different ball game." If Liam had been carrying some green face paint, he would have slapped it on at that moment.

"I wish we had some kind of layout of the house like in the movies," I said.

He was charged up on adrenaline. We both were. Which was a good thing, because if we took a second to seriously examine what we were about to do, we would have run screaming back down the mountain. But love makes you do stupid things. And the one thing in my life I was sure of was my love for Charlie Peters.

We made our way around to the back of the house. There was still no sign of anyone. The place appeared to be deserted. Liam crawled on his belly across the lawn. I dutifully followed. I got the strong feeling Liam was enjoying this a little too much. He was now relishing every minute playing the role of studly spy, although I suspected he might not have the brains to ever pass any kind of CIA entrance exam.

After a slow crawl to some trees we could use for cover, we both darted across the back lawn of the property to a sliding glass door that was adjacent to a shimmering kidney-shaped pool and Jacuzzi. Liam tried the door. It was open. He gave me a surprised look and then cautiously slipped through, his eyes searching for anyone wandering around. Not a soul in sight.

Once inside, we found ourselves in an immense memorabilia library that housed Uli's vast collection. We were both awestruck by the variety of TV and movie history that filled the room. There was Rhett Butler's coat from *Gone with the Wind*. The Rosebud sled from *Citizen Kane*. The wooden vat where Lucille Ball stomped grapes in *I Love Lucy*. Even Robin Williams's space suit from *Mork and Mindy*. I could have spent the entire day in-specting all the cool artifacts if I weren't on a life-saving mission. Liam, who was less of an entertainment junkie than I, wasn't nearly as impressed. He was already halfway into the next room when I snapped back to the business at hand and turned to fol-low him.

"Hello, Jarrod," a voice said from behind me.

I jerked around suddenly and found myself face to face with Philander, Uli's slender, young boy-toy assistant.

"What are you doing here?" he said.

"Well, we never got to finish our date earlier, so I came over hoping to find you. You know, so we could wrap up what we started."

Ouch. I was having a *Charlie's Angels* moment. Trying to se-duce the bad guy to get out of a tough spot. And he wasn't buy-ing what I was selling.

"I thought you came to find your boyfriend," he said with a steely gaze.

Where was Liam? Was he on the hunt for Charlie solo? Did he even realize I was no longer following behind him?

"Look, Philander, you've got to talk to your boss. Bring him to his senses. He's kidnapped a man. The police may be loyal to him, but they can't give him a free ride for something like this. Eventually his actions are going to catch up to him."

"It is not my job to question my boss. I am paid to service him."

"And I bet you do a bang-up job of it too," I said. "You must have very strong knees."

He did a slow burn. I was pissing him off big-time. Dumb move on my part.

"As for the police," he said, "their only interest is to keep the tourists coming. It's good for everybody. Talk of kidnapping would only scare people away. Notice that the Indian actor's murder hasn't blown up into such a big thing. That's because nobody really wants it to."

"Where's Charlie?"

"I don't know."

"He's somewhere in the house."

"My boss is in his study." Philander reached behind a Stetson from John Wayne's Oscar-winning classic *True Grit* and pulled out a .38 revolver. "Why don't we go ask him?"

"That's just a prop gun from the movie."

"No. It's real. Belonged to the Duke himself. And we keep it loaded just in case of times like this." He stepped forward. "Move."

I turned around, my arms in the air, and walked out of the room. Philander followed close behind me. As we passed through the door into a hallway, Liam jumped out from his hiding place, grabbing Philander around the neck and cracking his arm with a karate chop. Philander dropped the gun and it clattered across the floor. I quickly bent down to scoop it up and pointed it at Philander.

"Now I'm going to ask you again. Where's Charlie?"

Liam tightened his grip on Philander's neck. He winced. "I lied."

"About what?" I asked.

"It *is* a prop gun." Philander sneered, and then cried out, "Mr. Karydes! Help!"

Liam muffled Philander's cries with a hand over his face, but it was too late. The house erupted in a thundering sound as a stampede of guards rushed to the scene and surrounded us. Liam was yanked away from Philander, and we were both roughly led back into the memorabilia room where Uli Karydes himself soon joined us.

"I am so disappointed in you, Jarrod. To come here unannounced and recklessly endanger the life of the man you say you love. Such a shame." Uli paced back and forth. "What am I going to do with you?"

I shrugged, holding firm, trying to stay strong and act tough.

"You really scared the devil out of Khristos, Jarrod. You sent him home practically in tears. I'm quite impressed," Uli said, smiling.

"I don't like to be fucked with," I said, playing up the macho moment, hoping to knock him off guard a bit.

"Of course, Khristos never saw you in that Judith Light movie when you were in your early twenties, where you played the psychotic boyfriend of her daughter, played by Tori Spelling."

Damn it. Who knew they get the Lifetime Movie Network all the way out in the Greek isles?

"It was called *Stab in the Dark: A Mother's Worst Nightmare*. You threatened poor Judith with a knife. Recited some of the exact same lines you spouted off to Khristos."

Damn it. Damn it. Damn it. Caught again. My tough-guy act was history, and Uli knew it.

"Where is it?" Uli said, his voice low and threatening, as he drummed his pudgy sausage fingers in anticipation.

I couldn't tell him Laurette had broken the head off the Academy Award. He might fly into a rage and kill us on the spot, and then where would Charlie be? No. I had to think fast. Come up with another story that would buy us more time.

"It's Liam's fault we're here," I said.

Liam raised an eyebrow. He watched me curiously, wondering why I had suddenly decided to feed him to the wolves.

"He was just so devastated by his beloved Claire's death, he was desperate to hold on to anything connected to her memory. The Oscar was the most concrete tie to her sadly interrupted life. He just couldn't live knowing someone else had it. That's what brought him here to Mykonos. He was following the same trail as I was. He saw me take it from Akshay that day on Super Paradise Beach and he showed up at my hotel room with a gun and demanded I give it back or he'd kill me. I didn't have a choice. I couldn't rescue Charlie if I was dead. Once Liam got his hands on it, he wasn't about to part with it again, even for Charlie's life. So I had to improvise and try to rescue Charlie without it."

I was reasonably satisfied with that complete line of bullshit. So was Liam. He didn't open his mouth to refute it.

"And you? You got what you wanted. Why come here?" Uli said, eyeing Liam.

"I'm not a complete louse. He got me my girlfriend's Oscar back. I figured I owed it to him to help him get back his boyfriend," Liam said, having a far less difficult time selling the tough-guy act. "Besides, I get off on the thrill of danger."

"That way of thinking could get you killed."

"Hasn't happened yet," Liam sneered. "Luck of the Irish."

"Well, it seems your luck has finally run out. You have a very difficult choice to make," Uli said, stone-faced. "Either you give up your one little piece of your dead girlfriend's memory, or he gives up his whole living, breathing boyfriend."

I looked to Liam, who took his cue from me and spat out, "Forget it."

"Sacrificing someone you don't even know is one thing," Uli said, narrowing his eyes. "Sacrificing yourself is quite another. If you're the only person between me and my prize, I have no compunction about killing you right here."

Liam swallowed hard, trying to play the moment as best he knew how. He mustered up his limited acting skills, eyeing the armed henchmen with their guns trained on him, waiting for the appropriate beat before whispering, "Fine. You can have the damn thing."

Claire had seen some talent in the young Irish hunk. And she was right. He wasn't half bad.

"Excellent. Where is it?" Uli said, clapping his hands.

"My friend has it. We have to call her to meet us," I said.

"Fine," Uli said, handing me his cell phone. "But no more tricks. I'm out of patience. Now where is she?"

"The Andromeda Residence."

Uli punched in some numbers and handed me the phone.

"Look at this incredible collection. Why would you go to such lengths to get one stupid gold-plated statue?" I said.

"When you get to be my age and have my money, the whole joy in life is any kind of challenge. And the more difficult the challenge, the more fun I have."

"But kidnapping?"

Uli shrugged. He was a corrupt Greek shipping tycoon. The idea of morals and ethics was completely lost on him. I couldn't believe my boyfriend's life had been put in jeopardy over a piece of movie memorabilia. Only a gay thug would go to such extremes.

Delphina answered the phone. Her tone was gruff and short due to her being up half the night. I asked her to connect me to our room, and she did so without any pleasantries. After a few rings, Laurette picked up.

"Hello?" she said with a worried lilt in her voice.

"Honey, it's me, Jarrod."

"Omigod, Jarrod, I've been worried sick. Where are you? Did you find Charlie?"

"Sort of. I need you to bring me the Oscar."

"Jarrod, I stopped off at the pharmacy on my way back and picked up some glue. I put the thing back together again, but it hasn't had time to dry yet. The head may roll off again."

"Never mind that. You have to meet us. Charlie's life depends on it."

"And yours too," Uli added.

"And ours too," I said.

"Something's gone wrong, hasn't it?" she said.

"Please, Laurette, just meet us."

"Where?"

I glanced up at Uli, who was smiling. He was so close to that damn Academy Award he could barely contain himself.

"She wants to know where to meet us."

Uli snatched the phone from me and spoke to Laurette. "Delos Island. It's a few miles off the coast of Mykonos. You'll have to take a ferry to get there. Be there in an hour. Every minute you're late, your friends lose a finger."

He clicked off and broke out into a wide smile. "She sounds like a reliable sort. You may all just get out of this alive."

I looked at him skeptically.

"Really. I'm not a monster, Jarrod," Uli said as he picked up a gorilla mask from the original *Planet of the Apes* movie and put it up to his face. "Unless you make me one, and you surely don't want to do that."

# Chapter 31

Delos is a tiny, uninhabited island located in the middle of the Aegean Sea that was a major religious and commercial center of the ancient Greek world. It is the mythical birthplace of the god Apollo and boasts the impressive remains of temples, shrines, and sanctuaries. Among the many fascinating attractions on the island are three temples dating from the fifth and sixth centuries BC, and to the west, the Sacred Lake where Apollo was reputedly born. Standing guard over the lake are nine replicas of the famous marble lions. The actual remains can be found in the island's archaeological museum, which houses a breathtaking collection of exhibits, including statues, masks, and ancient jewelry.

On my last trip to the party island of Mykonos, I had hopped aboard a ferry for the twenty-five minute ride to Delos because as an actor, I was excited about standing amongst the ruins of a grand theater where audiences used to watch ritual orgies in ancient times. Sometimes we're just born too late.

Although I had been hungover from too much drinking and dancing at Pierro's, the island's premier gay club, the night before, I was struck by the island's beauty and all of its rich history, and my memories of the day were still stark and clear. So I took some comfort in the fact that I was familiar with where we were going and knew of some probable hiding places if Liam and I miraculously managed some means of escape.

We were hustled aboard Uli's speedboat, which was anchored at a small dock in a cove below his property, and ordered by Khristos, who took great pleasure in manhandling us, to sit quietly in the back of the boat. Uli joined us momentarily, along with Philander and Leandro, and after firing up the engine, we sped off toward the island of Delos.

Philander was at the wheel and seemed to be aiming the boat right for the waves so the sea spray would repeatedly splash me in the face. I guess he was still ticked off at me for getting him drunk and manipulating some key information out of him. Uli settled back with a martini cocktail in a silver tumbler, while Khristos and Leandro tried their best to wear intimidating scowls in order to keep us in line.

I imagined the panic and worry that had to be coursing through Laurette's veins right now. She was definitely cursing herself for abandoning her cuddly new boyfriend, Larry, to join me in London only to get mixed up in all this mayhem and murder. She was a real trouper, but I was a little nervous about how she might handle her latest assignment. As long as the Oscar's head stayed glued in place, we had a shot of surviving this dangerous escapade.

I recognized the island off in the distance, and as a ferry chugged past us, loaded with camera-toting tourists, I knew we were only minutes away from showtime. The boat circumvented the main dock and circled around to the other side of the island, where Philander drove the boat as far in as possible. When the bottom of the boat scraped across the pebble-coated shore, Leandro hopped into the water, which was up to his knees, and gripping a thick rope, pulled us nearly up on the beach.

Balancing what was left of his martini, Uli offered his hand to Leandro, who helped his portly frame down to the ground. Khristos pulled a gun out of the back of his pants and waved us to get off. Liam gave me a questioning look. What the hell was the plan? Since I didn't have one yet, I ignored him.

The six of us hiked along a dirt trail until we saw a gaggle of tourists streaming into the island's museum. A few others were scattered along the remains of some buildings where the island's wealthiest residents had built lavish houses with grand, colonnaded courtyards.

"Where's your friend?" Uli barked, anxious to get this little trade over and done with.

I raised my hand to block the harsh rays of the sun from my eyes and scanned the immediate area. At first I almost missed her. But after squinting to get a clearer view, I spotted Laurette in a bright orange tank top, printed green wraparound skirt, seashell necklace, and sandals standing in the middle of what was once the island's majestic amphitheater, built in 300 BC, which at one time had accommodated fifty-five hundred spectators. She looked like some resurrected goddess like Athena—except for the loud color of her ensemble, of course, and the black carry-on bag she clutched in her arms.

We trudged toward her, and as we got closer, I could see the fear etched all over her face. She was way out of her league on this one, but she was going to do what she had to do to get me and Charlie back safely.

Philander and Leandro broke apart from the group and casually circled around behind Laurette in an obvious effort to keep a tight rein over the proceedings.

Uli mustered up a sincere smile and stepped forward. "Thank you for not making this more difficult than it has to be."

She thrust the bag at him. "Here. Just take it. Can we all go home now?"

"Absolutely," Uli said, unzipping the bag. "But first let me just make sure you're not going to double-cross me like the dearly departed Akshay."

Uli gently lifted the Academy Award out of the bag. Laurette, Liam, and I held our collective breath. The Oscar had his head on straight. No obvious signs of damage. Things were finally looking up.

At that moment, I noticed a large group of tourists, all snapping photos of the various ruins and making their way toward us. Uli gave the group a cursory glance but then quickly returned to inspecting his newest, most prized possession.

Philander, eyeing the approaching group, leaned in to his boss. "Mr. Karydes, I think we should go now."

Laurette searched our party. "Where's Charlie? You promised to let him go."

"Don't worry," Uli said. "I have no reason to hold on to him anymore. He'll be back in time for you all to have dinner tonight at one of our fine gourmet restaurants. On me."

When I glanced over at the tourists, who were now only a hundred feet away from us, I was startled to see Delphina, our receptionist at the Andromeda Residence, among them. She was wearing a big, bright yellow floppy hat and sunglasses as a make-shift disguise, but it was definitely her. What was she doing here? She lived on Mykonos. Why on earth would she be touring Delos Island with a Kodak disposable camera?

The tourists began fanning out and pointing at several well-preserved mosaics that had been excavated since the archaeological dig of Delos began in the late 1800s. That's when I noticed that all of the camera-toting travelers in the tour group were Greek, which just raised more questions.

Uli noticed them too, and raised an eyebrow.

I suspected Delphina and her friends were here to help. "They're probably fans. I can't go anywhere without getting recognized."

Uli seemed to buy it, but then the unthinkable happened. The head on top of the Academy Award sagged to one side before rolling off entirely and bouncing off a rock. There was a stunned silence.

Uli's face flushed with anger; his mouth was open, but no words came out. He was about to blow with more fury than Mount St. Helens. We were done for.

What happened next unfolded so fast I didn't even have time to react. The tourists that had surreptitiously wandered up to us split apart, drawing guns from their camera bags. They screamed in Greek. I had no idea what they were saying, but Uli's men instantly raised their hands in the air and lowered themselves to the ground. I felt like I was caught up in some Greek version of *Cops*, except I wasn't wearing a wife beater. Liam, Laurette, and I immediately followed suit and kissed the gravel. Uli, defiant to the end, stood his ground as the gun-slinging Greeks closed in on us.

The shortest one, an olive-skinned badass with a goatee and shaved head that made up for his height, bellowed in English, "Hellenic Police, Mr. Karydes. I suggest you cooperate and lie down on the ground. Otherwise, I'll have my men help you."

Uli stared the officer down before quietly lowering himself to the dirt, spreading out on his belly.

Delphina threw off her yellow floppy hat and rushed over to us. "Laurette, Jarrod, you can get up. It's safe now."

Laurette stood up and threw her arms around Delphina. "Thank you so much. You promised to take care of things and none of us would be hurt, and you came through."

I was flabbergasted. Our hotel receptionist was some kind of cop? This was insane.

Laurette hustled over to Liam, who still was facedown on the ground, and smiled at the officer who was standing over him. "He's with us."

The officer stepped aside, allowing Liam to climb to his feet.

I turned to Laurette for an explanation as the group of Greek officers began handcuffing Uli and his men.

"Remember last night when Delphina offered us help if we needed it?" she said breathlessly, still reeling from all the drama. "Well, this morning, before you called me to come here, I got so worried I went to her."

"She woke me up again," Delphina said with a smile.

"It turns out Delphina's brother is a special guard with the Hellenic Police, which is a branch of the Ministry of Public Order in Athens," she said, pointing to the bossy short one overseeing the other men, who were busy securing the prisoners.

I had heard of the Ministry of Public Order. They were the ones who did such an impressive job of security at the 2004 Athens Olympics.

"My father was a special guard; my grandfather was also, as well as my great-grandfather. I would be one too if they allowed women to join," she said. "My brother was here with some of his buddies partying on Mykonos all week. So when I called and told him what was going on, he offered to bring along his friends and help out. The Hellenic Police have been keeping tabs on Karydes for years, trying to bust up his smuggling and extortion operations. He's very clever, and it's been a frustrating task for the government to try and find enough evidence for an arrest."

"If he has an Achilles' heel, then it's his obsession with his TV and movie collection," I said. "Seems he'd do anything to add another priceless piece like Claire Richards's Academy Award."

"Even kidnapping," Delphina said. "Karydes has reached a point where he believes a crime like that is not a big deal if it gets him what he wants. He's been so successful keeping the Greek authorities at bay for so many years that he started to feel he was above the law. When Laurette came to me and explained everything, I knew we had him."

"What about Charlie?" I said.

Delphina smiled and pointed to a helicopter off in the distance that was fast approaching Delos. "My cousin owns a chopper. He gives island-hopping tours three times daily. It was a slow day today, so I sent him over to Karydes's place to see if he could find your friend. He called me on my cell about twenty minutes ago and said he found a man locked up in one of the guesthouses on the back end of Karydes's property."

My heart pounded as the helicopter landed on a flat bed of rock well south of where we were to protect the surrounding artifacts. The passenger door flew open, and Charlie, weary, dirt smudged, and bruised, climbed out and crouched down to avoid the whirling blades of the chopper above him as he staggered forward.

I choked up as I ran toward him, my arms outstretched, bursting with relief that he was alive and well. I practically knocked him over as I grabbed him in a bear hug. He winced from the pressure I was inadvertently applying to his bullet wounds, and I quickly loosened my grip.

"Hey, babe, what took you so long?" he said with a warm smile.

# Chapter 32

As Delphina's brother and his pals carted off Uli and his band of thugs and began making excited calls to the home office in Athens about their big capture, Delphina's cousin with the helicopter offered three of us a ride back by air. I suggested Delphina, Liam, and Charlie go with him. Laurette and I could just take one of the ferryboats back. I wanted Charlie checked out by a doctor as soon as possible to make sure he was okay.

"I'm a little tired, but I'm fine," Charlie said. "We've been apart long enough, Jarrod. I'm going back on the boat with you."

Laurette was more than happy to go back to Mykonos on the chopper. It would give her an opportunity to squeeze in next to the strapping Liam, who was happy to have the Oscar back, one of the few remaining connections to his dear late lover.

Charlie and I clasped hands and made our way toward the dock, where a large number of tourists were already lining up to board the boat back to Mykonos port.

I had so many questions for Charlie, but I didn't want to overwhelm him so soon after our joyous reunion. He knew me well enough to know it was in his best interest to tell me everything now. Otherwise, it would be an impossibly long cruise back to Mykonos.

"After you stormed out of the room that night, Akshay called and asked me to meet him down at the bar. I was just pissed enough at you to take him up on it. Besides, I didn't want to sit around the room stewing all night, so I went down for a cocktail. Apparently, Uli's guys were staking him out and saw us drinking together. They caught Akshay trying to make a pass by pawing my knee under the table."

My back stiffened, but Charlie smiled and massaged the knots with his hands. "I pulled away, don't worry, and told him I wasn't interested. But it was too late. The guys had already reported back to Uli that Akshay had a boyfriend. On my way back up to the room, they got on the elevator with me and chloroformed me with a rag. That's the last thing I remember. Next thing I knew, I was on a private plane with a massive headache. And I wound up here. I didn't know what the hell was going on."

We waited in line to board the boat, and I noticed the middle-aged Little Rock couple from the Music Café where Laurette and I first met Uli standing in line ahead of us. They were straining their ears trying to eavesdrop on our spicy conversation.

"That entire first night I was held captive at the compound, I tried convincing Karydes his guys had made a colossal mistake, that I barely knew Akshay and I had no knowledge of what kind of schemes he was involved in. Of course he assumed I was just trying to save my own ass, hoping he'd let me go. But I finally started to get through to him, and after he did a little checking on his own, he realized I was telling the truth. And that you were my boyfriend. At that point, it dawned on me that I might have been stupid. He could've just driven me out to sea on his boat and dumped me into the ocean. Luckily for me, Uli Karydes may be a lot of things, but he's no killer."

"So Akshay agreed to make the trade anyway?"

"He at least had a shred of decency. He felt responsible for my predicament, so he agreed to swap the Oscar for my immediate release."

"And the e-mail you sent me?"

"That was Uli covering all his bases. He didn't want you snooping around, so he sat me down at the computer and forced me to write it. When word got back from his guys that you were undeterred in finding out what happened to me, he made me call you. I figured my one shot was sending you a message that something was wrong, which was why I got Snickers's gender wrong. I knew you'd pick up on that, and it would just fire you up to keep searching for me. I knew in my heart you'd never give up, babe."

I reached up and kissed him full on the mouth, much to the consternation of the conservative red-state couple in front of us who had craned their necks to get a good look at us while we talked.

We boarded the boat, never letting go of each other's hands, and settled in for the twenty-five minute ride back to Mykonos. As we pulled into the dock, I noticed a small commotion. Laurette, Liam, and Delphina were all there, as well as a few of her brother's Special Guard buddies and some very uptight-looking, pasty-skinned officials. As passengers disembarked down the plank to the dock, I made eye contact with Laurette, who was looking very worried and uncomfortable. Uli Karydes had been arrested for Charlie's kidnapping. Liam had Claire's Oscar back. Charlie was safe. What could be wrong now?

I gripped Charlie's hand tighter as we ambled up to the assembled group waiting for us. That's when I saw them. Detective Inspector Sally Bowles and Detective Colin Samms. The two British cops who were so convinced I was hiding something and were trying to pin Claire's murder on me.

Bowles marched forward like an angry den mother who had

accidentally lost one of her charges on her watch. "Skipping the country has done nothing to alleviate the perception of your guilt, Mr. Jarvis."

"I'm not concerned with perception since I'm innocent," I said.

Samms scowled. "That's not what they're saying back in England."

Detective Colin Samms unfolded a Fleet Street tabloid for me to see the blaring headline. *Former Child Star on the Run after Poisoning Claire Richards!*

"Yeah, well, that paper also said Princess Di faked her own death and is now living in a cult of Tibetan monks."

"Why did you flee the country, Mr. Jarvis?" Bowles said.

"There was a small matter of rescuing my boyfriend from a crazed Greek shipping magnate with an Academy Award fetish."

"Well, you did yourself no favors back in London. Her majesty's government has gone to great expense to come here and retrieve you," Samms said with that intimidating fixed scowl on his face.

"There were no charges against me. I was free to go where I wanted to, and I wanted to come here."

"You were advised to not leave, and you disobeyed that request," Bowles said.

"I don't get what the big deal is," I said. "You're acting like I was under arrest when I left London. And we all know that wasn't the case."

"Yes, you're right about that," Bowles said. "But that was then. This is now."

"What are you talking about?"

"Circumstances have changed," Bowles said with a smirk. "We now have enough proof to substantiate our suspicions."

She removed a pair of handcuffs from the belt looping around her business-suit skirt and slapped them on my wrists. "I'm placing you under arrest for the murder of Claire Richards."

I turned to Charlie, who stared at me in disbelief as the elation from our all-too-brief reunion quickly melted away and Inspector Bowles and Detective Samms led me off to a waiting car.

# Chapter 33

Upon our return to London, I was escorted directly from Gatwick Airport over to Inspector Bowles's precinct for further questioning. Charlie was able to accompany us most of the way but was shut out from any further contact with me once Bowles and Samms got me into an interrogation room. The last words I heard from him were, "Don't worry, babe, I'll get you out."

This was insane. I was being tried in the press, and in the court of public opinion, I was already guilty. I knew Liam would stamp out any lingering questions about my sexual involvement with Claire. Not only that, I was in plain view during the entire opening-night performance. I was completely clueless as to what kind of proof they had that would warrant my arrest.

I didn't have to wait long. Inspector Bowles took a sip of her bottled water and stared at me like a satisfied cat that's just cornered a frightened mouse. I shifted uncomfortably in my chair, eyeing her and the grinning Detective Samms, who was feeling very virile after collaring such a supposedly high-profile killer.

"So are we going to sit here all day, or are you going to tell me what kind of ridiculous evidence you have against me?" I said, trying to maintain my cool although I was ready to burst into tears.

"I was prepared to cross you off our list of suspects, Jarrod, but then you fled the country so abruptly it forced me to revisit you all over again and take a closer look," Bowles said, never taking her eyes off me.

"I've told you twenty times why I left London. Talk to the Ministry of Public Order in Greece. They've got my boyfriend's kidnapper in custody."

"We already did," Samms said. "We know why you went."

"But while you were off on your little Greek adventure, we had some very interesting developments in the Claire Richards case," Bowles said, putting on her reading glasses and picking up a file. She flipped through some pages and pulled out a lone sheet. "I assume you know Susie Chan, the well-respected coroner from America."

"And my boyfriend's ex-wife. Yes, I know her," I said. "I called her to ask for her help when you first began to suspect me. She said she knew a British doctor who might fax her Claire's autopsy report."

"Oh, he did indeed. He's already been reprimanded for breaching the hospital's confidentiality policy."

"Susie must have been a blast in bed for him to risk a formal reprimand," I snorted, but neither of them bothered to respond.

"After studying the report, Ms. Chan found some inconsistencies with the purported cause of death and what was found in the victim's system. As we already established, Claire Richards did not die of an allergic reaction to peanut oil," Bowles said.

"I know that already," I said. "So did Susie find what really did kill her?"

"Ricin," Bowles said, lowering her glasses to the bridge of her nose as she read from Susie's fax. "A natural toxin found in castor beans. Very cheap and easy to produce. It can be manufactured as a powder or can easily be turned into an aerosol that can be inhaled."

"Seems Dr. Chan worked on a case last year in Los Angeles where a trophy wife replaced her cheating husband's deodorant with a spray bottle full of the stuff. He was dead in less than two hours," Samms said, taking a long sip of the steaming hot coffee that another officer had brought in to him and Bowles. I wasn't offered any.

Bowles took off her glasses and stared me down. "It doesn't take much to kill a man. Just one to ten micrograms of ricin per kilogram of body weight. We had a case here in London back in 1978 where a trace of ricin on the sharpened tip of an umbrella was enough to kill the Bulgarian dissident Georgi Markov. Happened right on the Waterloo Bridge."

"It's also virtually undetectable in an autopsy, unless you know what you're looking for. Because of Dr. Chan's history of identifying the poison, the Richards autopsy immediately raised alarm bells," Samms said.

"Especially since Ms. Richards was taking medicine for her peanut allergy and the doctors determined the oil that was in her make-up wasn't sufficient enough to cause a serious reaction, let alone death," Bowles said.

"Akshay Kapoor was right," Samms said. "He did see Ms. Richards's understudy assist her in applying her make-up on the night of the murder. And Dame Sylvia Horner did, in fact, see her mix a foreign substance into the pancake base. But the girl never intended to kill Ms. Richards. Her goal was to make her sick enough so that she could take her place in the show. She had no idea Ms. Richards's allergy wasn't very strong and she was taking medication that would leave her virtually unaffected."

"That's all well and good and puts Minx in the clear. Somebody else murdered Claire with the ricin," I said, sitting up in my chair, itching to take on my accusers. "But that someone is not me. Where on earth would I get my hands on a poison like ricin?"

"It's everywhere. A big stash was even found in the caves of Afghanistan some years back. They weren't making stew with it," Samms said.

"Check my passport," I said. "I haven't been to Afghanistan recently."

"It doesn't matter how you got it," Bowles said. "The fact is, we found traces of it on the flowers you gave Ms. Richards that night."

"What?" I said, my stomach churning.

"That's right. You delivered flowers to her dressing room. The poison was sprayed on the peach carnation in the bouquet. Ms. Richards came in close contact with that particular flower and breathed in the poison. Unsuspecting, she went onstage to do the show. By the time the curtain came down at the end of the performance, she was dead."

"Wait just a minute! Did you say a peach carnation?"

"Yes," Bowles said. "Why?"

"There wasn't a peach carnation in the bouquet I gave her. She hated them! She made that very clear. I would never risk getting yelled at by making such a stupid mistake. I saw how mad she got at Liam when he tried to give her some."

Bowles and Samms exchanged a look. They didn't know whether I was desperate to save my hide or telling the truth.

"But there *was* a peach carnation in the bouquet I gave to Sir Anthony Stiles! I went to his dressing room right before Claire's. He could have sprayed the poison on his peach carnation, then switched vases when Claire was distracted," I said, my mind reeling from the implications. "He also knew Claire hated peach carnations. He knew she would immediately remove it from the vase and come in contact with the poison!"

That was it. It was Sir Anthony. But why? What motive did he have to kill Claire? I turned to Bowles and Samms expectantly. Was I free to go?

Bowles folded her arms and said halfheartedly, "We will be sure to check your story out in due time."

My heart sunk. "You don't believe me, do you?"

Samms smirked. In his mind I was already tried, convicted, and on my way to the British big house.

Sir Anthony. It was Sir Anthony. Now all I had to do was negotiate my freedom, come up with a motive, and uncover enough evidence to clear my own name. A tall order considering I was under arrest for murder. And if I did go down for the crime, the worst thought of all was that it would be due to the diligence and expertise of Charlie's ex-wife, Susie Chan. That bitch. I could almost hear her laughing all those thousands of miles away.

# Chapter 34

After an all-night interrogation by Bowles and Samms, I was escorted by car over to the Magistrates' Court, where I was formally charged. Thoughts of living out my days in an English prison terrified me, but I kept my cool, trying to maintain a sense of dignity, not to mention innocence, about me. My hair was disheveled, my clothes were wrinkled and smelly, my eyes bloodshot. As the officers escorted me up the steps inside the court building, the crush of paparazzi blinded me with their flashes. I looked a mess and braced myself for the onslaught of photos that would hit the tabloids and make those unfortunate wild-haired mug shots of Nick Nolte, who was pulled over for drunk driving a few years ago, seem downright refined.

Charlie and Laurette met us inside and followed my entourage of police escorts into the courtroom.

I twisted my head around as far as it could go and called out to Charlie, "I love you."

He forced a smile that didn't hide his worry. "I love you too, babe."

"Did you send the flowers?" I said.

He nodded as I was hustled into a room. Bowles looked me over suspiciously.

"Sending more flowers?"

I sighed. "To Akshay Kapoor's family. He recently passed away, and I was rather fond of his mother."

"Shot in Greece, as I understand," Bowles said. "Interesting coincidence."

I didn't have the energy to refute her insinuations. I was distracted by the judge making copious notes on the bench. He was decked out in a black robe and long, white, curly wig that made him look like a character out of Monty Python. I never knew judges today actually still dressed up like their forefathers.

Charlie had been on the phone all morning trying to drum up a lawyer. There was a handful anxious to take on such a high-profile case, but we were unable to pick one before my arraignment. The judge reviewed my charges, I pleaded innocent, and then he kicked the whole case up to the Crown Court, a higher-level court that takes on the most serious indictable offenses. The murder of one of the queen's most beloved subjects certainly warranted the top guns. After the prosecution trying the case argued vehemently that I be denied bail due to my recent side trip to Greece, the judge overruled their request and granted me freedom for a mere one hundred thousand dollars. I was stunned by the number and thought I would sit out the time leading up to trial in a jail cell with some scrappy, young street hustler right out of *Oliver Twist*, but Charlie miraculously came up with the money within an hour and I was finally released. My passport, however, was confiscated until after the trial.

We escaped the onslaught of reporters and photographers waiting outside the police precinct and squeezed into a taxicab.

"How did you get the money for bail?" I said.

"Don't worry about it," Charlie said.

"Do we still have a home to go back to in LA?"

He smiled and nodded. I guessed he had borrowed the money from our retirement account. All my residuals from *Go to Your Room* are directly deposited into a personal IRA for our golden years. So we shaved off a few of those golden years so I wouldn't have to rot away in prison while awaiting trial. Worked for me.

Now that I was charged with murder, I was no longer welcomed at most of the chic London hotels, but Charlie and Laurette had managed to rent a flat in north London using Laurette's name. We paid the driver an extra twenty-five pounds to ditch the motorcycle-driving photographers on our tail, and soon we were rolling up a back alley to the rear entrance of the building. We were finally going to get some peace and quiet.

The flat was a one-bedroom, cramped space with scuffed and banged-up appliances, a weathered couch, and no heating. I didn't care. It was out of the intense glare of the media spotlight, and I could shower and change and get some sleep. Charlie tucked me in, kissed me lightly on the forehead, and told me everything was going to be all right. Laurette had dashed out to buy us some food.

When Charlie flipped off the light and left me alone in bed to rest, I just lay there wide awake. I kept thinking about Sir Anthony Stiles. I had to talk to him. I had to find out if he stuck a poisoned peach carnation in Claire's bouquet. But if I confronted him directly, he would deny it. I had to be stealthy and sneaky about it. I was certain there would be some evidence socked away in his flat somewhere. It was early evening by now, going on seven o'-clock. I slid out of bed and padded over to my bag and fished around for my cell phone. I double-checked the cast sheet for his number and rang him up. He picked up on the second ring.

"Sir Anthony, it's Jarrod Jarvis."

"My dear boy, I'm watching you on the news right now. You look ghastly. At the very least, one of those officers could have offered you a hairbrush."

"It was dreadful. But I'm free on bail and hiding out at a flat in north London."

"You poor darling," he said.

"I didn't do it, Sir Anthony, I swear it."

"I believe you."

"You're the only one. No one will have anything to do with me except for the press. Those vultures won't leave me alone. It's as if everyone in the world has already tried and convicted me."

"People are demanding to know the identity of Claire's killer so they can finally put the matter to rest. Be strong, Jarrod. The truth will come out in time. It always does."

"You're such a good soul, Sir Anthony. Talking to you makes me feel better already."

Come on, Sir Anthony. Take the bait. Take the bait.

"I'm always here if you need me, love."

Bingo.

"Do you really mean that, Sir Anthony?"

"Of course I do."

"Because of everyone I've met since I've been here in London, you are the most genuine, the most sincere, by the far the most decent and good-hearted."

"Really? Well, I'm flattered you feel that way."

"So you don't mind if I come over now?"

"I beg your pardon." Sir Anthony's tone abruptly changed.

"I've been under such pressure, and my future is so uncertain, and I could really use a friend right now. My boyfriend, Charlie, just doesn't understand what I'm going through. But you do. You're a high-profile actor. You get it."

"I do, Jarrod, I do, but I am expecting a student tonight. He's coming around at eleven—"

"Oh, I won't stay that long. I'll be gone by ten, I promise. Thank you, Sir Anthony, thank you. I'll see you soon."

I quickly hung up before he could say another word.

I walked back out into the living room. Charlie was watching the news coverage of my arrest, but when he heard me shuffling toward him from behind, he scooped up the remote and quickly flipped to an old comedy sketch show starring Stephen Fry and Hugh Laurie.

Laurette wasn't back yet. I was about to tell Charlie about my suspicions surrounding Sir Anthony, but if I even hinted to him that Sir Anthony was Claire's murderer, Charlie would never allow me to go over there.

But Charlie never saw the expression on Inspector Bowles's face that I did. She couldn't have cared less about investigating my claims about Sir Anthony. In her mind, the killer had already been caught. No. I had to have proof. And I had to get it any way possible. Even if it meant lying to my boyfriend.

"I'm going to go for a walk," I said.

"Are you crazy? Someone might spot you."

"It's already dark outside. And it's cold. I'll just cover my face with a scarf. I'll look like one of Michael Jackson's kids."

Charlie chuckled, but it was clear he didn't relish the thought of me going out alone. I would have told him where I was heading and asked if he wanted to come along, but he had been through such an ordeal, and he was in a weakened state from his gunshot wounds, I just didn't want to take any chances with his health.

"I'll be back in a while."

I walked to the door and turned around to see Charlie frowning. He really didn't want me to go anywhere.

"You're going to be here when I get back this time, aren't you?" I said.

Charlie grinned. "I'm always going to be here, babe."

I winked at him, pulled the scarf around my face, and walked out.

It didn't take long to hail a taxicab, and after a speedy twenty-minute drive to Sir Anthony's flat, I was ringing his doorbell.

Sir Anthony opened the door and welcomed me inside with a warm embrace. Any reservations of my sudden visit were wiped away by the drama of it all. Actors adored being in the eye of a crisis. It gives us good sense memory material to work with later.

Sir Anthony had tea and crumpets waiting for me. It was only a little after eight in the evening. I had plenty of time to pump my host and case his flat for clues before the arrival of his boy toy at eleven.

I peppered him with questions about his longtime friendship with Claire, their history together at the Royal Academy of Dramatic Arts, their one movie together and multiple stage productions. He appeared genuinely saddened by her passing, and it suddenly became difficult for me to picture him spraying a peach carnation with ricin and stuffing it in Claire's bouquet. But he was an actor, and quite possibly he could be giving the performance of a lifetime. I could make no assumptions based on his demeanor.

As Sir Anthony poured more tea, I noticed the wilting, dried-out flowers that I had given him on opening night displayed on an end table.

"I'm surprised you didn't throw those out by now," I said.

Sir Anthony at first didn't understand what I meant. But he followed my gaze to the flowers and nodded with a smile. "I've been so busy, I just haven't had the chance. And perhaps a part of me wants to hold on to them. After all, they're the last tangible connection to our final night with Claire. Once they're gone, we will only have our memories."

Genius. If he did kill her, he was putting on a damn good show.

"I thought I put a peach carnation in there," I said, eyeing Sir Anthony for any change in his demeanor.

He never skipped a beat. He looked the flowers over and shrugged. "Frankly, my dear boy, I hardly remember if there was one in there or not."

"I remember because I was careful not to put one in Claire's bouquet. She despises peach carnations."

"That's right. I do remember that. She was very particular about her tastes," he said, shaking his head and amused at the memory.

He wasn't going to crack. I needed to regroup and think of another tack.

"Sir Anthony, may I use your little boys' room?"

"Of course, go right ahead. Second door down the hall on the right."

I stood up and headed down to the bathroom. I saw him check his watch. He was nervous I might overstay my welcome and still be around when his young protégé arrived.

Once inside, I bolted the door and looked around. Nothing out of the ordinary. I opened the medicine chest and perused the row of white bottles, not seriously expecting to find one marked with a skull and crossbones and labeled "Ricin." But I was desperate. I didn't have a concrete plan coming over here, and a part of me felt that if I left the flat empty-handed, my fate was sealed and I would be serving out the rest of my days in prison.

I plopped down on the toilet seat and buried my face in my hands. What was I thinking, racing over here hoping to expose a killer? What did I seriously hope he was going to do? Pour me some tea and then jabber on about how he pulled off the perfect murder? I was feeling pretty dumb when my eye caught something. It was a magazine sticking out of the bottom cupboard below the basin of the sink. I recognized the masthead instantly and pulled it out. It was a copy of *Playboy*, a Christmas issue with a buxom redhead on the cover wearing a Santa hat and little else. Maybe Sir Anthony was interviewed inside. But after flipping through the pages, I saw nothing about him. I opened up the cupboard and found stacks and stacks of men's magazines, some *Playboy*, some *Hustler*, and even more hardcore porn titles. This was interesting. What was the flamboyantly gay Sir Anthony doing with this kind of bathroom reading material? I walked over and opened the door slightly. I heard Sir Anthony in the kitchen piling some more crumpets onto a plate. I slipped out and scurried quietly to the bedroom. There was nothing unusual in the room. Mostly pictures of Sir Anthony's many theatrical triumphs and one larger framed photograph of him being knighted by Queen Elizabeth. There was a cabinet in the corner. I walked over and tried to open it, but it was locked. I searched his bed-side table drawers, finally turning up a key. I tried the key in the lock, and it clicked open. I stumbled back in shock. Rows and rows of DVDs. All porn. All straight porn. Not a gay title in the bunch.

"What are you doing in here?"

I spun around to confront an ashen-faced Sir Anthony. He held the plate of crumpets in his hand, which was now shaking. He had been caught.

"Omigod," I said. "You're straight."

"No," he said in a last-ditch attempt to hide the truth. "I am as gay as Graham Norton, believe me."

I picked out one of the DVDs in the cabinet and looked at the cover. "*A Midsummer Night's Wet Dream*? *As You Lick It*? Lots of highbrow Shakespeare here. But not a pretty boy in sight. All plucky young girls with big jugs. If you're gay, then so is Russell Crowe."

Sir Anthony shifted and sighed, desperate to figure a way out of this, but the evidence was far too overwhelming. "All right, yes, I prefer women. No crime in that."

"But why?"

"My career was dead. It was Sir Anthony Hopkins this, Sir Peter O'Toole that. People were forgetting who I was. I had to do something dramatic to get people talking again."

"So you pretended to come out of the closet?"

"Of course. Look at all the old English queens who come out, get loads of attention from the press, and more importantly, find themselves getting cast in the best movie parts. Take that bitch Ian McKellan."

"Sir Ian McKellan."

"Bollocks. There's nothing about that poof that remotely says 'sir.' After he declared himself a homosexual, not only did he get an Academy Award nomination playing a gay film director, he also landed two plum parts in a pair of huge franchise movie series. Why wasn't I considered for *Lord of the Rings*? I could have played the villain in those blasted *X-Men* movies! It is unfair, I tell you! I am every bit the actor he is! So I decided it was time to shake things up a bit. And I will tell you this, Jarrod, coming out has done wonders for my career. I am suddenly back on everyone's radar. And because of that, I am very close to landing a juicy role in a big Hollywood film."

"You lied about everything. All those boys, the late-night tutoring sessions, it was all an act to revive your career."

"And it worked beautifully."

"How far will you go, Sir Anthony, to keep up this charade?"

"What are you implying, Jarrod?"

"If someone found out the truth and threatened to expose you, what would you do? Would you risk all your hard work at creating this illusion by letting that happen, or would you take steps to ensure that person never had the opportunity to tell anyone?"

"Are you suggesting . . . ?"

"Claire somehow found out you were lying. She was going to blow everything. And you panicked. You got your hands on some ricin and sprayed it on the peach carnation that was in the bouquet I gave you. When Claire removed it, she was exposed and died a few hours later. Now no one could ever stop you from becoming the film legend that in your mind you were destined to become."

"No! Claire did know about me. How could she not? We have been dear friends and frequent costars for years! She knew my history with women. We even dated in our younger years at the Royal Academy. But she loved the idea of me creating this charade! She thought it was brilliant! And she did anything she could to talk me up to the press as being a much better actor since accepting my supposed truth! I did not kill her! I could never kill her!"

"What about the missing peach carnation from your bouquet? How did it reappear in Claire's bouquet sprayed with poison?"

"I don't know. But I never saw Claire before the show. After you presented me with the flowers, I went directly to make-up for final touches. Both Minx and Dame Sylvia were there at the time. Not to mention the make-up girl and several stagehands. I have plenty of witnesses to back me up. I was never anywhere near Claire's dressing room. I could not have switched the flowers."

Then who did? Who else was backstage and in proximity of Claire's dressing room? Suddenly it hit me. Of course. How could I have missed it? There was one person that night who did have the opportunity to switch the flowers—the mysterious "acting student" that Sir Anthony was entertaining in his dressing room. But if Sir Anthony was indeed straight, then the boy must have been a woman. And there was only one other woman seen milling about backstage that fateful night.

# Chapter 35

"Wallace Goodwin wasn't the only one having a secret affair with someone in the cast," I said, staring Sir Anthony down. "So was his wife, Katrina. She was sleeping with you."

Sir Anthony didn't respond. He didn't have to. A key was inserted into the door, and it swung open. Katrina Goodwin flounced in, wearing a heavy fur coat and high heels.

"Darling, I thought I would surprise you and show up a little early," she said.

Sir Anthony stood frozen, his eyes popped open, desperately trying to signal her, but she blathered on, not realizing I was standing to her left, out of her line of sight.

"Why not make the most of our last night together before we bid adieu," she said, dropping the fur coat to the floor and revealing her stark naked and remarkably well-preserved body.

"Those Pilates sure have paid off, Katrina," I said.

She whipped her head around to face me and let out an audible gasp. "Jarrod, what . . . what are you doing here? I thought you were—"

"In jail? Arrested for a murder *you* committed?"

"Me? What are you talking about?"

She looked to Sir Anthony for some help, but he was so stunned, so flabbergasted at having been outed as a straight man, he didn't know what to say in Katrina's defense.

"I know what happened now. You discovered that Wallace was having an affair with Claire Richards, and it drove you wild with rage. All those years you stuck by him when he was nothing, all those years you were the architect of his career, you pushed him and pushed him to be the best that he could be, and then he committed the ultimate act of betrayal. He strayed. And with a woman much older than you, which made it even worse. You didn't know it was just a forgettable one-night stand. Claire made a point of building it up to be much, much more than that, didn't she? She didn't like you and wanted to screw with your head, so she made it sound like she and Wallace were going to run off together to the south of France or something. Only thing was, she was gloriously happy with Liam. He was much more of a stud than Wallace. The only reason she slept with Wallace was to make sure he worked hard to keep her role in the play the most colorful and interesting. God forbid that Dame Sylvia get all the best lines. But you didn't know she wasn't serious about Wallace. You thought all your years of sweat and sacrifice to turn Wallace into a successful Hollywood writer and renowned playwright were for nothing. You had to do something. You had to take action. You had to kill Claire to save your marriage."

"You're not making any sense, Jarrod," Katrina whined as she reached down and picked up the fur coat to cover herself. "You're delusional."

"No, I'm afraid not. You remembered my long-standing tradition of delivering gifts to my fellow castmates every opening tape night of the first show of the season when we did *Go to Your Room*. You knew I always gave my leading lady fresh flowers. That was when you formulated your plan. You were certain I'd give Claire flowers, and you knew that Sir Anthony's dressing

271

room was next to Claire's. It would be logical that I would stop by his room first. During rehearsals, you befriended Sir Anthony, hoping you'd become pals and he'd invite you to visit his dressing room. But you hit pay dirt. You found out that the flamboyant Sir Anthony was only pretending to be gay. It would certainly explain him always leering at you. So you used that new information to seduce him. It wasn't some act of revenge on Wallace for cheating, it was a coldly calculated strategy to be in his dressing room before the curtain. You told Sir Anthony to play up his love of flowers in front of me so that I would be sure to give him a bouquet as well."

Sir Anthony was shaking, not knowing what to do or how to react. Katrina stood her ground, eyes narrowed, face like stone.

"I played right into your hand," I said. "I gave both Sir Anthony and Claire fresh flowers. I included a peach carnation in his because he made such a point of telling me he loved peach carnations. After Sir Anthony left for make-up, you sprayed the peach carnation in his bouquet with poison, and knowing Claire abhorred the flower, you managed a last-minute switch while she was distracted. Claire went to remove the carnation, inhaled the poison, and died a few hours later."

"This is all fantasy, Jarrod. You're making this up as you go along," Katrina said. But there was no passion behind her words. It was an automatic response. She knew I was on to the truth.

"You were certain Sir Anthony would never tell a soul that you were in his dressing room that night. It would raise too many questions about the exact nature of your relationship. He couldn't have that because he was afraid it would expose his secret. And you were even more afraid it would expose yours."

Sir Anthony kept glancing at Katrina. He was a bundle of nerves and on the verge of collapse.

"When you ran into me at the Savoy a couple of days later, you used that opportunity to solidify your story. You made a big point of telling me you had only just found out that Wallace was having an affair with Claire. That way, if you were in the dark about your husband's infidelities at the time of the murder, there would be no motive for you to kill her. It was the perfect murder. Except for one hitch. Akshay Kapoor."

Sir Anthony furrowed a brow, confused, obviously unaware of this wrinkle in Katrina's plan. Katrina continued to stand firm and give nothing away.

"Akshay saw you leave Sir Anthony's dressing room that night. It was the luckiest break he could have hoped for. He owed Uli Karydes thousands of dollars and had no way to pay it. So he tried blackmailing you for the money, thinking he could alleviate some of his staggering debt. He knew Wallace had socked away a lot of his earnings from his heyday as a sitcom writer. You were understandably upset and incensed. How dare this second rate Bollywood star mess up your perfect plan? And even if you did pay him off to keep quiet, what would guarantee that at some point he wouldn't piss away the money and call on you again for another payday? He could haunt you for the rest of your life. You'd always be looking around, waiting for him to show up at your door or send an e-mail and threaten to tell the police what he knew if you didn't write another check. No. That was unacceptable. Especially since Wallace was back on track and you fully expected him to be a huge success in the theater and perhaps one day even break into movies. Akshay had to be dealt with immediately. So you pretended to be returning to the States, but instead you followed him to Greece. You waited for your opportunity and then gunned him down on Super Paradise Beach. You are, after all, a good shot. Wallace told me at Starbucks that you fared better than he did on the firing range while re-searching his play."

Katrina finally flinched. The accusations were dead on and wearing down her stoic resolve.

"When you returned to London, the press was screaming for my head. It was perfect. You never liked me anyway. I always got all of the attention when we did the show back in the eighties. Wallace took a backseat to me for five years. You saw it as poetic justice that you got what you wanted and I would pay the price for it. You found Wallace, probably a blubbering mess, at the hotel. I'm sure it was a wildly romantic scene. He was so lost without you. You grandly announced your change of heart. This, I'm sure, was followed by lots of kissing and hugging and hours of lovemaking. You were both ready to resume your life together, with Claire out of your hair forever and Akshay no longer a threat to your future."

Katrina flipped back her hair and laughed. "What a compelling and fascinating piece of fiction you've come up with, Jarrod. With not one shred of evidence to suggest that any of it is real."

"Oh, I'll leave that up to the police. I'm sure your passport will have a stamp from Greece on it. A gun in Mykonos will turn up eventually. And then, of course, there is Sir Anthony."

"Sir Anthony would never back up these pathetic lies," Katrina said, eyeing him warily.

"Oh, yes, I believe he would when he thinks about it," I said.

Sir Anthony looked at me curiously.

"He's an actor, and if there is one thing I know, it's actors," I said. "Once Sir Anthony reviews the situation more carefully, he will understand that a story this rich with drama, this potent with scandal, can only help his career. Especially if he's in the red-hot center of it. Think about it. Actor pretends to be gay in order to compete with his rivals for the juiciest roles. But this little white lie, the most innocent of offenses, gets him embroiled in a sinister murder plot. And the victim? A fellow thespian, a dear, beloved colleague he's known for years. He would have to step forward, confess the truth about himself, and testify in court against his beautiful secret lover."

Sir Anthony's eyes lit up with the possibilities.

Katrina boiled with rage as she spun around to face Sir Anthony. "No! All you will get is ridicule from the press and public and possibly a charge of obstructing justice."

"No, what he will probably get is a book deal and a role as the villain in the next James Bond movie," I said.

That was all it took. Sir Anthony couldn't contain himself.

"You were right. Katrina was in my dressing room the night of Claire's murder. I think you might be right about everything."

Furious and desperate, Katrina began pounding Sir Anthony about the face and chest with her fists. I bolted across the room and pulled her off him. She fought me like an alley cat, but I managed to hurl her to the floor, where she finally gave up and began sobbing. Sir Anthony was now the second man after her husband to betray her.

Sir Anthony called a press conference the following day to confess his bad judgment about misleading the public regarding his sexual orientation and admit his indiscretion with the wife of a promising playwright. He denied any knowledge of the murder plot, and in a surprisingly bold move, announced his retirement from acting. Everyone knew this was just a ploy, and after a huge outcry from his fans, he graciously accepted a costarring role opposite Ian McKellan in a new comedy about an aging gay couple, together for thirty years, who sue to get married. It was a perfect comeback vehicle. And Dame Sylvia Horner even signed on to play Sir Anthony's doddering aunt, who fires off a barrage of sharp-tongued zingers.

All of the charges against me were dropped and my passport was finally returned to me. Charlie and I booked a flight home immediately. As for the state of my own career, that would remain a mystery for now. Whatever momentum I had hoped to gain from my West End theater debut had been clouded by all the allegations and scandal, but at this point I really didn't care. I just wanted to go home and see my friends and my dog Snickers and hike in the Hollywood Hills with my soul mate, my Charlie.

Laurette had flown back to the States a few days earlier and was reunited with her boyfriend, Larry, who came back from Maui armed with a new script that surprisingly sold to Universal in the high six figures. Lucky bastard. And back in the office for only a day, Laurette called with a firm acting offer for me. A small comedy troupe was mounting a show called *Go to Your Room Live on Stage* where the actors recreated the original scripts from my sitcom word for word. It's fun and nostalgic and has worked for several other shows ranging from *The Brady Bunch* and *The Facts of Life* to *The Golden Girls*. They wanted me to play myself at twelve years old. The idea of me, at thirty-four years old, playing myself at twelve struck me as hysterical, and since no other offers were forthcoming, I agreed. Why not? If you can't live down your past, then play to it.

For the first time in my life, I was not going to worry about the sorry state of my career. Too many other facets in my life were heading in the right direction. Katrina Goodwin was losing the man she had made a life with, the man she loved, and was driven to desperate measures. At one point during this challenging ordeal, I too thought I had lost the most important person in my life. I will never forget that chilling phone call from him in the middle of the night, his flat voice explaining to me that he was leaving me for Akshay. It was the most devastating moment of my life. The idea of losing him was unthinkable, and it forced me to contemplate a future without him. There were no guarantees in life. There was always the possibility of some crazy man shooting Charlie again in the line of duty, and this time the bullet might strike a vital organ. I hated to even think about that happening. Or of the possibility that one day either of us could somehow fall out of love. There were so many variables, so many possible outcomes in this unpredictable game of life.

Our plane taxied down the runway for takeoff, and Charlie and I sat side by side in our seats, holding hands. A conservative, middle-aged woman across the aisle sniffed with distaste at the sight of two men showing affection for one another. But I didn't care. Love is love no matter who it happens to, and some day the world will understand that. Charlie Peters was the love of my life, and we were about to begin a long journey home together, and for right now, at this moment, and for however long God allowed it, I was going to stay right next to this wonderfully compassionate force of nature. My man. My Charlie.